The Devil Shops on Sunday

Angela Corbett writing as
Destiny Ford

The Devil Shops on Sunday

Angela Corbett writing as
Destiny Ford

Copyright © 2024 by Angela Corbett

Cover design by Kat Tallon at Ink and Circuit Designs

All rights reserved. No part of this publication may be reproduced, distributed, or transmitted in any form or by any means, including photocopying, recording, or other electronic or mechanical methods, without the prior written permission of the publisher, except in the case of brief quotations embodied in critical reviews and certain other noncommercial uses permitted by copyright law.

This is a work of fiction. Names, characters, places, and incidents either are the product of the author's imagination or are used fictitiously, and any resemblance to actual persons, living or dead, business establishments, events, or locales is entirely coincidental.

ISBN: 978-1-965228-10-4

Published in the United States of America by Midnight Sands Publishing, LLC Utah

Dedication

For our sweet little furball, Pippin the pom. He was my constant companion from the beginning of my author career, and sat by my side for every book I wrote...but he wasn't here for all of this one. I miss his adorable little face, walk demands, kisses, and the cheese tax he required me to pay daily. I think of him every time I write Gandalf, and a little piece of Pip lives on through Kate's pup.

Chapter One

The white powder covering the ground and everyone in the vicinity wasn't what surprised me. Branson Falls is in Utah, after all, and our state is known for its powder. Soft snow often covers the ground, but not usually during the first week of November. During the rare times it does snow this low in the valley, this early, it usually doesn't stick. The powder I was witnessing was definitely sticking. Judging by the scene in front of me, it would probably be stuck for months.

The strange thing wasn't what appeared to be a culinary disaster that would make any of the popular bake-off show hosts cringe. The real shocker was the woman screaming, her cherry red face visible even through the puffs of white splattered on her forehead, cheeks, and nose—as if this particular pantry staple had developed a raging vendetta against her. I hadn't seen her this furious since gay marriage was legalized.

Her entire body was covered in all-purpose flour, particles flying in the air as she yelled and shook her fists at the police officers who were attempting to wrangle her. I'd gone to high school with some of those officers. They'd been cowboys who worked on family ranches and could rope a calf as easily as they brushed their teeth. They looked like they were considering breaking out a line and tying the woman up in the grocery store parking lot.

I stood back, watching the scene and trying to take it all in—it was a lot to process. There were plastic bags and groceries scattered all over the asphalt. Milk was dripping off a water softener salt display like blood, and while I was certain milk splatter experts didn't exist, I felt like there was now a need. It looked like a whole pallet of flour had exploded in front of the grocery store's exit, and given that we'd recently had the town's actual sugar factory explode, I wasn't ruling that out.

The store still stood, however, so a bomb hadn't gone off…but something had. It seemed that Branson's only grocery store had been booby-trapped, by what appeared to be a baker…or someone with access to a lot of wheat and an industrial strength grinder.

Liz Green, a woman who lived a few blocks from my house, came over to me as I took photos and tried to mentally piece the puzzle of this story together. Liz was wearing a forest green skirt and a pale pink lacy blouse, like she'd just come from church—she probably had. She was one of the few people in the vicinity who weren't covered in baking product. "You didn't get hit with flour?" I asked.

Her expression was a bit unfocused as she shook her head, like she was trying to make sense of what she'd witnessed. "I was pulling into the parking lot when it happened."

"What did you see?"

She pointed toward a man who was currently handcuffed and being helped into the back of a Branson Falls police cruiser. The guy was dressed in a black three-piece suit that was smeared with white marks from the flour. He had a patterned green tie around his neck, and he was wearing a winter mask that covered his whole face and made him look like a Sunday's-best bandit.

For a minute, I wondered if he was part of the Speedy Superheroes, the group of well-meaning do-gooders that had recently formed a league in Branson Falls. They dressed up in costume and patrolled the town looking for crime, miscreants, and, to be honest, something to do.

Branson Falls is usually a quiet, small town located in the Rocky Mountains, that prides itself on faith, family, and community—and expects everyone in town to share the same values. Everyone knows everyone, Mormon Church membership is used to decide whether someone can be trusted, and gossip is currency—and something I was often the subject of thanks to my lack of church attendance, my vocal opinions, and my dating life.

Flour littered the ground in front of the automatic sliding glass doors that acted as both entrance and exit for the grocery store. An industrial strength fan, the kind usually used by disaster clean-up crews to dry out homes after a flood, was on the ground, about twenty feet back from the door, and still running.

"When I pulled up, I saw this guy holding a bag of flour and blasting it in front of the fan every time someone walked out the door. He flour-bombed a lot of people," Liz explained.

My brows lifted. "He did all this with one bag?"

"No," she said, pointing to the ground by the fan where there were multiple bags of flour stacked like they'd been brought in on a pallet. "He had flour reserves."

He certainly did.

"How many people were hit?" I asked.

"I saw at least five. Some kids too. He was unrelenting."

It sounded like it. It also made no sense. I saw Officer Bob standing by the grocery store door. "I'm going to talk to Bobby and see if he knows what the flour attack motive was."

Liz nodded and followed me.

I walked over and gave Bobby a big smile. "Bet you weren't expecting this today," I said. Bobby and I had grown up together and he'd learned to love me, or at least tolerate me most times, since I'd moved back home to Branson Falls six months ago and had become the editor of the town newspaper, *The Branson Tribune*.

Bobby's expression indicated he was perpetually trying to not be annoyed with the state of the world. "If there's anything this job has taught me, it's to expect the unexpected."

I felt the same about my career. "What happened here?"

Bobby took a deep breath. "Jack Pine was upset about the grocery store bein' open on Sunday."

There had been a town controversy about stores opening on Sunday. The predominant religion in Utah was The Church of Jesus Christ of Latter-Day Saints, formerly, and more well-known, as the Mormon Church. They'd even had a multi-million-dollar ad campaign about Meeting the Mormons, and trying to tout Mormon diversity. And their main religious text was called *The Book of Mormon*, so the focus shift away from the Mormon name was confusing on many levels. But according to current church leadership—who deeply despised nicknames—referring to the church or its members as "Mormon" was "a major victory for Satan" so I would continue to do so.

THE DEVIL SHOPS ON SUNDAY

Members of the Mormon Church weren't supposed to spend money or do business on Sunday. It was supposed to be a day of rest when no one worked. It always amused me because anyone who had devoted any time to being a church member knew that wandering the halls of a Mormon Church Ward house was as good for networking and business dealing as hitting balls on golf courses, or holding parties to recruit new members to their MLMs. And people don't stop getting sick or needing milk because it's Sunday.

The argument had been made that the grocery store needed to stay open for emergencies, even if the Sabbath was a little less holy because of it—another major victory for Satan, surely. They'd tried to close the grocery store on Sunday for a hot minute. It lasted a few weeks and there was so much complaining from people who needed necessities, like medicine, and those who preferred to shop on Sunday, that they reopened it.

I was grateful since Sunday is when I, and all the other gentiles—the non-members among the Mormons who Mormons are either forced to contend with, or convert—allocate time for grocery shopping. It's the day most of the faithful population stays home and you get wide aisles and fresh baked doughnuts all to yourself. Truth be told, the store was still plenty busy on Sundays with heathens like myself, and Mormons who had forgotten things like diapers, toilet paper, and diet soda to name a few. There were also those active Mormons who didn't care about the letter of the law, made up their own rules, and were fine with shopping on Sunday. They were looked down on and judged for it, but it didn't stop them. After today though, it might.

Bobby continued, "Jack decided to tag everyone who went shoppin' today so people would know they were sinners."

My mouth dropped. "You've got to be kidding me." Hester Prynn and her chest emblazoned with "A" had nothing on Branson Falls religious zealots and their creative ways to shame people.

"Nope. Got a lotta people before we arrived."

I slid Bobby a confused look. "The police station is literally a block away." I pointed in the direction of the station house. "Like, it's right across the street. I can see it from here."

"I know." Bobby's exasperated expression indicated I wasn't the first to point that fact out. "The calls we got indicated there was an active shooter. We're a small-town police force and had to secure multiple areas. All the people in the area and inside the store didn't help either. Ever since everyone started movin' in, the grocery store is way busier on Sunday."

That was the truth. It was still less busy than the mayhem of a Saturday night grocery run, when everyone was trying to shop before Sunday struck at midnight, but I used to be able to shop on Sunday and not see another soul for aisles. That wasn't the case anymore. Utah was experiencing exponential growth, and a lot of Utah residents, especially in small towns like Branson Falls, weren't happy about it. They didn't like change, and didn't want the culture to shift around people who had different thoughts and ideas than they did. Confirmation bias was real, and people in Branson Falls, and many rural Utah locations, were holding onto it like a lifeline.

They only wanted to be surrounded by people who were like them. Many believed that differences were dangerous instead of a learning opportunity to open their minds and critically think. It was one of the reasons I'd decided to move back home. Being forced to interact with people who had different opinions and ideas could alter someone's thought patterns and help them understand other perspectives. I'd seen it repeatedly in my work as a journalist in other parts of the world. Embracing different perspectives and trying to understand one another was essential. I knew the ability to adapt would be a marker for Branson's future success or failure. If this scene was any indication, it wasn't looking great.

"How many people were hit?" I asked Bobby.

He looked around at the crowd. "Probably twenty-five before we got here. Some didn't stay because they didn't want to give statements or let people know they'd been shoppin' on Sunday, so we aren't exactly sure on the count."

Of course they left the scene of the crime so they wouldn't be implicated over the pulpit.

"And what about this situation," I asked, gesturing to the woman the officers had been trying to wrangle when I got there. She was sitting in a chair, fanning herself, the ruffles on her pastel blue blouse drifting with the air. She looked like a monumentally angry ghost.

The woman covered in flour was none other than Mrs. Olsen, winner of the award for most judgy woman on the planet. She had chastised me for almost every move I'd made since I'd relocated back to Branson Falls. The same woman who, according to her religious beliefs, should *definitely* not be buying things on Sunday. Or judging people. It seemed the universe had decided to take notice. A satisfied smile crossed my lips at the Karma.

Bobby made a face that was part cringe, part annoyance.

"She was shoppin', walked out, got hit with flour, and turned into a rabid jackal."

The corners of my lips twitched. "Have you seen a lot of rabid jackals here in rural Utah, Bobby?"

He shot me a look back. "More than you realize," he said in a way that let me know he often had to deal with people who behaved like wild animals. He continued, "She took out the perpetrator all by herself, with her groceries."

I cocked my head to the side with both suspicion and interest. "How did she do that, exactly?"

Bobby's brows crept up on his forehead and I knew this was going to be quite a story. "The flour hit her and she was stunned. Witnesses we've interviewed so far said it looked like she was momentarily frozen in time. It took her a minute to get her bearings, but once she did, she lasered in on the guy mannin' the fan and flour, and took after him like one of those heat-seekin' missiles that are built not far from here. She started grabbin' her groceries, one-by-one, and threw them like ammunition. The guy had to dart behind the fan and softener salt to avoid her potatoes, zucchini, chicken, and Metamucil."

My eyes widened to a degree I didn't think they were capable of opening to. Mrs. Olsen had to be around one thousand years old…okay, she was probably in her late eighties, but was still not someone I would have pegged for having a throwing arm, let alone being accurate with it.

Bobby noticed my skepticism. "She's a pretty good shot. Played softball on a church league when she was young."

Of course she did. Church sports weren't as common anymore, but for years they'd been one of the only ways for people who were supposed to be perpetually kind and perfect, to take out their aggression. Young women got to play softball and volleyball. Men played basketball. It was Mormon Ward vs. Ward. Relationships had been destroyed over the teams, and movies made about the competitions.

"The guy couldn't move fast enough," Liz said, confirming Bobby's story since she'd actually been there when it happened. "It was like watching dodgeball being played with food, and he was taking a produce beating."

That dodgeball quote was going straight into the article. I jotted it down with my other notes.

Bobby nodded in agreement with Liz. "Mrs. Olsen ran out of groceries in her bag and the perpetrator still wasn't down, so she decided on more drastic measures."

"More drastic than grocery bombing?" I asked. "What did she pull out? A gun?" It honestly wouldn't have surprised me. A lot of Branson residents started learning how to shoot as soon as they could hold a firearm.

"Worse," Bobby said. "She grabbed her gallon of milk, clutched it in the nook of her arm, spun twice to get momentum, and chucked it at his head."

My jaw dropped. "She shot-put a gallon of milk at his skull?"

"Like an Olympian," Bobby confirmed. "He ducked down just in time, but barely. We were able to get him while he was on the ground. You can still see the milk mess." He pointed toward an area that I thought was more flour, but could now see the dry ingredients congealing with the wet milk like someone had interrupted a cooking class being taught on asphalt.

I turned back to Bobby. "So, you were assisted in your flour bandit capture by a carb-covered senior citizen who should apparently be on some professional team for both dodgeball and the shot-put?"

Bobby shrugged. "Pretty much."

I sighed deeply, knowing what I'd have to do next. "This means I have to go get a comment from Mrs. Olsen." I tried to avoid interacting with her at all costs.

Bobby's mouth spread into a grin. "Given her feelings about you, I hope she's calmed down, and that she doesn't have any more groceries to throw."

I did too. I walked over to where she was sitting on a folded chair that someone had brought for her, still doused in flour, and looking spectral. And not in a "nice friendly ghost" way, but one of those "attach to a person's soul and torment them for the rest of time and all eternity" way.

"How are you doing, Mrs. Olsen?" I asked, willing my voice to be as polite as possible. It was a struggle.

Her voice came out more crackly than usual, and the way her dark eyes narrowed between her mask of white flour made her seem like some sort of demon who had just walked off the set of a horror movie. I expected her irises to start glowing blood red at any moment. "How does it look like I'm doin', Kate Saxee?"

It looked like she had an axe or ten to grind, but I wasn't going there. "I hear you helped stop the man who was throwing flour at people."

Her body tensed and I could tell she deeply disagreed with my summary of events. "He wasn't throwin' it," she said, her voice lowering to an octave that matched the demon makeup she was sporting. "He was assaultin' people with it."

Okay then. "The police said you helped them with the capture."

"Well, someone needed to. They certainly weren't doin' their job!"

I gave her a knowing smile. She hadn't said a word about why she'd been hit in the flour attack. She was trying to deflect from the fact that she was shopping on Sunday with comments about the lack of talent in the police department instead. "Well, it's a good thing you were here," I said. "And on a Sunday even!" I couldn't help myself.

Her eyes slitted like she was about to turn into an actual agent of Satan and not just try to imitate one. "I needed things, Kate Saxee. Don't you dare try to spin this like I was doin' somethin' wrong. I know you and your mainstream media type. Always tryin' to make everyone into the bad guy to advance your liberal agenda."

I managed to refrain from rolling my eyes. Deflection as a defense was a tried-and-true Branson Falls coping method, and one I'd become an expert at beginning with childhood and my introduction to my Mormon Ward primary class where any question that couldn't be answered was quickly turned around on the person asking it. Luckily, I'd been raised observing it and being taught to practice it, and could spot it from a mile away. As for her accusations, number one, I had no agenda and wasn't trying to advance it. It would be futile in a place like Branson Falls. Number two, it was interesting she thought people who shopped on Sunday were "bad" since she was one of them.

"Do you want to make any comments for the paper?"

She glared at me. Hard. "I do not."

I'd expected that. I pressed my lips together and nodded. "Okay. You know where to find me if you change your mind before the paper goes to press."

She said nothing as I walked over to the police car where Jack Pine, the flour bandit was currently cuffed and sitting in the back seat. I leaned down to talk to him through the open window. I identified myself and asked, "Why did you blast flour at people getting their groceries?"

"They know why," Jack answered, his voice gravelly.

I stared at him, waiting for him to elaborate. He didn't.

"Did you think you were doing a good thing?"

His chest puffed up and he sat taller. "I was," he stated, his tone full of righteous indignation and authority. "People need to be punished for not followin' the rules."

The rules, meaning the rules that he believed in and wanted to impose on everyone else instead of letting them make their own choices—a concept that went completely against the Mormon Church's "Free to Choose" foundational teachings.

"Did someone encourage you to do this, or did you come up with the plan all on your own?"

He paused before answering, "No one else was involved."

I wasn't sure I believed him, but it was good to know there wasn't a flour bandit attack team that future Sunday shoppers, myself included, would have to be prepared to defend themselves against. I didn't want to have to wear a parka to get groceries, and my standard shopping list of cereal, bread, butter, cheese, coffee, and creamer wouldn't have the impact that Mrs. Olsen's milk had.

I finished taking notes and getting photos, then got in my car and drove home. It was the weekend, and it was supposed to be my day off.

I pulled up to my house, a white bungalow with navy blue shutters and a detached garage. The brisk fall weather had started to strip the leaves from the trees and shrubs, and the house looked a bit bare because of it. I'd been renting the house since moving back to Branson Falls, but given what was happening with property values across Utah, I felt like I might need to figure out a way to buy soon.

I walked to the front door to unlock it and stopped abruptly to stare at the gorgeous arrangement of flowers in a magenta-colored vase sitting on my porch. There were a dozen bright roses with heavy blooms that practically dripped decadence in various shades of pink. They could be from anyone, but there were two men in my life who were front-runners for the delivery. One of them I was happier with at the moment than the other. I eyed the petals suspiciously as I contemplated whether I currently had the emotional capacity to read the card.

"Pretty flowers, Kate!" my neighbor and reality TV show watching cohort, Phyllis, said with a wave. She was wearing a red and white dress and her hair, which was most often in curlers, had been styled for Sunday. "They were delivered about an hour ago."

An hour ago? On a Sunday? The sender either called in a favor, or sent them from out of town because unlike the grocery store, flowers were not considered a necessity and neither of the two florists in Branson delivered on the Sabbath.

"I've been watchin' 'em for ya so no one would steal 'em!"

I gave her a warm smile. "Thanks for always looking out for me, Phyllis."

"You bet! We girls have to stick together." She said it with a twinkle in her eye indicating she thought we were part of some sort of gang, and I supported that.

"Did you see who delivered them?"

She picked up some trash that had blown into her yard. "Yep, but it wasn't anyone I recognized and there wasn't a business name on the car that drove up."

That meant the flowers probably came from one of the bigger cities, or a private delivery service. Which didn't help me figure out who had sent them. Both Hawke and Drake spent a lot of time outside of Branson Falls, and had business contacts in many locations.

"Are we still on for watchin' the premiere of Homemakers of the Beehive State?" A popular reality show franchise had decided Utah was an excellent spot to highlight for their next series. I couldn't blame them. Utah was a world of its own full of perfection, scandal, and all kinds of sins from people who claimed that they strived to be sinless. I anticipated a lot of pseudo-swears, some real ones, yelling, fighting, and copious amounts of Botox, filler, and plastic surgery. I was also excited for the hashtag: #HOTBS. I wasn't sure if they'd thought that abbreviation through and done it on purpose, or by accident. But Hot BS amused me either way. It described a lot of Utah culture perfectly.

"Of course! I can't wait to watch!" I'd been at some press events for the show and met a couple of the women being featured. I wouldn't miss it.

Phyllis waved and I took the big vase of flowers inside and put them on my kitchen table. I stared at them for a solid five minutes and decided to make myself an emotional support grilled cheese before reading the note that came with them. My adorable little black and grey dog, Gandalf, approved of the cheese plan and sat on the kitchen rug, waiting for me to drop something.

I finished cooking my sandwich and then pulled out the card.

"I didn't get enough of you the other night. I never will."

My heart sped up and I immediately dropped the card on the table. It wasn't signed. But I could guess who it was from. It had been a memorable night, and I hadn't seen the flower giver since. Not for lack of trying, and I was bit annoyed about it.

I took a long inhale of the roses, then grabbed my laptop, went to the living room, and flipped on a baking show. It seemed like appropriate background noise to write a story about Sunday sinners being baptized with flour.

Chapter Two

"Forever in Blue Jeans" started belting out of my phone's speakers at a volume that should be solely reserved for bad news and booty calls. I loved Neil, but it was way too early in the morning for this BS, and I meant the real words those letters stood for, not "Beehive State."

I hit the green button on my phone and mumbled, "Hey, Spence."

"Hey," his sleep-laced voice answered. At least we were both on the same page about early morning emergencies that resulted in phone calls at the butt crack of dawn. "A body was found on what used to be the Barret Ranch. The one with the new housing development going in. Police are on the scene."

Gandalf squirmed beside me, also annoyed at the sleep intrusion.

"A body?" I asked, sitting up and rubbing my eyes. It was way too early on a Monday for murder. People died of natural causes in Branson Falls, and we occasionally had suspicious deaths, but a dead body being found on what used to be someone's private property wasn't especially common in a town this small. Then again, Branson was growing, and the town was uniquely placed for interstate crimes—something I'd learned while covering a story a few months ago.

"That's what the police scanner said. An excavation crew was doing dirt work on the new development and came across the bones. They thought it was an animal at first until they found a very human looking skull."

I cringed as I walked to my closet, Gandalf following close behind. "That's a morbid discovery for a Monday morning."

"I can't argue with that," Spence said. "According to the preliminary info, it looks like it's been there a while."

Ah, I thought, as I pulled on a pair of jeans and a sea green sweater that brought out the lighter tones of my blue eyes. I'm about 5'7" and an average build, but I know how to work with what I have. Gandalf appraised me and based on the fact that he didn't barf, seemed to approve of my outfit choice. It might also be that he was hungry and didn't want to upset the person who procured his food. "So, they're bones that used to be a body, and probably a lost hiker or something," I said.

Branson Falls is nestled in the beautiful Rocky Mountains and people often get lost or hurt while recreating. Occasionally, people who don't know better and haven't done their research, go hiking without the proper gear and don't realize they need things like water, or warmer clothes at higher altitudes once the sun sets. They frequently require rescue if they're in a place with cell phone coverage. And if they're not, they often become a missing person.

"Could be," Spence answered through a yawn. "The police are examining the scene at the ranch now."

"The Barret's owned a farm, but I don't think the Barret

property is technically a ranch. Ranches are much bigger than that."

"Fifty acres seems pretty big."

I grinned at his assessment. "That's because you didn't grow up in a farming community."

"Thank God."

I laughed. "I'll leave as soon as I'm presentable." Spence mumbled something in the affirmative before I hung up.

I grabbed breakfast and fresh water for Gandalf, and started the coffee maker. I was going to need a barrel of it this morning. While I waited for Gandalf to eat and my coffee to brew, I cleaned my teeth, then ran a brush through my shoulder length wavy light brown hair and pulled it into a ponytail. I moisturized, sunscreened, and slapped on some mascara, foundation, and blush. I grabbed my coffee tumbler and Gandalf so I could drop him off at my parents' house, and left to find out more about the dead body on the former ranch that wasn't a ranch.

I pulled up to the Barret—now developer's—property and was met with the entire force of the Branson Falls police department. I really hoped no one else was committing a crime this early because the police wouldn't be able to respond.

The area was sectioned off with yellow tape. A white pop-up police tent shaded the ground where the bones had been found. The tent had sides so I couldn't see the area where the body had been uncovered. A giant yellow and black excavator was sitting idle near the spot, the arm of the machine looking like it had been stopped mid-claw.

I walked up to Bobby, who was talking to someone I didn't recognize. Bobby saw me and wrinkled his nose. "I should've known you'd be here soon."

"I'm surprised the Speedy Superheroes didn't arrive before I did."

Bobby fought hard to not roll his eyes. The Speedy Superheroes had been "helping" the Branson Falls police force by patrolling the town in costume and finding criminals. It was a relatively new development, and I got the feeling the police weren't particularly happy about it. I couldn't blame them. If some group rolled in and tried to start helping me do my job, I probably wouldn't be too happy about it either.

"I hear you found a body," I said.

Bobby nodded. "The developer, Grant Kimball, is over there talkin' to one of my officers." He pointed to a man across the field with light brown hair and a lanky build. He was probably about 5'10", and he looked to be in his early forties. Bobby tilted his head in the direction of the guy he'd been talking to when I arrived. "This is Jory, the excavator who found the bones."

"Hi Jory." I smiled and held out my hand. "I'm Kate Saxee, editor for *The Branson Tribune*."

"Nice to meet you," Jory said.

"I bet you're getting a lot of work right now," I observed. With the population boom, the housing supply was in sharp demand. Inventory was incredibly low, and prices were high. Developers were buying land at a record pace, and trying to get as many homes built as quickly as possible. There was no shortage of work related to the construction industry.

Jory nodded. "I ain't complainin'."

"Can you tell me what happened?" I'd seen large excavators work before. They got a high-level view of things as they dug, but they probably wouldn't know they were hitting something unless it was large enough to be a boulder. "How did you even know you'd uncovered a body?"

"My son was with me and saw the bones as I dug. He waved for me to stop."

If his son was with him, he was probably a subcontractor. "So, you're not an employee of the developer?"

"Nope. I've been playin' in the dirt for twenty years. I own my machine and my business. When people need dirt work done, they call me and I contract with them for what needs to be moved."

I'd always thought the developers or home builders owned the excavating equipment. But they subcontracted everything else out to other companies, so it made sense they would hire a company to move the dirt as well.

"Do you live in Branson Falls?" I asked. I hadn't seen him around before, which is uncommon in a small town. I had a good memory for faces and even if I didn't know him directly, I probably would have recognized him if I'd seen him in Branson.

"I live in Rowe."

So not Branson Falls, but still the same county. It would make sense to hire someone close to Branson since it probably wasn't cheap to transport that excavator.

"What happens now?" I asked Bobby.

"We'll seal off this area, take photos, and have forensics come in. They'll take the remains to be examined and we'll hopefully get a better idea of the cause of death, and how old the person was. If we're lucky, we'll also get an identification."

"How long will that take?"

THE DEVIL SHOPS ON SUNDAY

Bobby lifted a shoulder. "Could take days, or weeks. It all depends on the state of the body and if we have DNA, fingerprint, or dental records that match it on file."

"Do you have any ideas about how the person died?"

Bobby crossed his arms and lowered his head deliberately. "Are you tryin' to get me to let you see the body?"

I crossed my arms to mirror him. "If Hawke was here, I wouldn't even have to ask."

"Probably not," he admitted. "But we're keepin' the area secure and as undisturbed as possible until forensics arrives."

"You won't give me any hints at all? You have to know a general idea of how long it's been there. Do you think it was a hiker?"

Bobby hooked his thumbs through the belt loops on his pants. "Could be, but we ain't sure yet. Based on the decay, it's been a while."

That wasn't a lot to go on, but at least I now knew the body had been there long enough to decay, and I should have more answers as soon as the medical examiner did—or as soon as I could get ahold of Hawke.

Bobby turned to answer a question from one of the other officers, and motioned for Jory to come over. The three of them stepped aside.

I was trying to eavesdrop when I heard a shrill voice behind me and attempted to pretend I hadn't. This particular person was one I avoided almost as much as Mrs. Olsen. I had no clue why she was here unless she'd heard the police scanner and decided her very early morning needed some excitement.

Jackie Wall, the ringleader of The Ladies, a group of women so judgy and gossipy that they'd decided to organize in order to wreak even more havoc. We hadn't been friends when she'd tormented me in high school, and we certainly weren't friends now. She and her cohorts had strong opinions about everything in my life, especially the men I dated, and my decision to leave the Mormon Church.

Jackie came over, white flecks sprinkled through her hair and all over her clothes like she'd gotten in the way of someone spray painting. My eyebrows pushed together in puzzlement and then a lightbulb dawned.

She stopped right in front of me, planted her feet, and curled her mouth into a sneer. "What are you doing here?" she demanded, her tone accusatory.

I gave her a look that matched her attitude. "My job," I answered dryly. "What are you doing here?"

She put her hands on her hips, and straightened her spine, standing a little taller like the additional half an inch might impart more authority. "I'm dating one of the owners of this development," she said, her nose turned up in the air. I was surprised by this since she'd been sending me laser glares at the Halloween Carnival when she saw me with Drake. She must have decided to expand her horizon of potential suitors and I wondered how long she and Grant had been together. Grant and Drake were polar opposites in the looks department so she didn't have a physical type, but she definitely had a preference for bank account size.

Few things were more revered for women in Utah and the Mormon/LDS Church than marriage and motherhood, and you weren't supposed to have one without the other. So, there was an immense amount of pride for some women in catching the interest of a man, and even more pride in catching the interest of a man with money so women could be stay-at-home moms and raise their kids without having a paying job. The idea irritated me for many reasons, including the fact that women should get to decide their roles, not have those roles dictated by their church, and the invisible labor that went into raising kids and managing a household should pay them all far more than what their husbands made at their high-income jobs.

Mormon women who had careers, even if the jobs were in the home, were judged for it. I thought it was a ridiculous barometer for faith, and it was almost impossible to afford to raise a family by today's standards without a two-person family income. The idea that a mother needed to stay home and work for free seemed antiquated...then again, most of the ideas preached by the religious majority in Utah felt the same. I'd always been the type of woman who wanted a successful and meaningful career, and firmly believed in women saving themselves, so the suggestion of finding a man to take care of me did not appeal at all, but it did to a whole slew of patriarchy-indoctrinated women. And Jackie Wall was one of them.

"So, you heard about the body and decided to come out here with your boyfriend?" I asked.

She folded her arms across her chest. "Yes," she answered curtly. "This is a problem, and could affect his project. I didn't want him to face this trial alone."

I could respect that she wanted to support him but I had other, more pressing questions, I needed answered. "What's the white stuff on your shirt?" I asked, already pretty sure I knew the answer because I'd seen several people similarly coiffed and attired at the grocery store yesterday.

Her eyes widened like a deer in headlights and everything

seemed to freeze for several seconds. She finally came around with an obvious lie cloaked as denial. "What white stuff?" she sputtered, and tried to cover her guilt with a cough. "I don't know what you're talking about."

I leaned over and brushed some flecks off her shoulder. "The flour that's all over your clothes." I paused long enough to make her nervous. "Jackie Wall," I said, like I was saying tsk, tsk tsk. "Were you at the *grocery* store? On a *Sunday*?"

"What?" she said too quickly. Then followed it with, "That's a ridiculous thing to say and you're a ridiculous person, Kate."

Calling me ridiculous was the nicest insult she'd ever given me. I also noticed she didn't answer "no," which was an indicator that someone was lying through their teeth. My lips curved into a slow, knowing smile. "Really? Then why do you look like you walked through a flour tornado?"

She stood firm and doubled down on her lie. "No one walks through tornados and saunters out of them, Kate. And I was baking. I must have gotten some on my clothes."

"Baking at six in the morning?"

"Yes," she bit out. "Breakfast. Ever heard of it?"

"The flour is also in your hair," I said, gesturing helpfully. "It looks kind of like dandruff. For a minute I thought you'd died it gray."

She released a horrified gasp at both of those observations. The Ladies were obsessed with looking young and superior, and wouldn't tolerate dandruff, gray hair, or anything less than perfection. "That…that…that's a new dry shampoo I'm using!" She stammered, pleased with herself at coming up with another lie on the fly.

"Do you know how dry shampoo works?" I asked.

"Because this," I said, gesturing to her hair and whole ensemble, "isn't it."

She sneered and opened her mouth to say what I was sure was something extraordinarily kind and neighborly like she was instructed to do by her faith, when Grant walked up behind her, nodding to Bobby who was about ten feet away. "How are things going?" he asked, gesturing to the dig site and the police working the scene.

Bobby left Jory and the other officer and walked back to our group. "Nothing new to tell ya," Bobby said. "We'll get the body moved and once we have the clear, you can start workin' over here again."

"How long will that take?" Grant asked.

"Depends on what we find. Could be a day, could be a week."

Grant took a breath and I could see his jaw work. "Okay. Let me know. This is phase one of our development. We want to work on this area as soon as we can."

Bobby nodded. "I understand. We'll try to get ya up and runnin' again as soon as possible."

"We can work on other areas though, right?" Grant clarified.

"Yep," Bobby said. "Just not where we've taped off."

Grant nodded, looking a little more relieved. I was sure the delay was causing him stress, and I'd be even more stressed about the fact that he might have to disclose the dead body information when he tried to sell that lot. Someone was going to get a really good deal.

I stepped up and put my hand out. "Hi, I'm Kate Saxee, editor for *The Branson Tribune*."

"Grant Kimball," he said. "I own GCR Development with my partners, Chris, and Ryan. We're the property developers."

I nodded as I asked for the spelling of his name and business, and wrote it down. "I remember hearing about your project approval in the City Council meeting several months ago. Your company has a few development projects in the area, doesn't it?"

"We hope to. We're in negotiation on some other properties. This is the first, so we're eager to get the excavation done and be able to start the rest of the process."

"How many homes are going in?"

"One-hundred-twenty-five in this area. A mix of large one acre estate lots, and smaller single-family lots."

I nodded and looked around the property. "It's a great location." And it was. The property was situated higher in the mountains on the benches, and provided outstanding views of the valley and the western range beyond it. It was hard to find large pieces of land for development in Utah anymore. It was common for eight or more homes to be squished onto one acre. What had once been farming land or cattle grazing property was being sacrificed to real estate because the land was worth more with a house on it than it was with crops in a field. That fact was going to make the Branson Falls teens who took dates to watch *Children of the Corn* in a corn field sad since there weren't going to be many more corn fields left.

"It is," he answered. "We were lucky to get it."

"What's your timeline for building?"

"We're doing the initial work and infrastructure now. Utility lines, water, streets, curbs, that kind of thing. Once that's done, we'll start building the first phase of homes."

"How will this situation affect your timeline?" I asked, gesturing to the area that had been cordoned off.

"There are no good delays," he answered, his breath shallow. "Hopefully we'll get answers quickly, and we'll keep working on other areas until this spot is clear."

He didn't seem too concerned about the person who had died, but maybe he was worried about his business.

Jackie slid her hand over his forearm and squeezed it in what I imagined was supposed to be a soothing gesture, but from my perspective, looked a lot like a python strangling its prey.

Another guy in a suit walked up, a bit taller than Grant, with a more robust stomach and blonde hair cut in a traditional Mormon "missionary" haircut—which meant short and clean so they'd seem trustworthy. "Hi, Chris," Grant said.

"Any news?" Chris asked.

Grant nodded and the two of them stepped away to talk.

Jackie's expression was one of concern until the exact moment when Grant was no longer paying attention, then she snapped her glare to me. "This project is one Grant's been working on for a long time. It would be unfortunate if anything bad was said about him, or the property, in the paper."

I tilted my head to the side, appraising. "Why would I say anything bad about him? Is there something I don't know?"

She put her hands on her hips and huffed in an exasperated way. "No. I'm just saying you should stick to the facts."

That seemed like an odd thing to tell me to do, and made me even more suspicious. She'd guaranteed I was going to look up Grant Kimball on my background check service at the *Tribune*. "I always do."

"Make sure of it." She brushed some flour from her shirt before shifting her eyes up to mine. "I expect you to be professional about this," Jackie said.

"Which part?" I asked. "The body that was found on your boyfriend's property development," a slow smile stretched my lips, "or the fact that you stayed the night at his house and were so caught up in *whatever* you were doing after you got floured while shopping on a Sunday, that you didn't even think to clean up your hair, or wash your shirt?"

Her face reddened and for a moment, I thought steam might actually start coming out of her nose and ears. "You don't want to aggravate me, Kate Saxee."

That seemed a lot like a threat. And I'd stopped allowing Jackie Wall to terrorize me years ago.

"I know you didn't go to college," I said, "but if you had, you'd understand the walk of shame, and realize you just completed it."

I walked away from her before she tried to assault me with something more than words, and I got the rest of the interviews and photos I needed. I left to go back to the office right as the Speedy Superheroes drove up. I could see Bobby rolling his eyes all the way from my Jeep.

It was still early in the morning by the time I finished at the Barret's old property, and I felt like I'd been awake all night. I yawned as I pulled onto the main road and decided I was in desperate need of another coffee.

I turned my car toward Beans and Things, the only coffee

house in town. Coffee was outlawed in the Mormon Church because it was against the Word of Wisdom, which said members weren't allowed to partake of things like hot drinks and tobacco—a revelation the Mormon prophet and church founder, Joseph Smith, had come up with after his wife—one of them at least—Emma, had gotten sick of cleaning up the tobacco mess made by church members. A coffee shop opening in Branson was the equivalent of the first of the four horsemen showing up, and the Beans and Things business approval had made Branson residents certain that the apocalypse was nigh at hand—something they'd been believing and using as a fear tactic since the beginning of the Mormon Church in 1832, or 1835, or 1838, or 1842 depending on which different version of Joseph Smith's First Vision a person believed. And the coffee shop had opened months before the tattoo shop, so the Second Coming was bound to happen any day.

As I pulled into a parking spot, I noticed that a crowd had gathered out front near the patio seating. In most places, that would be considered normal since it was morning and people needed their coffee, but in Branson, it was uncommon because most people got their caffeine from soda instead of coffee—or made coffee at home that could masquerade as hot chocolate. And also, it was the first of November and mornings were becoming more chilly so the patio wasn't the first choice for gathering in fall and winter months. I got out of my Jeep as a brisk breeze whipped across my face. It had stayed relatively warm so far this year, but the morning air was a reminder that a cold change was coming soon.

I walked up to the front door and saw Kelcie, my favorite

barista, scrubbing the beige siding. Royal blue paint was sprayed across it in a nonsensical way. It looked kind of like a snowman with no face. It had three stacked interlocking circles that were supposed to be symbols of some kind, but I had no idea what the images meant because I didn't speak graffiti.

"Hi, Kelcie," I said. "Interesting morning so far?"

She glanced up. "Hi, Kate." She blew a piece of hair out of her eyes that had escaped her pony tail during her scrubbing. "Yes, we found this painted on the wall when we arrived."

"Any idea what it means?" I asked, pulling out my camera and taking some pics of it. I hadn't meant to accidentally get a story with my second morning coffee, but a lot of things that happened in my life were unintentional.

"It's a symbol for a hate group. I've seen it before. We called the police, but they haven't made it over here yet. We took photos and they told us to go ahead and start cleaning it up if we could."

"The police are at the old Barret farm dealing with a situation there," I supplied for her. "Do you have security cameras?"

"We do, but the people were wearing masks."

"Like Halloween masks?" Halloween hadn't been that long ago. And then there were the Speedy Superheroes still running around in full-on costumes. They were in the business of catching criminals though, so I didn't think they'd be joining one in vandalizing the coffee shop.

"Ski masks," she answered. "Like they were playing cops and robbers."

"But they didn't try to break in?"

"Nope. They spray painted this and left."

They must have known the cameras were there. "It looks like it's coming off."

Kelcie nodded. "Slowly but surely. Our insurance broker gave us some tips for removal so we could try to do it ourselves before making a claim."

I looked at the people on the patio and wondered if that was the order line and if I should go home and make myself more coffee instead. "Are you the only one here today?"

She shook her head. "No, we've got two more baristas inside. Most of the people out here aren't waiting for coffee, they're just nosy." She tilted her head toward the door. "You shouldn't have to wait long."

"Thanks!" I said, walking to the door. "Next time you're vandalized, I hope they put someone else on scrubbing duty so you can make my coffee because you make it best."

Her lips spread wide. "That made my day a little better."

I smiled back and walked in the cute shop. It had brightly colored flooring in a herringbone pattern that alternated between shades of blue, green, and teal. White quartz countertops sat on black cabinets, and various sized wood tables were scattered around the perimeter of the shop. An eclectic array of art work hung on the walls.

I walked up to the front, said hello to the baristas working —my second and third favorite coffee suppliers—and ordered my drink.

"You're good to go," Bran, the barista, told me after he rang it up.

I pushed my bottom lip out slightly, confused. "I haven't paid yet."

"I know. Someone else paid for your drink for you."

I looked around the store and didn't recognize anyone who would have done that. "Who?"

He shrugged. "A secret admirer? All I know is that this drink is free." He handed my credit card back to me without swiping it.

I was immediately suspicious because it wasn't like I had many friends around town. Half the town saw me as a sinner, the other half a liberal, and a good portion of those two groups overlapped. The "pay it forward" trend was popular in cities, but I hadn't seen it much in Branson Falls and wasn't sure it would catch on here. The community was pretty cliquish, and those cliques originated around church membership—and most members avoided anything that even hinted at the words "mocha" and "latte."

"Do you know who paid for it?"

"Can't say."

I eyed him. "Can't, or won't?"

He smiled back.

"I thought we were friends, Bran," I said, stepping aside to let someone behind me order.

He laughed and I moved to the end of the counter to wait for my salted caramel latte with lots of milk and sugar. When it came out, I grabbed the silver container labeled "chocolate powder" because I liked it with a hint of chocolate. What came out of the container was white, and definitely wasn't white chocolate.

I grabbed the cinnamon container as well and dumped some out. It was full of the same thing.

I lifted my cup to my lip to taste the drink and confirm my suspicions. I made a face as I sipped. Hilarious. Someone had put flour in the flavor containers. And it was now in my coffee. Probably some teen pulling a prank after they heard about the Sunday shopping flour attack. I took my drink back to the front and waited while they made me another one. This one, I paid for.

Chapter Three

I pulled my dark blue Jeep Grand Cherokee into the parking lot behind *The Branson Tribune* office. I walked in the back door and crossed the charcoal-colored high traffic carpet with various shades of green specks scattered throughout it. I passed the archive room where our volunteer archivist, Ella, spent most of her time, and walked through the open work area with tables for *Tribune* correspondents—and doughnuts. My desk was in the main room and when I got there, I found a box of my favorite chocolates, gift wrapped. I pulled the card from under the ribbon and read it.

"For the sexiest Amazon alive. I can't wait to see you, and that outfit, again. And take it off."

I recognized the handwriting and I hadn't seen him since the Halloween party either. It had been a week with hardly a word. I wasn't happy about that. I wasn't happy about a lot of things, to be honest, and needed to do some thinking about my future and what I wanted.

"How's your morning going," Spence asked from his office. It was the only office with walls in the entire building, and it was across from my desk.

I glanced up at him and away from the card, message, and thoughts of the muscles that had written it. "It started with a dead body, an unpleasant encounter with Jackie Wall, and me pouring flour into my coffee instead of chocolate."

"It sounds like you need more sleep."

I gave him a solid glare. "Maybe if people would stop finding bodies at the butt crack of dawn and my boss would stop calling me to cover the story, I could get it."

His lips lifted slightly, amused. "Did you get more non-floured coffee?"

"No, the barista at Beans and Things did for me, though. Right after I interviewed his co-worker about the graffiti they found on the side of the building this morning."

Spence's brows shot up. "I didn't hear about that."

"Probably because the entire Branson police force is at the Barret's old farm. Dead bodies trump vandalism."

"What happened with the body?" Spence asked, taking a sip from his black mug—full of coffee, not hot chocolate, because he was a sinner like me. "The chatter on the police scanner indicates they think it was probably a hiker, like we thought."

"That's what Bobby told me, but we won't know until they do the autopsy and some forensic testing. It could take anywhere from a couple of days, to eight weeks or more, to find out who the body belonged to."

"It sounded like it had been there a while."

"Bobby said it looked like it, too. They had a tent up shielding the area so I couldn't see the scene." I put my bag down and sank into my chair. It was only ten in the morning but it felt like it had been a whole day.

"How does the body discovery affect Grant and his development company? I assume this slows down their home build timeline?"

"Bobby told Grant and his partners they'd get out of his way as soon as possible. Probably twenty-four hours, but it could be up to a week. Until then, they can work on different areas of the property so they don't have to stop completely."

"I'm sure Grant was happy about that."

I gave Spence a curious look. "Do you know him?"

Spence lifted his shoulder a little. "Kind of. We've met before, back when he was initially trying to get the development approved."

"You'll never guess who he's dating."

Spence tilted his head slightly. "Who?"

"Jackie Wall."

Spence's eyebrows shot up. "I would not have made that guess. Jackie is a lot for someone as mild-mannered as Grant."

I agreed with his assessment. "She was there with him this morning and tried to give me some thinly veiled threats about how I should write the *Tribune* article so people don't perceive Grant poorly. She was also covered in flour, which tells me she was hit by the flour bandit while shopping on Sunday yesterday and she didn't go home afterward."

Spence made a tsking noise. "She's going to have to repent."

"Probably more than once. For multiple things." A tenet of the Mormon faith was taking responsibility for your wrongdoings by telling a Mormon man in a position of authority about your sins. Always a man. It had felt icky when I was a kid, and felt even more icky and manipulative as an adult now that I understood how easily people could be taken advantage of and hurt in those situations.

"How was your weekend?" I asked Spence. We traded off being on call for stories each weekend and the last one had been mine—hence the flour bandit coverage.

"Not too eventful."

I scowled. "Why is it that when it's your weekend to be on call, things are calm, but when it's my weekend, all hell breaks loose?"

He lifted his shoulders. "Just lucky, I guess."

Lucky, or something. "How are things with Xander?" Spence had been seeing a new boyfriend. He'd been keeping it on the down-low though because people in Branson Falls were not the most accepting of different sexual orientations, and most refused to even attempt to wrap their brains around pronouns. There was little respect for things Branson residents didn't view as familiar and comfortable.

Spence's lips spread into a wide smile and his eyes softened. He was twitterpated in every sense of the word. "They're amazing. We have a concert coming up in Salt Lake in a few weeks. It should be fun."

"I'm glad there's a place you feel you can be together and still be safe."

"Salt Lake and Park City. That's about it. Maybe we'll come out to people in Branson one day, but not anytime soon."

I didn't blame him. People would legit cancel their subscriptions to the *Tribune* if they knew Spence was gay and acting on it. That was the key phrase there, "acting on it." Different lifestyles were tolerated as long as LGBTQ+ people lived their lives without relationships, companionship, sex, intimacy, love, or all the things that made life worth living. Mormons could forgive Spence for not being part of their church, barely, but they wouldn't forgive him for being actively gay.

There were some progressive Mormons who wanted the church to change, but there were a lot of traditional Mormons who felt like the leadership had already adapted too much, lost its way, and needed to go back to its roots. Those roots were extremely problematic—and that was putting it nicely. The treatment of people who were different, like Spence, was a shitty situation all around, and I felt horrible for him and anyone the church viewed as a sinner instead of a human. "I hope things will change and be different here soon."

"Who knows," Spence said. "With all the new blood moving into Utah, maybe they will."

I had high hopes for that as well. In my dreams, Utah would become a state where compromise and seeing other perspectives was valued, instead of demanding everyone be the same. With the transplants from other cities and states migrating here, and their different opinions, that might actually happen. Though even if it did, the state legislature would gerrymander the voting lines until they made sure the state stayed exactly like they wanted it to, just like they'd gerrymandered the districts in Salt Lake to make sure all of Utah's congressional representatives stayed that way as well. But a girl could dream.

I spent the morning and most of the afternoon working on the flour bandit story, and writing a draft about the remains of the assumed hiker.

I also looked up Grant's company, GCR Development.

They'd been in business for twenty years, and had developed properties for home and commercial real estate all along the Wasatch Front. The Barret property acquisition was their first foray this far from Salt Lake City. Grant, Chris, and Ryan all had an equal partnership. They also owned pieces of other companies that helped with land development, like landscaping companies and home builders. They funded a lot of projects on their own, but also frequently got investors to help fund as well.

I updated all the *Tribune* socials with info from the articles I'd been working on, and then I got a text from my mom saying she had cookies, and asking if I wanted to stop by for a late lunch. I texted back and said I'd be there shortly. I'd dropped Gandalf off there on my way to work this morning, but I'd been so tired, I'd barely said a word. Puppy cuddles, a homemade lunch, and especially cookies sounded like exactly what I needed.

I pulled up to my mom and dad's house. Their giant witch display from Halloween was still up with three six-foot tall inflatable witches. My mom was the mom who fully dismantled the Christmas tree and all decorations the day after Christmas, so I was surprised her spooky decorations weren't already safely tucked away for the year.

"Your witches are still glowering at people," I informed her as I came in the door, just in case taking them down might have been an oversight. The house smelled like freshly baked heaven, and I took a moment to close my eyes and breathe in the scent of sugar comfort. Gandalf came bounding over to me, jumping all over my legs and licking my arms with little kisses. I sank to the floor to give him pets and snuggles, then threw a ball for him. He chased after it and brought it back.

My mom's eyes screwed up, and her lips pursed into an expression I'd often seen as a kid. The expression could go one of two ways: exasperation that turned to humor, or exasperation that made the person witnessing it feel inclined to run for their life. I wasn't sure which way this was headed. "Oh, I *know* my witches are up! And they're going to stay up!"

It was the "run for your life" one.

"Why?" I asked slowly, my brows pinching together. I threw the ball for Gandalf again.

"Because my neighbor is absolutely ridiculous and complained to the city!" She huffed and mumbled some things that sounded like pseudo-swears as she motioned for me to come into the kitchen. I walked by the counter and grabbed one of the chocolate chip cookies crammed full of three different types of chocolate. It tasted like joy.

She was standing at the stove, making lunch. I grabbed a glass of milk and leaned against her granite countertop as I took a drink. "Someone complained about the witches?"

"Yes!" she said with a stomp of her foot. She flipped my sandwich over to finish toasting. "That Gladys Simpson is a rabble rouser and she's been trying to turn the whole neighborhood, and the Ward, against me!" My parents were still technically members of the church, but they weren't active, and didn't really believe it. I thought they stayed because it was just easier in a place like Branson Falls. My mom continued her tirade, "And *then* Gladys called the city! *The city*! She said my decorations are *Satanic*! Can you believe that utter nonsense?"

Actually, I could. Mormon Church boundaries were divided into "Wards." People within a specific address boundary went to different Wards. I'd covered a story earlier in the fall with some local Wards arguing that Halloween shouldn't be allowed because it was a Satanic holiday. None of them seemed to realize it was originally a Pagan holiday, and Paganism was an actual religion that was far older than Christianity—and not Satanic. And that if they weren't celebrating Halloween, they also shouldn't be celebrating Christmas—another holiday that was co-opted from Pagans.

One problem with Utah is that people are so surrounded by other people who believe like they do, that they don't take the time to learn history—even their own—or find out about other belief systems. Being a thorn in their side who was different from them but still a good person was one of the reasons I'd agreed to move back to town—that and my ex cheated on me, but it was mostly the thorn in their side part. I'd felt a deep obligation to show Branson residents that not everyone is one thing, and people can have different beliefs. It seemed like people in town didn't really appreciate my efforts though, especially if they were complaining about Halloween decorations still being up when Halloween had just happened.

I took my drink to the table and sat in one of the chairs. "What did the city say?"

My mom gave a slow, conniving smile as she put a sandwich down in front of me. "They said there's nothing in the city ordinances that prevents me from having my witches on display. So now I'm going to leave them up all the time and decorate them for different seasons."

Of course she was. My mom was nothing if not persistent, and she liked to make a point, even if it was done passive aggressively. "That will cause some controversy," I said, taking a gooey cheesy bite.

"Good! I hope it does! I have nothing to worry about. The police officers said I didn't do anything wrong."

I tipped my sandwich half at her and grinned. "The same police officers you bribe with treats?"

"Don't be silly," she said, adjusting the towel that was always on her shoulder. "I don't *bribe* them. I bring them goodies to thank them for all their hard work."

My mom also excelled at justification. I tilted my head and gave her a look because it was a bribe and we both knew it, but I didn't have the energy to argue.

"Where's Gandalf?" I asked, wondering where he'd run off to after I'd thrown the ball the second time.

My mom glanced out the window over the kitchen sink that faced their sprawling back yard. It was carpeted with grass that still managed to be emerald green even as the seasons were changing, and the leaves on the trees and shrubs were vibrant shades of red, yellow, and orange. "He's playing in the back yard." The yard was fenced and my parents had bought him a little obstacle course. I didn't think he cared about the course as much as he cared about having wide open spaces and freshly cut grass to run around on and stain his little paws green.

She gave me another plate complete with a sandwich, chips, and a fresh cookie. "Why don't you take this out to Hawke."

I froze with my own sandwich halfway to my lips. "Hawke is here?"

I hadn't seen him since the night of the Halloween party. I

didn't even know he was back in town. And I definitely hadn't seen his car in the driveway.

My mom nodded like it was the most normal thing in the world for Hawke to be hanging out at their house. "Your dad needed a part for his Mustang and Hawke had it. He brought it over, helped your dad with some stuff for the car, and he's been playing with Gandalf since. I told him I'd make him lunch."

I stared at her. "A little warning that he was here would have been nice."

She looked at me like I'd lost my mind. "He's here a lot. Am I supposed to call you every time he comes over?"

I stared back. "Yes!"

"You don't call me when he comes to your house."

"Because you're not in a maybe-relationship with him."

She raised an eyebrow. "So now you're in a relationship?"

"I said *maybe*!" I paused. "And no. Not yet. Maybe not ever. I'm still figuring things out."

She raised the other brow.

"I don't know what it is," I said, waving off the theories I knew were already going through her head, and finishing the last of my sandwich. "We haven't defined it and given how my last relationship went, I'm not sure if I'm ready to."

"I heard that you were defining *something* at the Halloween party. But I heard you were *defining* it with multiple men."

I pursed my lips. "I haven't defined anything, with anyone. Who did you hear that from anyway?"

She put her palms down on the counter. "Kate, you of all people should know better than to try and keep anything secret in this town. You were at a public Halloween party, and you were dressed as an Amazon superhero showing a lot of shoulder, cleavage, and legs. That kind of outfit was bound to cause tongues to wag, even at a costumed event. You were very recognizable. However, there's quite a bit of debate about the two men you were with, and who was who."

I groaned, closed my eyes, and felt like if I'd been a dragon, steam would have been shooting out my nose. We'd been in public, and we hadn't cared who was watching. But I should have known plenty of other people would. "I haven't heard any rumors."

"Because you aren't friends with the right people."

"Or maybe I am, and you're the one who's not friends with the right people if they're talking about your daughter behind her back."

She gave an offended little snort. "Are you kidding me? I'm basically your own personal spy! I keep you informed!"

"Apparently not, since the Halloween party happened more than a week ago and this is the first I'm hearing about these rumors."

I heard Gandalf giving happy little play barks in the yard. "And it's also the first I'm hearing about Hawke being here and spending so much time at my parents' house!"

I could tell she wanted to roll her eyes, but refrained. That was fair since I often wanted to roll mine and scream at the same time when I was around her. "I'll take Hawke his food."

I grabbed the plate and checked my reflection in the window as I opened the door to the patio. Gandalf jumped up from playing tug-of-war with Hawke and ran over to me, bringing me his ball. Hawke stood from where he'd been crouched on the ground, his long sleeve black t-shirt was painted to his substantial shoulders and wide chest. He was wearing grey cargo pants that did nothing to hide his massive thighs, and his feet were protected by heavy black boots. I watched Hawke as his eyes raked over me slowly, starting at my face, traveling down to my chest, then waist, and lower where his gaze held before moving back up. I could practically see the sins he was thinking about going through his head. I wasn't opposed to any of them.

"I didn't know you were here, Kitty Kate," Hawke said, walking toward me.

"I didn't know you were here, either, *Ryker*," I answered back, using his first name since he was in a little bit of trouble. I threw the ball Gandalf had dropped at my feet.

Hawke arched one brow at the use of his first name and waited for me to keep talking because he wasn't going to respond and potentially implicate himself.

"My mom asked me to bring you lunch." I put his plate down on the cedar patio table with matching chairs and got a whiff of his scent—salt, sand, and the beach. It almost distracted me from my annoyance. Almost. "I wasn't aware you regularly dined at Café Saxee."

He gave me a look. "It's a nice place, but I'm much fonder of dining off their daughter."

Heat immediately started rising in my cheeks. "Number one, that's never even happened—"

"—Yet," he cut in.

I took a steadying breath and in quiet voice continued, "Two, you can't say that stuff. My dad is, like, right here... somewhere." I looked around, wondering where exactly he was, and if he really had overheard Hawke's comment.

Hawke grinned. "I'm surprisingly unconcerned."

I pointed at him. "You're lucky you're his Mustang parts dealer."

Hawke inclined his head. "Your mom is the reason I stay fed." He washed his hands off in the outdoor sink before sitting at the table and taking a bite of his food.

"I didn't realize she was your personal chef."

His lips tipped up. "I stop by every now and then. She texts me sometimes."

I wondered what exactly they were talking about in those texts. "I got your chocolates," I told him. "Thank you."

He took a drink and let his tongue slide slowly over his lips. "I thought something sweet was fitting since the last time we were together, I was tasting something sweet. You."

My gaze darted around the yard for spies of any kind, including the Lady and animal variety, before I whisper-hissed, "You can't say those things here, Hawke!"

His eyes sparkled, amused. "Why not? We were in the middle of the parking lot where anyone could watch us. It's not like we were being covert." He'd once told me that when the sex is good, you don't care if people are watching. I'd disagreed at the time, but then he'd started to prove his point.

I waved to the house, trees, and the whole universe. "Parents! House!"

He pulled his bottom lip back with his teeth. "Do you think they don't know you're an adult with a sex life?"

I gaped at him. "I think I don't want them thinking about my sex life at all! And I don't want to think about theirs! It's a mutual agreement!"

He chuckled.

"Also," I said, continuing my whisper, "We haven't had s-e-x."

He grinned again at my spelling. "I'm pretty sure your

parents know how to spell. And since you're alive, they understand the mechanics of the word."

I glared at him.

"We've had almost sex," he pointed out, lifting a chip in his hand like the fried potato was helping him to make his point. And he still wasn't lowering his voice. "Many times."

"Almost sex isn't sex."

"You're right. We should do something about that and have sex. The mind-blowing kind."

I was about to scream. "You have to stop saying that word! My parents could come out at any minute!"

"That would be a shame because I have plans for you and this patio table." He ran his hand slowly over the finish and I knew I'd never be able to look at it the same way again. My parents were going to have to get a whole new table.

I had to change the subject STAT. I folded my arms across my chest. "Where have you been? Your departure from the Halloween party was abrupt."

He pressed his lips together. "A work situation came up."

Yeah, it had. In the middle of something that was headed way past almost-sex and rocketing to mind-blowing, with me braced against the side of his '67 Shelby Mustang, my corset askew and threatening boob release, and his hand way up my very short Amazon superhero skirt.

"You said that when you left me hot and bothered."

He pressed his lips together like he was trying to decide what to say next and landed on nothing.

I have no problem with confrontation, so I pressed on. "And you've been gone ever since?" It was a question because I wasn't sure when he'd arrived home. "I didn't even know you were in Branson."

"I just got in," he said. "Your dad texted me while I was away, so I brought the part on my way back into town."

My mouth fell open. "You texted my *dad* but not me?"

He tilted his head and gave me a look like I was overreacting.

I was not.

Hawke sighed. "I got his text and picked up the part on my way back into town, but I didn't text your dad back either. It wasn't safe."

Hawke had a dangerous job that he'd purposely left rather undefined, but I was pretty sure killing people wasn't off the list of his business offerings. He was former military, and seemed to be a highly sought after mercenary who got paid well for his skills, though I'd never been able to confirm that with my own investigations, or even by asking Hawke directly. I knew he helped a lot of people, but like most things, how people viewed his help likely depended on what side of his skills disbursement they were on. He specialized in grey areas, and had an exceptional understanding of selective ethics.

"I'm not sure that makes me feel any better." The safe part, or the fact that he couldn't text because of it. "Did it have something to do with the job you were working on a few weeks ago with the auction?"

He pressed his lips together before answering. "That particular issue is ongoing."

"But not something you can talk about?" I said to clarify. "And whatever call you took at the Halloween party kept you from contacting me for over a week?"

I could see his jaw pulsing like he was trying to figure out how to respond. He settled on, "My work is unpredictable and sometimes dangerous. There are things I can't talk about."

I ran my tongue over my lips in thought. "That makes things difficult. For a lot of reasons."

He caught my eyes and held them. "My job matters. A lot. So do you."

I took a breath and held his gaze. "Which matters more?" I asked. It was a question I'd been wondering for a while.

He was saved from answering that question by my dad's voice, "There's the man who rescued my restoration work this morning." My dad smiled as he shut the door at the back of the garage. It was a good thing we hadn't been utilizing the patio table like Hawke suggested. Hawke might not find himself with an open-door invitation anymore if we had.

"What part were you missing?" I asked as my dad moved a hose in the yard to water some plants. Gandalf followed him from plant to plant, trying to attack the water like it was a toy.

"A piece for some welding I needed to do. I wanted sheet metal from another '66 Mustang, not reproduction metal. It's hard to find, but Hawke knew someone."

I gave Hawke a speculative look. "Hawke seems to know everyone, and have connections everywhere."

"Guilty," he said, winking at me. He finished his food and took his plate and glass inside.

I followed him.

"I have to get back to the office, but thanks for lunch," I said to my mom.

"Yes, thank you for the sandwich, Sophie. It was delicious, and I'll have to spend extra time in the gym tonight to make up for the cookies."

I almost snorted, but caught myself. I could see the outline of Hawke's many abs through his shirt and it was clear his metabolism could handle as many freaking cookies as he wanted.

My mom smiled at the compliment as she handed each of us a plate of cookies. "You're both very welcome."

I grabbed a cookie off the counter for the road.

"I'll walk you out," Hawke said. "Thanks for the food, Sophie." He poked his head out the back door, "Thanks for the car talk, Damon. Let me know if you need anything else."

My dad raised the hand not watering plants in the air in acknowledgment and said, "Thanks, Hawke!"

It was so weird to hear Hawke in my childhood home, talking to my parents like they were friends. Because they were. And Hawke was…something of mine. I wasn't sure what, and wasn't sure what I wanted.

Hawke walked me to my Jeep and I realized I hadn't noticed his vehicle when I pulled up because it was parked on the side of the house. He had his matte black motorcycle that looked like hell in the best way, and conjured up all kinds of leather and motorcycle gang fantasies.

Hawke noticed my attention. "Want to take a ride?" he asked, not even trying to hide the insinuation.

I wanted nothing more than that, but I was working, and I was also still salty about being abandoned in the parking lot during the Halloween party. "Last time I was made promises like that, I was left disappointed."

Hawke prowled toward me until he was inches away. "I can make that up to you. More than once."

My heart started a rapid acceleration that had nothing to do with all the coffee I'd consumed today. "I can't at the moment. It's the middle of the work day."

"What about tonight? I could pick you up and take you to my house." His voice dropped down even lower than usual, "I have a large patio table."

I licked my lips and his eyes followed.

I had no idea what my plans for the night were, but I wasn't opposed to including Hawke in them. Especially when he looked like wicked incarnate. I opened my mouth to answer when "Forever in Blue Jeans" started playing from my pants. Which wasn't exactly representative of my current mood since kicking my blue jeans right off was a top priority. "Hi, Spence," I said, my voice wistful as I thought about Hawke, his very private, well-protected, Lady-proof house, and his patio table.

"More remains were found on the Barret farm."

My jaw dropped. "You've got to be kidding me?"

"Nope," Spence said. "The excavator was working on another area while police were analyzing the scene from this morning. The excavator found more bones."

One body could easily be excused as a hiking accident, but two bodies on the same property was a whole different story.

"I'll go check it out," I said, ending the call.

I turned to Hawke. "I guess it's my phone and my job interrupting us this time. I have to go."

"Did I hear Spence say there were more remains found?" Hawke asked.

I nodded. "GCR Development bought some property and they're starting to excavate the area to build homes. The remains of a body were found this morning, but police thought it was a lost hiker. Now it seems there's another body on the same property."

"The old Barret farm?" Hawke asked. "I heard about the

remains this morning, but didn't have a chance to stop by the scene."

Of course he already knew about it, despite the fact that he hadn't even been in town. Hawke knew everything, and probably had his team of fellow maybe-murderers monitoring the police scanner and informing him of anything they thought he needed to know.

"Yes," I answered.

"I'll follow you there."

I lifted a shoulder, wondering what Hawke's interest in this case was. "Okay," I said. I got in my Jeep as Hawke pulled his bike out and followed me to what now seemed to be a growing crime scene.

Chapter Four

When I arrived at the Barret property, there were far more police officers on scene than there had been this morning. Which was odd since the entire Branson Falls police force had been on hand for the first discovery of human remains. They must have called for backup when it looked like a second body was found. I drove by the white tent that had been erected earlier, and kept going to where the majority of cars were parked, and most people now stood. I got out of my Jeep and went over to the crowd.

Bobby was standing on the north end of the development this time, and was pointing at an area of disturbed dirt. He was talking to another officer I didn't recognize.

"Long time no see," I said, walking up to Bobby.

He put his hand to his temple like he had a headache. I had that effect on him sometimes, but this time, I didn't think it was just me. Bobby finished giving instructions to the other officer.

"Have you even left here today?" I asked, as the other officer walked away.

"No. I haven't had breakfast, lunch, or coff—hot chocolate, and dinner looks unlikely too, so you can imagine my mood."

I winced at that. "I'm sorry. I would be stabby and probably adding to the body count if I were you." Hangry is a real thing, and that's without the added stress of trying to uncover human bones and figure out who they belonged to.

"You ain't kiddin'," Bobby said.

A group of four people walked by us and I overheard them talking about the remains.

"There are a lot of official looking people here," I said to Bobby. Some were dressed in vests, others had coats on.

"We needed additional support so we called in some officers from Rice to help. We'll see what happens next, and if we need to expand and ask for more assistance."

"What would make you need additional assistance?" I asked.

"Lotsa things. But if it looks like the deaths are suspicious, that'll require other agencies."

That made sense. "It's definitely odd to have two bodies on the same property. What does your gut tell you?"

He looked at me like there were a lot of things he wanted to say and couldn't. "That it's odd to have two bodies found on the same property."

Good to know we were in agreement. "The land was in the Barret family for a long time, wasn't it?" I asked.

Bobby nodded. "We're lookin' into that. It's been in their family for decades. The matriarch, Georgia Barret, is older now, and in assisted living. With property values goin' wild, the family made the decision to sell. The developer had connections so he was able to get approval on the project fast."

"Have you talked to the family? They have to know something about the history of the land. Could this have been a family cemetery, or an old Mormon pioneer graveyard?"

Bobby kicked at a rock on the ground. "We haven't talked to 'em yet. Been a little busy diggin' up bones. But the Barret family is on our list as soon as I can get away." Bobby said. "We don't know what happened here, but it looks like more than a couple of lost hikers, and the bodies aren't in plots like a graveyard. Somebody, somewhere, knows somethin'."

"What's the next step? I asked.

"We'll bring in cadaver dogs," Bobby said. "See if there's more bodies on the property. This crime scene has expanded and we need to know if there are other unmarked graves."

"I didn't realize cadaver dogs were so effective," I said, noticing Hawke wandering around the second pile of dirt, talking to people he clearly had an acquaintance with. When I said Hawke knew everyone, I wasn't kidding. The freaking governor had hired him for a personal situation six months ago, and that investigation had been the reason Hawke and I met. I had a feeling Hawke could probably get an audience with the President of a country if he wanted to.

Bobby followed my gaze and coughed to get my attention. He gave me a knowing look before explaining the dogs in more detail. "The dogs are amazing. They can find a body that's years old."

I stared at Bobby. "Seriously?" I asked. "I had no clue that was possible."

"Yep. They're highly trained, and the level of decomposition doesn't really matter. There are dogs for all kinds of things. Bomb sniffin' dogs, drug dogs, bed bug findin' dogs."

"Bed bugs?"

"Yep."

I was going to have to do a feature story on service dogs because I was fascinated by Bobby's info. So fascinated in fact, that I didn't even notice Drake until he started walking toward me with his signature swagger, looking very professional in black pressed slacks, a long sleeve button-down pale-yellow shirt, and a dark blue tie that brought out the cobalt in his eyes. His midnight-colored hair looked ruffled from the breeze, and he was wearing a black, unbuttoned jacket that matched his slacks. He was dressed like he'd come from church, but it was a weekday. While Drake looked very dapper and elegant in his expensive suit, I'd seen him without the jacket, tie, and shirt, and preferred the raw, muscle-filled, half-naked version.

Given his outfit, I was certain he was here in a professional capacity.

He flashed me his full smile that was imbedded with all his charm. Not the same smile he gave to kids and twitterpated women when he was campaigning. A real smile that made me feel like I mattered.

An officer came over to grab Bobby and he stepped away as Drake arrived.

"Hey, Katie," Drake said, standing close enough that I could clearly smell his clean fresh scent that always reminded me of the mountains in summer. His voice was a deep pitch that made my sacral chakra dance.

"Hi," I said with a smile, trying not to give my feelings away on my face. I hadn't seen him since the Halloween party either, and some things had been left unresolved.

"Busy morning," he pointed out.

"Busy few days," I answered.

"And nights," he added.

My cheeks flushed and I was glad Bobby had been pulled away to talk to another officer.

"What are you doing here?" It was a strange place for him to be unless he was representing someone, and I wanted to know who that was.

He put his hands in his pockets and glanced at the team of people under the newest white tent. "I know the owners of the development. Grant Kimball called me this morning when the first body was found, and called me again when more bones were recovered."

Dylan Drake wasn't only a politician and Branson Falls' representative for the Utah State House of Representatives. He was also a lawyer, and a very good one at that. Some women might find that attractive, and as a package, I couldn't deny Drake's appeal, but I'd known too many politicians, lawyers, and men for that hypnotism. It made me immediately wary because his schooling had taught him how to argue, his politics taught him how to manipulate, and his religion taught him how to use both skills to sell belief. Because of that, I wasn't sure who exactly Drake was. Drake had spent a significant amount of time trying to convince me he wasn't like everyone said and the rumors about his own love life weren't true. He'd done a pretty good job of proving himself, but all things considered, it made me wonder if I would ever truly be able to take him at face value and trust him. And given my relationship history, trust mattered a lot.

Drake had networks all over the state, so it was no wonder that he knew the developer and they wanted someone with legal standing here on-site to represent them. The fact that

Drake was from the area and had connections would have made him even more appealing to retain.

Grant Kimball, the property developer, walked up with his partner, Chris. Grant's face was lined with worry and he looked like he hadn't slept in a week. I could relate. This day had started way too early. "Thanks for coming," Grant said to Drake.

"Glad to help," Drake replied. He gestured toward me. "You know Kate Saxee, editor of *The Branson Tribune?*"

Grant nodded. "We met this morning."

"I'm sorry this is happening," I said. "Have you gotten any additional information on the bodies?"

"No," Grant answered. "They'll rush the tests to try and figure out what caused the deaths, and then we'll go from there."

"How long will this set you back?" I asked.

"No clue," Grant said, shaking his head.

"We hope it won't be long," Chris answered.

"The police don't like to hold up commerce, but it really depends on what they find," Drake added. "We'll do our best to get you back to work as soon as possible." His tone was reassuring.

Grant's other partner who I'd seen this morning, Ryan, came over. "We need to take this call."

Grant nodded and glanced at Chris, whose mouth was set in a tight line. They both looked like the call was the last one they wanted to take. "Excuse us, Drake and Kate."

We both nodded and watched them walk off.

Hawke looked over from where he was standing with some of the officers working the scene and caught my eye. I watched as his gaze tracked from me, to Drake. Then Hawke started moving our way.

"What are the chances they'll actually get back to work as soon as possible?" I asked Drake, watching Hawke stride closer.

Drake lifted a shoulder. "It depends on what the police find."

"I've heard that a lot today."

"Two bodies aren't good," Hawke said, walking up. "The officers I talked to suspect foul play, and it's a good assumption, which means they'll have to bring in teams from Salt Lake."

"Good to know," Drake said, flashing a smile. "I'll tell my clients."

"Drake," Hawke said looking him in the eye before his gaze deliberately shifted to me and tracked over my body with a possessive heat. It was how he'd looked at me at my parents' house, and how he looked at me every time he saw me really, and it made me feel like I was on fire in the best way. He could have done something like slide his arm around me in an obvious gesture to make Drake jealous, but he didn't even need to. It was like his intentions were written across his expression in testosterone ink, and any man who wanted to come close was immediately warned via pheromones. He turned his attention back to Drake. "I can't imagine your clients don't already know."

Judging by Drake's pinched expression, he got Hawke's messaging about me loud and clear. "Hawke," he said, his tone tight. "You think my clients had something to do with this?"

Hawke gave him a very neutral look and because I knew

Hawke, I felt that look spoke volumes. "I have no idea. That's why the investigators are investigating."

Drake shot him a glare like he hoped Hawke would wither and die. "My clients have investors and a lot of money in this project. They wouldn't have bought the land if they'd known there were bodies on the property."

Hawke folded his arms across his chest and shifted his stance so his legs were shoulder width apart. "I find people are capable of making a lot of poor decisions," Hawke answered. "Especially when the profit margins are favorable."

Drake gave Hawke a smile that wasn't really a smile and moved closer to me, reaching over to touch the gold bracelet I'd put on before I left this morning, and letting his large hand linger on my wrist. The fact that I'd managed accessories that early was a shock even to me. "This looks like the one you were wearing at the Halloween party."

I saw a muscle in Hawke's jaw pulse at that information. I hadn't told Hawke that I'd gone back to the party after he'd abandoned me in the parking lot. Hawke had needed to leave for work, but I'd seen no reason to go home and wallow in self-pity. It's not like Hawke and I were exclusive. We hadn't had anything close to that kind of discussion. He could be off banging half the women in the country, or multiple countries, and I wouldn't know it, or be able to expect any sort of loyalty because that wasn't our arrangement…at the moment.

Annie had invited me to the Halloween party and I'd planned to stay, so I did. Drake had stayed as well. In fact, I realized in a sudden lightbulb moment, Drake always stayed. That was one thing about him—he was consistent and could be counted on. So could Hawke, provided he was in the same state, or country, as I was. And really, I was perfectly fine on my own and didn't need to count on either one of them. But if I was going to be in a relationship, I wanted a partner one hundred percent of the time, not sixty percent of it.

I pulled my wrist back because it felt weird to have Drake touching me in front of Hawke. "The one I was wearing at the Halloween Party was part of a costume. This is a bracelet, not a bullet deflector."

Hawke's expression turned contemplative. "I didn't think the bullet deflector had survived the side of my car. Didn't it fall off with the other parts of your costume?" He was deliberately trying to stake his claim in front of Drake, and that also felt weird.

I tilted my head and let the challenge show in my eyes. "I picked it up after you left me in the parking lot. Before I went back inside to continue...socializing."

Hawke licked his lips and gave a slow smile like I'd challenged him and he was accepting it. "Next time, I'll have to be more thorough, Kitty Kate."

"Next time, you'll have to stick around," I pointed out.

"You left her in the parking lot?" Drake's jaw went slack and he looked absolutely appalled. "Nothing would have been able to keep me away from Katie."

Hawke's attention shot to Drake. "Some of us have actual jobs where people's lives depend on us. You wouldn't know anything about that though, so I don't expect you to understand."

"I'm on a job right now," Drake said, inclining his head toward the police and gesturing with his hand at the tents covering the human remains. "And I still make time for Katie."

Hawke's smile turned sharp. "I've heard you have plenty of time for lots of women, and you're personally trying to resurrect the doctrine of polygamy...the one on earth, not the afterlife, since you already believe polygamy will definitely exist once you're dead. So, are you trying to make Kate your first wife here in the mortal existence? Or are you planning to add her to your celestial harem of Goddesses when you die, become a God, and get your own planet?"

A vein near Drake's temple looked like it might legitimately explode.

Personally, I was surprised at Hawke's grasp of LDS doctrine considering he wasn't a member of the faith. A lot of practicing Mormons didn't even know about afterlife polygamy, or the whole becoming a God of your own planet bit. It was Hawke though, so I wouldn't be shocked if he knew the actual location of Kolob and the throne of God. He'd probably sat on it.

Drake opened his mouth to say something cutting back. This was going to keep escalating between them, and would not end well so I was going to end it. "How long are you two going to go on like this?" I asked, interrupting and waving my hand between them. "Neither one of you strike me as the type of man who would be okay with the woman they're interested in dating other people. But I'm going to be honest. The last man I dated was a shitty human. I'm more than hesitant to get into another relationship, and I'm definitely not taking that dive until I know a lot about the person I'm jumping in with. You could both have your pick of women, so if you're expecting me to make a decision today, or tomorrow, or next week, it's not happening. I need time."

I breathed out and felt immediately lighter. I hadn't been planning on having this conversation today, but it was a discussion that was needed. I'd been trying to figure out my feelings and felt guilty for not making a choice, but now I had—I chose to take time, and take care of myself. It felt good to set boundaries because I hadn't done that early enough in my last relationship.

But truly, I was dumbfounded by Drake and Hawke's interest. They were two of the most eligible bachelors in the state. Like a lot of women, I had my fair share of confidence issues, and I wasn't sure why these two alphas were continuing to fight for me when they could date anyone. Part of me felt like it was about more than me, and if that was the case, I didn't like it. I wasn't okay with being a pawn in whatever game they were trying to play. This wasn't the Serengeti, and they weren't lions competing for dominance.

"We just met six months ago, Kitty Kate," Hawke answered, rocking back on his heels, unconcerned. "I'm not in a rush."

It was true. I'd only moved back to Branson Falls six months ago. But six months was practically a millennium in Utah time. Mormons often married within one to three months of meeting each other…mostly so they could have sex without committing the sin next to murder—sex outside of marriage. That's probably why Hawke wasn't concerned about timelines. He knew Drake likely wouldn't have sex with me before marriage. But I wasn't so sure about that.

"I met her decades ago," Drake said in response to Hawke. I frowned at that because he'd just made me feel exceedingly old. "And I've known her almost my whole life," Drake continued.

I slitted my eyes. "That's a stretch."

He ignored me and kept talking at Hawke, "I've been

waiting years for this relationship, but I'll keep waiting, because she's worth it."

Hawke walked closer to Drake and gave him a smile that wasn't a smile at all, it was an absolute threat. "On the point of Kate being worth waiting for, we can agree. And to be very clear, I have no problem waiting either." He turned to me. "I'll see you tonight, Kitty Kate?" Hawke asked, starting to walk backwards, away from us both.

That was awkward. Drake was right there. And that was exactly the reason Hawke had asked it. I didn't like that. And didn't like being played by either one of them. "I'll text you," I answered. Hawke gave me a grin full of so much insinuation that I heard a woman ten feet away from me gasp, and then he turned and walked back to the police officers he'd been talking to earlier.

Drake looked like he was about to say something that I was certain wouldn't be complimentary, when Grant called his name. Drake took a deep breath to prevent his head from exploding. "I have to go," Drake said, his eyes still tracking Hawke in a calculating way before they settled on me. "But you and I aren't finished."

I'd heard that before, too.

Drake walked away and I was able to get back to my actual job. I took my phone out and jotted down some notes in my notepad app, then took some photos before going back to my car. I grabbed what I needed and went back to Bobby. I handed him the plate of cookies that I'd taken from my mom and dad's house. "You need these more than I do."

His eyes sparkled with the first bit of life I'd seen today. "Are they your mom's cookies?"

I nodded.

"If it wouldn't land me in The Ladies crossfire and get me a post in their Facebook group about the two of us doin' unseemly things, I'd hug you right now."

"I'll take that as a 'thank you.' I hope you get home sometime tonight, Bobby."

"Me too."

By the time I finished at the potential crime scene, it was after dinner. I ordered some cheesy breadsticks with extra cheese from Sticks and Pie, and picked them up on my way home after I retrieved Gandalf from my parents' house…and got more cookies. I was happy to share my treats with Bobby, but wasn't about to go home without some of my own.

My phone started playing the seductive notes of "Play Me," Hawke's ringtone.

"Hey," I answered.

Hawke responded with a frustrated sigh. "This is not the call I want to be making, especially given how we left things this afternoon, but I'm going to be here helping police for the rest of the night."

Of course he was. "So, you're not picking me up?"

He paused. "Not tonight, but soon. And I'll carry you right to the patio table."

"Promises, promises," I said.

"Just you wait," he answered, his voice deep and rugged.

"Good luck. I'll talk to you sometime, I guess." Between my job and Hawke's job, our schedules might prevent a potential relationship someday all on their own.

"Sometime soon," he said and hung up.

I pulled a breadstick out of the box and put it on my plate when my phone lit up with a call from Ella, our *Branson Tribune* volunteer archivist, and vice empress of shenanigans—my mom was the empress. "Holy heavens!" She exclaimed as soon as I answered the phone. She didn't even say hello. "The whole town's in an uproar and everyone's talkin'! We've got bodies everywhere!"

"Hi to you, too, Ella."

"Bodies! Everywhere!" she repeated.

"I mean, "bodies everywhere" seems like a stretch," I said, biting into my food. I closed my eyes and took a second to enjoy the cheesy goodness. "There were two bodies, on the same piece of property. Bobby's supposed to get me more information as soon as he can."

"You better tell me right away once he calls!" Ella said. If I'd been there with her in person, her amber colored eyes would have been the size of saucers. "What if it's a serial killer, Kate?"

I pushed my brows together. "That also seems like a stretch. This is Branson Falls, Ella. It's rural Utah. We don't have serial killers."

"Not so much anymore," Ella pointed out. "But you never know. That notorious serial killer, Jeff Zundy, lived in Utah for a while. And he had lots more victims than they know about."

I'd forgotten about that, but Jeff Zundy living here was Utah state folklore. There are many unique things about Utah, but one of them is that almost everyone has a story about a time that the Mormon Holy Ghost, part of the LDS Trinity of God, Jesus, and the Holy Ghost—all separate beings—prompted them not to do something, and it saved their life or prevented something horrible from happening…and I'd heard many of those stories involving Jeff Zundy. He'd lived in Salt Lake City and attended college there as far as I knew, but I supposed he could have traveled Branson's way at one point or another. "I guess we'll see. My dinner's getting cold so I'll talk to you at the *Tribune* tomorrow."

Her voice took on a determined tone. "I'm goin' to bed with a weapon."

I paused with another piece of breadstick half-way to my mouth. "I don't know if that's wise."

"I ain't gettin' murdered in my sleep and dropped in a shallow grave only to be found in forty years when someone needs to build a mansion there, Kate. I have a stun gun and I know how to use it."

I sighed. The only consolation in her statement was that she was going to sleep with a Taser instead of an actual gun. "Night, Ella."

"Night, Kate."

Ella was right. By the time I finished my breadsticks, the Branson Falls town Facebook page was already full of theories about the two bodies.

Chapter Five

I was at my desk the next morning, drinking hot, white chocolate flavored coffee from my thermos, and working on an article about the bodies at the Barret property. My phone rang and the caller ID gave me Bobby's name. I answered and Bobby went straight to business. I grabbed the pad and pen on my desk to take notes. "The first body we found yesterday mornin' was a male. We're still waitin' to see if we can identify him but so far, we think the guy was in his sixties or seventies."

"That's a quick turnaround on the gender and age," I pointed out. Especially since he'd said it could take anywhere from a couple of days to eight weeks or more.

"We have a lotta people workin' on this, and they're gettin' us the information as fast as possible."

"How do you know the first body was male?"

"You can tell some things by the size of bones."

There was a dirty joke in there begging to be stated, but somehow, I managed to refrain.

"How do you know his age?"

"Somethin' that was found with the body."

"Something like a driver's license?"

"No, and I can't tell ya more right now."

I sighed. "You know I'm not a patient person, Bobby."

Bobby continued, pretending I hadn't said anything, "Like I said, it will take time to get full identification, but I wanted to let you know the gender on the first body, and that we're workin' as fast as possible."

In other words, he wanted me to report that information in the *Tribune*. I slitted my eyes at the phone like Bobby could see me. "It's not normal for you to give me more information than you have to, especially when you don't have all the information yet." I'd covered a lot of crimes and the scenes usually took time to process. Authorities would hold back information until they knew as much as possible, and then they'd be selective about what they revealed. And they would want to be thorough.

"We're holdin' up a whole property development right now. We can't release the scene until we know what we're dealin' with. Things are bein' escalated so we can get the contractors back to work."

That made sense, and I had a suspicion that Drake and his legal maneuverings were helping to put pressure on the police for his client, GCR Development.

"Do you still think the first body belonged to a hiker?"

"Don't know," Bobby said. "Hopefully we'll get more details soon."

"What about the second body? Do you know anything about it yet?"

There was a long pause. "We're still waitin' on that info, too."

The pause made me pause. "You found the two bodies within twelve hours of each other. How do you know information about one, but not the other?"

I could hear crickets, but not Bobby's answer, because he wasn't answering. I knew him well enough to know he was holding something back and I didn't try to hide my suspicion. "What aren't you telling me, Bobby?"

He made a huffing noise like I'd exasperated him—it was a noise I heard often. "Things I can't tell ya! Yet. I'll call about it as soon as I can."

If Bobby wasn't telling me something, there was a good reason and I wouldn't press harder—right now. Patience wasn't one of my core strengths, but I would persevere. "Did you finally get some food last night?" I asked.

Bobby sighed. "Yeah, thanks for the cookies by the way. They were just what I needed to make it through until Hawke sent a food truck to feed us all."

"He commandeered a food truck?" The surprise was evident in my tone. "Where did he find one?" Branson Falls had a handful of restaurants, but none were on wheels.

"Don't know. Salt Lake City, maybe? He must've called in a favor. He knew it would be a long night, and he was out there too."

"That was nice of him," I said, and meant it.

"Hawke knows what it's like to be stuck somewhere, tired and hungry."

My ears perked up at that tidbit. "How do you know that?"

"You hear things."

Even more intriguing. "What else have you heard?"

Bobby snorted. "Do you know who your boyfriend is, Kate? 'Cause I ain't gonna start talkin' about him and piss him off. I don't got a death wish."

I tapped my fingers on my desk in an attempt to channel my frustration. "I'm trying to find out who he is! That's why I asked what you know. Also, he's not my boyfriend."

Bobby gave a short laugh like I'd said something funny. "That's not what people are sayin'. And I heard you're datin' both Drake and Hawke, like reverse polygamy."

I made a psssh noise. "Have you spent any amount of time with Drake and Hawke? They could never be brother-husbands. They'd kill each other."

I took Bobby's silence as agreement on that.

"If you know something about Hawke that I don't know, I'd like to know, Bobby."

"You should ask him. I ain't sayin' nothin'."

"Story of my life." Hawke said he told me what he could, but I knew there was a lot of information I still didn't have—and might not get. And aside from that, both Hawke and Drake refused to say anything about why they hated each other. It was like this weird man code. Really, I suspected they each had information that the other didn't want revealed, so there was an unspoken mutual agreement of omission between them. "Thanks for the info about the bodies. Call me when you can tell me what you're not telling me about the crime scene."

"I will."

I hung up and leaned back in my desk chair, twirling a pen between my fingers. The fact that the body was male would likely put it out of the running as a Zundy victim since Zundy's victim profile was to go after young women he could date and charm before he killed them. But it didn't completely rule him out. If Zundy was in the mood to murder and couldn't find anyone else, maybe he would have killed a man. It also didn't rule out other possible murderers. We'd had more than one serial killer and mass murderer in Utah, and there were likely a lot of murderers that we didn't even know about. It was unusual to have two bodies found on one property, and that anomaly made me think the same person had put them there.

I'd already done a search on Grant Kimball's GCR Development company yesterday. He and his two partners, Chris, and Ryan, were well known in Utah as developers and businessmen, and they'd been able to push everything through with the Branson Falls city council quickly. Their business was worth hundreds of millions of dollars, and they knew what they were doing. They didn't strike me as the type of people who would buy a piece of property without knowing everything they could about it. Drake had mentioned the project had investors, which was common, but I couldn't find anything about who the investors were, and Grant's company wouldn't have to disclose that information.

I pulled up a property history search and typed in the address of the Barret farm and scanned the information on the page. Like most land in Branson Falls, and the surrounding farming communities, it had been in the Barret family for generations, passed down from family to family—which confirmed what Bobby had told me yesterday. I pulled up a background check and searched the Barret family as well. Saul Barret had been married to Georgia Barret. They had two kids together—Bethany and Jordan. Saul passed away twenty years ago from a heart attack and Georgia kept the property. A public records search confirmed she put it into a trust. Georgia was now struggling with dementia, and living in an assisted living center.

I tapped my pen against my notepad, wondering what the terms of the trust were. Bobby said the family had made the decision to sell the property when land values exploded in Utah. That would mean the Barret children were overseeing the trust and had the authority to approve the sale even though Georgia was still alive. It seemed like they'd probably still need Georgia's consent, unless they'd accounted for all of that legally. Grant Kimball's company and its investors wouldn't have bought the property without completing due diligence. At least, that's what I hoped. And if Drake had been their lawyer for the land acquisition as well, he would have insured proper inspections and disclosures were done.

Then again, a lot of shady things happened in Utah real estate. Around sixty percent of the Utah state legislature was composed of people with ties to real estate and development in their day jobs. They frequently passed laws that favored companies and developers over homeowners. They pushed for small government because it made it very difficult for homeowners and property owners to get protection in the event something went wrong.

I had a lot of unanswered questions and needed to talk to the Barret family and find out more about why they chose to sell. I also wanted their take on why two bodies had been found on their property, and to find out if they knew anything about the remains. Georgia Barret only had two kids, which was a small number for rural Mormon Utah, especially with a farm the size she and her husband had owned. Multiplying and replenishing the earth was one of the most important tenants of the Mormon faith, and Mormons took it seriously and were even shamed for not having more. It wasn't odd to see a family with eight kids, some even had twelve or more. Georgia's kids still lived in Branson Falls: Jordan Barret, the oldest, and Bethany Barret, Georgia's youngest child. I put Jordan's name in my search software and got his phone number. I called and it sent me straight to voicemail so I left a message telling him who I was, and asking if I could schedule a time to talk to him. After that, I called and left a message for Bethany.

As I hung up the phone, Ella came in and dropped a box on the desk for me. I picked it up, turning it over in my hands as my brows formed a line. "What's this?"

She put her hand on her hip, like that would give her some extra authority. "A stun gun, silly! You live alone and there's a serial killer on the loose. You've gotta protect yourself!"

I opened the box, revealing a piece of equipment that looked a lot like a flashlight. I was afraid I'd confuse it for a real flashlight and accidently tase myself during the next power outage. I pulled it out of the packaging. "If it's a serial killer, they're not a very good one since they've only killed two people."

Ella crossed her arms over her chest. "That we know of. And it only takes three different kills over a long time period to be a serial killer. They're one body away and the killer could still be active!"

Fear was the backbone of conspiracy. "I wish you would have brought doughnuts instead." Frosted Paradise had the best doughnuts in the state and when I'd moved away from Branson Falls, I'd longed for their glazed and chocolate frosted goodness. I'd take sugary dough over a weapon any day.

Ella pointed at a box of doughnuts on the treat table and my eyes popped wide. "How did I miss those?" I made a beeline for the snacks.

"I brought 'em when I got here this mornin'."

I grabbed a glazed doughnut frosted with chocolate and topped with finely chopped peanuts. I bit into it, savoring the experience. "This is exactly what I needed," I said around my bite.

"It really does make the day better," Ella agreed.

"Do you know the Barret family?" I asked her as I continued to eat. Ella was around the same age as Georgia, and I was sure they knew each other.

Ella nodded and took a bite of her own doughnut. "Sure do. It's sad Georgia isn't doing well. She was quiet when she was younger, but I suspect that had to do with her jerk of a husband. She seemed to come out of her shell more once Saul died. She was more social, at least."

That was curious. I wondered what Georgia and Saul's relationship had been like—it sounded like her husband might have been a bit controlling, though that wasn't uncommon for Branson Falls, or men in the predominant religion. "Did you know Saul?"

She took a drink from her cup of water to wash down the doughnut before answering, "Not well, but I knew him enough. Had a mean-streak, that one."

"Maybe he's the one who put the bodies on their property," I said, offhanded.

"Wouldn't put it past him," Ella answered with a shrug. "But my money's still on Zundy."

I took a drink of my coffee before informing her about my news. "Bobby called me."

She planted her hands on my desk, eager as a child. "Is it a Zundy victim? It's a Zundy victim, isn't it?"

"I can't say much because the info hasn't been released yet, but I don't think it was Zundy unless Zundy had a pattern change we didn't know about."

She looked slightly crestfallen, but only for a moment. "Coulda been someone who got in Zundy's way, or tried to stop him. He killed lotsa people and we don't even know about most of his victims. I'm not rulin' Zundy out." She put a finger up to her cheek, thinking about it. "Or maybe it was another serial killer. There are lots of 'em."

"Another serial killer? One who lived around Branson?" I'd entertained that idea myself, but wanted to hear Ella's perspective.

She shrugged. "Who knows? It could've been anyone, really. Zundy's just the obvious culprit 'cause he visited here a lot."

I went very still, stunned. I knew Zundy had lived in Salt Lake City for a couple of years, and had even converted to the Mormon Church. I also knew he had killed in Utah—probably more than any of us knew the extent of—but I'd never heard that he'd been to Branson Falls. "I'm sorry, what? Zundy visited here?" I waved my hand around in a circle. "*Here* as in Branson Falls?"

Ella nodded nonchalantly as she cleaned up some trash on the treat table. "He knew some locals and would visit sometimes."

I stared at her for a solid twenty seconds. "How have I never heard this before?"

She lifted her shoulders. "Maybe you're too young. You weren't alive then, but most people my age remember he was here. Lotsa people met him."

My heart started to pick up speed the way it always did when I got a tidbit of information that could lead to a bigger story. This changed a lot of things. Before, I'd dismissed the idea of a serial killer being responsible for the bodies because it seemed crazy. But now, knowing that one of the most infamous serial killers in history spent time in Branson Falls… maybe there was something to it. "Do you think anyone who knew him would talk to me?"

Ella's eyes sparkled. "See. Now you're startin' to believe the remains found were Zundy's victims too. I'm sure some people who spent a lotta time with him would be willin' to talk. Let me ask around."

I tapped my fingers on my desk as my mind started racing. "I don't know what I believe, but I'd like to ask some questions to people who knew him."

She nodded. "Personally, I think it could've been any serial killer! Zundy was here, but statistically speakin', the FBI says there are between twenty-five and fifty serial killers active at any time, and there are between two and four thousand serial killers alive right now. There's at least one serial killer for every fifty thousand people and there are eight billion people in the world so…do the math."

I stared at her. "I don't think I want to know how you know those statistics."

She lifted her shoulder in a slight shrug. "I listen to a lot of true crime podcasts."

Of course she did. A voice crackled across the police scanner announcing a disturbance at Bubbly Sweets, the soda shop, and requesting police. I wasn't sure what could possibly be causing problems there, but they had caffeine and cookies, and I needed a break from being at my desk and computer. I grabbed my bag. "Bring me back a large Sweet Berry Pie!" Ella yelled as I walked out the door.

I waved at her in acknowledgment and got in my Jeep.

Chapter Six

Soda shops had become a popular fixture in Utah culture, and they'd become especially popular with the religious residents of the state since members of the church couldn't drink coffee. For many years, church members thought the "no coffee" rule had to do with caffeine, but the church had clarified saying caffeine was fine, as long as it wasn't hot. This led to the advent of Utah's soda culture, and people who liked their pop "dirty."

The obsession started with a random soda shack in Southern Utah. The shack was known for their pink frosted and smashed sugar cookies, and their sugary soda drinks with an army of flavors and clever names. Locals knew about the shop, and after a while, people were making special trips to try the soda concoctions laced with different flavored sugar and cream. And the ice in the drinks was always pebbled, not cubed. Pebbled ice *mattered*.

Realizing the shop might have appeal outside of the tiny town, the business eventually expanded into larger metropolitan areas of Utah, and then into neighboring states with high Mormon populations. It did so well that other soda companies immediately opened in Utah, copying the business model and selling similar items, with different versions of drink names, and different treats to accompany the drinks. Other states had coffee shops, but Utah had soda with copious amounts of sugar.

I pulled up to Bubbly Sweets and the line of people both in the drive-through, and standing in the building, was even longer than usual. I wasn't sure if the owners realized that most people outside of Utah equated "bubbly" with champagne or dessert wines, not carbonation. But maybe that's why they'd named it the way they had. Instead of "avoiding the appearance of evil," they were capitalizing on it.

A police car was parked in front of the store as well; the officers made it before I did this time.

I walked into the store and it was complete chaos. Bobby was trying to hold back a red-faced, irate woman with curly shoulder length brown hair who was yelling at a twenty-something male store employee. The employee was wearing a black apron, covered in flair, something Bubbly Sweets was known for. All their employees picked buttons to reflect their personalities. Judging by his, he really liked fantasy movies, video games, and telling people what to do. He didn't seem the least bit concerned by the woman's outburst.

I saw my friend, and my mom's personal EMT, Annie, standing in a corner, drinking her soda with wide eyes like she was watching a reality show play out in front of her. I sidled over to her. "Hey, Annie."

She looked at me and flashed a wide smile. "Kate! You got here right in time."

"What's happening?"

She pointed at the woman Bobby was holding back and spoke in a hushed tone. "Cary Ferro ordered a drink and they refused to make it for her. She told them they couldn't refuse to serve her something on the menu. They finally made it, but they *poisoned* it."

My eyes went as wide as a rodeo champion's belt buckle. I thought I was here to cover a misunderstanding at the soda shop, not attempted murder. "Shouldn't you be helping her?" I asked. "You're an EMT!"

Annie waved a hand in front of her like it wasn't a big deal. "It wasn't anything lethal, and she's calmed down quite a bit."

If this was calm, I was curious how she'd been acting before.

"That Cary Ferro is Satan in human form!" the familiar, scratchy voice of Mrs. Olsen said, butting into my conversation with Annie. Mrs. Olsen somehow managed to be everywhere…like the ghost she'd appeared to be at the grocery store on Sunday.

"Satan seems like an overstatement," I observed.

"Are you kiddin' me? That *gentile*," Mrs. Olsen said the word like she was talking about dog poop, and to her, they were probably one in the same, "has been drinkin' since seven am!"

That also seemed unlikely. Mormons don't drink alcohol, at least not publicly. It was a sin serious enough to require a confession to their bishop, and one that could get a Mormon temple recommend revoked. Few things were worse among church members than not being able to flash a card to show their faithfulness and prove their worthiness. It was notoriously difficult to sell alcohol in the state, and being bestowed with a liquor license in Utah was almost the equivalent of winning Willy Wonka's golden ticket. The soda shop didn't have a liquor license, so Cary couldn't have ordered alcohol. "What has she been drinking?" I asked.

"Diet Coke with espresso!" Mrs. Olsen hissed. She made it sound like the drink was straight cocaine. "Probably mixed in with some of those other sweeteners and cream. This is her second drink chock full of caffeine! It's downright evil! I knew that coffee shop would bring all kinds of sin to town and look at it!" She waved her hands about in a frenzy that almost took out two women standing behind her. "Just look!"

I directed my attention to Cary Ferro. She and her family were recent transplants to Branson, so I didn't know her well. Her hair was a bit frazzled, and she did seem a tad jittery, but I couldn't see an issue other than that. She looked like every other tired mom in the world. "She seems fine to me."

Mrs. Olsen's eyeballs seemed like they were going to pop out of her head. "She's high on caffeine and she's sugar wasted!"

I pushed my lips out in a thoughtful expression. "Sugar wasted" was not a term I ever thought I'd hear coming out of Mrs. Olsen's mouth.

Bobby had moved Cary off to the side. "I'm going to talk to Cary," I said. Annie looked like she wanted to throttle me for leaving her with Mrs. Olsen. I mouthed "sorry" as I walked away. Annie's expression promised retribution.

Cary was standing by the wall while Bobby and another police officer talked to the store employee and the store owners. Poisoning was a serious offense.

I extended my hand to Cary. "Hi, Cary. I'm Kate Saxee, Editor of *The Branson Tribune*."

She looked at me with suspicion. If I'd recently been poisoned, I'd do the same. "I've read your work."

I nodded. "Can I ask you some questions?"

Her hands were shaking and I wasn't sure if it was from the ordeal, or the caffeine. "Crazy people, that's what. We thought we were moving to a nice, quiet town, but it hasn't been that nice or quiet recently."

I couldn't argue. I thought I was moving back to cover stories about parades and high school dances, not murders and poisoning, but here I was.

"What happened this morning?"

She glared at the flair wearing employee. "*Someone* wanted to try and make a point and show me that he controlled my drink choices instead of letting me decide what I wanted."

The employee was a man in Utah, so that tracked.

"I ordered a 'Dirty Devil'—Diet Coke with espresso and cream. The kid looked at me like I was scum, then went to make my drink. He was acting weird so I was suspicious and watched him. It looked like he was making everything right, though. When he handed it to me, I tasted it and immediately wanted to vomit. It tasted like sour milk."

I looked up from taking notes. "So, he put expired cream in your drink?"

She gave me serious side-eye. "Not just expired. It smelled like manure and had actual chunks. Like it was deliberately left out of the fridge for a week."

"Why would they do that? It would be a major health violation, and could even put them out of business."

She looked at the Bubbly Sweets employee who wasn't standing far from us. "Yes, why would you do that," she glanced down at his name tag and in a disgusted voice said, "Hyrum?"

Hyrum was a popular Utah name, based on a historical religious leader. So, I had a strong suspicion about what religion Hyrum belonged to, and what his answer was going to be. She said she'd ordered a drink with a shot of espresso. Bubbly Sweets was newer to the soda shop biz and had expanded their menu to include some coffee drinks to help attract non-Mormons to the soda culture as well.

"We have a tolerance for how long after the expiration date we can use dairy products," Hyrum answered without even the hint of apology.

I tilted my head and gave a slight nod. "That's good to know. I'll make sure to put that in the article so people are aware that Bubbly Sweets serves sour milk."

His face lost some of its color. "We didn't do it on purpose."

Cary's eyebrows shot up her forehead. "You didn't do it on purpose, yet you knew it was expired? Who else got the expired milk, Hyrum?"

He pursed his lips and didn't answer. Kylee Smart, a Branson resident about ten years older than me, who was wearing a tank top and shorts that were leagues higher than the three inches above the knee Mormon modesty standard limit, came forward. "My drink also tastes like ass."

Jess Berk, a Branson resident with bright tattoos circling her forearm, nodded. "Mine does, too." I looked at the three of them and it seemed pretty evident to me who the people getting sour milk were. All three of them did not conform to the predominant religion's standards.

"Did you all order different things?"

"I got espresso in mine," Cary said, clearly noticing the same similarities I did between the sour milk group.

Tank top Kylee and tattooed Jess both ordered espresso shots as well. They were drinking coffee, and based on how they looked, and what they'd ordered, I was certain Hyrum had made a judgment that they didn't share the same beliefs he did. I'd made the same observation, but the difference was I had no problem with either side living their lives the way they thought was best—though on a personal note, I was excited to find some fellow coffee drinkers, and wondered if we should start a club.

"Did you not want to serve coffee?" I asked Hyrum.

He hedged for a minute and then seemed to make a decision. He squared his shoulders and stood a little taller, thrusting out his chest. "I would prefer not to. It goes against my beliefs."

One of The Ladies was standing in the crowd and walked up to give Hyrum a little pat on his back to let him know she was in support of his decision to make choices for others.

"Did you know you would have to serve coffee when you applied for the job?" Kylee asked.

He crossed his arms and his lips formed a sneer. "I knew it was on the menu, but didn't think I'd have to make drinks with it. Most people in town believe the same way I do." That last part was added with a heaping scoop of judgment, and a side of superiority complex.

I held back a sigh. Hyrum's line of thinking was a big part of the problem because not everyone believes the same things.

"You serve energy drinks though, and you don't have a problem with that, correct?" I asked.

He furrowed his brow like he didn't understand my point,

and maybe he really didn't. "Energy drinks are fine. Everyone drinks them."

"Why is it okay to order an energy drink with three times as much caffeine as coffee has in it, but it's not okay to drink coffee?"

"Because the church hasn't said not to drink energy drinks. But they have said not to drink coffee."

Mormons weren't banned from drinking caffeine, but it was looked down on, and one of those grey areas between what church members believe is doctrine, and what is really doctrine. Most of them had no real understanding of what the Word of Wisdom actually said. Technically, church members shouldn't be consuming any addictive substances, like sugar filled soda, or even eating meat often. It mentioned hot drinks, which was interpreted as coffee and tea, but it didn't say a word about coffee.

I routinely asked active church members why the Mormon Church didn't allow members to drink coffee and every time, I got a different answer. Some said it was simply because they were doing what the LDS prophet said to do and they didn't question it; others said it was an obedience test. Others told me it was because church leaders had higher knowledge and there was something unhealthy in the bean. That, despite all scientific evidence to the contrary, and the fact that one of the reasons the Mormon pioneers survived crossing the plains when others didn't was *because* they drank coffee. They were boiling water every morning to make hot bean water and that boiling stopped many of them from dying of dysentery.

"So, you decided that it was your right to push your own beliefs on a customer?" Kylee asked.

"I…I…No," Hyrum stammered. "That's not what I did."

She gave him a look. "Isn't it?"

Kylee was not wrong.

"How would you feel if I came in here and forced you to drink coffee?" Kylee asked.

His lip curled up and his jaw hardened. "You can't do that. It's against my beliefs."

"Exactly. And it's against my beliefs to be sabotaged by a kid hiding behind his religion," Kylee said. She'd lived here a lot longer than Cary, and had no qualms about standing up to people who were trying to push their beliefs on her.

This was going to keep getting messier. And not just with this soda situation. Branson Falls was growing and it wasn't going to stop. People had to learn to accept others, and not invoke the LDS church as a defense for prejudice.

Bobby came over and separated the women from Hyrum. The women talked among themselves and Bobby turned to me, closed his eyes, and took a deep breath.

"How are you doing, Bobby?"

"Every day's an adventure."

"I'm surprised you're not at the GCR development with the bodies," I said.

Bobby shrugged. "We've got lotsa people out there workin' on things, and the police department still needs to run."

"Were you able to talk to the Barret family?" I asked. I'd left a message for Jordan, but hadn't heard back.

"I got in touch with Bethany and Jordan. They don't know anythin' about the bodies, and weren't able to tell us any new information. I'm sure I'll follow up again as the investigation continues."

"Are you able to tell me more info about the second body, yet?"

He ran his hand over the back of his neck. "Cripes, Kate. I just told ya that this mornin'. You gotta learn to be patient."

I breathed a long-suffering, exaggerated sigh. "I figured since you'd left the scene, maybe things were calming down and you could tell me more."

He shook his head. "I had to come back in to release Jack Pine, the flour bandit."

"He's out of jail?"

"He made bail."

"That's unfortunate," I said. "Who knows what he'll attack people with next. What if he chooses milk? Or Anthrax."

"Anthrax ain't easy to get."

I'd talked to the flour bandit for less than five minutes and I wouldn't put it past the guy.

Bobby took Kylee, Jess, and Cary aside for statements. I talked to a few people, got quotes and pictures, and stopped next to Annie before walking out the door. "You're lucky they didn't serve you spoiled creamer too," I pointed out. "You could have been judged for your hair." It was a bright shade of teal today.

"My tattoos are covered, or I probably would have been served it too."

She was probably right, unfortunately. Annie was an active member of the Mormon Church but she saw the flaws and firmly believed that people shouldn't be "othered" for being different. She'd told me there were a lot of things she disliked and disagreed with about Mormonism, but she appreciated the community aspect of it. She felt the most important part of any religion was showing love and kindness to *everyone* and too often, people forgot that.

"People are funny," Annie said. "Our very Mormon, and

very single male neighbor is under the impression that the three women who moved in across the street are three college girls and he's about to have his pick of them all."

"He's not?"

She shook her head very slowly. "They aren't what he thinks they are, and he's so sheltered that he doesn't even realize it."

"What are they?" I asked, hoping for something scandalous. "A coven?" I loved real witches almost as much as my mom loved witch inflatables, but real witches would blow the minds of the people of Branson.

"More scandalous than that."

I made a fanning motion with my hand, gesturing for her to go on.

"Proper lesbians in a throuple."

"Holy. Shit." My eyes were wider than belt buckles now and I didn't think that was possible. I said the swear louder than I realized and got some glares. I was sure my swear would be reported in The Ladies Facebook Group shortly. "A lesbian throuple might get its own Facebook group and kick interest about my life down a notch. Why in the world would they move to Branson Falls?"

Annie took another sip of her drink. "Probably the same reason everyone is moving here. It's cheaper to buy property, and you get more of it."

I wondered if Spence knew about this. If other people who didn't fit the norm were moving in, maybe he and Xander would feel comfortable coming out in Branson Falls as well. Not that they needed to. It was no one's business but their own. But I hated seeing them have to silence a part of themselves, and didn't think it was fair. They deserved the same right to be authentic as the rest of us.

I closed my notepad app and put my phone back in my bag. "Phyllis and I are watching the premiere of HOTBS tonight if you want to come."

"HOTBS?" Annie asked.

"Homemakers of the Beehive State. They dropped that acronym right in my lap and I can't not use it."

Annie laughed. "I've been looking forward to seeing it! I'll be there! What should I bring?"

"Phyllis will make some snacks. Popcorn and hot chocolate for sure—with fresh milk, not spoiled. I'll bring some treats. Grab something that sounds good that you want to share."

"I'll be there!" Annie smiled and waved on her way out.

Another woman I recognized walked into the soda shop as Annie left. She had light brown shoulder length hair that was styled stick straight, and parted down the middle. She was rail thin, and moved with the gracefulness of someone who had been trained in dance. She was forty, a fact I knew because of the research I'd done on her family. Bethany was the youngest daughter of Georgia Barret, and one of the Barret family members I wanted to talk to. I recognized her from some photos I'd found online while looking up information about the property. "Hi, Bethany." I reached out my hand. "I'm Kate Saxee, editor of *The Branson Tribune*."

"I've read your articles," she said, shaking my hand, not too firm and not too soft. Kind of like Goldilocks. "It's nice to meet you."

"It's nice to meet you, too. I've been wanting to talk to you about your family's old property and the human remains that were found on it. Are you free in the next few days."

"Sure," she said tucking her hair behind her ear. "I'll tell you what I can, but my mom would be the better person to ask."

"I was under the impression she has memory issues and is in assisted living."

"She is, but she's on meds that are helping her memory and she has some moments of clarity. Why don't you meet me at the assisted living center in town tomorrow morning around ten. She does better earlier in the day."

"That sounds great. I'll see you tomorrow."

Before I left, I ordered Ella her Sweet Berry Pie, and warned them not to use spoiled milk. I decided against a drink of my own. I'd stop by the coffee shop and support them instead, and not risk getting spoiled milk.

As I stepped outside, I heard a commotion on the road and it looked like a small parade had spontaneously started. Several mini vans and SUVs drove down Main Street honking their horns, with music blaring from the vehicles. They looked like they were part of a mom-car caravan of some kind. As they flew by, I noticed one van had a sign on the side that said something about *murder*, with big eyes staring at me. I watched in stunned silence as they passed. What in the world? I shook my head, got in my Jeep, then grabbed a coffee from Beans and Things, before going back to the office.

Chapter Seven

"Heard more bodies were found," Ella said as I handed her the Sweet Berry Pie drink she'd requested. "And that the first body was a man."

Bobby had indicated that the gender information wasn't public yet, and I hadn't told Ella when I was talking to her earlier. "How did you know about that?"

Ella waved her hand around in front of her chest. "It's in the wind."

"What does that even mean?" Then my brain backtracked and caught up with what she'd said. "Wait, did you say *bodies*? As in more than the one body that was found yesterday morning, and the second body found yesterday afternoon?"

"Two bodies were found yesterday afternoon," Ella informed me, popping a piece of leftover Halloween candy in her mouth, and moving her head a little like the combined sugar from the candy and her drink had inspired a dance. I stared blankly at her and felt pressure rapidly expanding in my head.

"That's not what I was told." And I was there when the

second body was found, with Drake, Hawke, *and* Bobby. And I'd talked to Hawke and Bobby multiple times since I'd been at the property for body number two. So, if more bodies had been found yesterday afternoon and I didn't know about it, I was going to be pretty damn pissed off at all three of them.

Ella popped another piece of candy and pointed at me, "Better check your sources," she advised.

I'd known Bobby was keeping something from me, and he'd said there was more info that he couldn't tell me yet, but how would Ella have found out the information before I did? "Seriously, where did you hear about that?"

"Online." She lifted her shoulder like it wasn't a big deal. "The Murderoonies are here."

I blinked. "What the hell are Murderoonies?"

Ella stared at me like I'd started growing a carrot from my ear. "The famous podcast! The badass women who investigate true crimes. They're here because it's an ongoing investigation and people think it could be a serial killer, or Jeff Zundy's victims. It's a great story, and we're in the middle of it!"

"The story broke two days ago! It's not even really a story yet because we don't have any idea what's going on." How the hell had these people who didn't even live here, or have the connections I had, scoop me on the extra body? I was baffled.

"It's all over the true crime socials," Ella said, taking a long drink from her Bubbly Sweets cup. "Everyone loves a good mystery and The Murderoonies solve crime in real time. It's their tagline."

Of course it was. I took a deep breath. "Who exactly are they?"

"Amateur investigators who try to solve crimes."

We already had an amateur group like that—the Speedy

Superheroes. I wasn't sure the town, or Bobby and the police force, could handle another one. "Why are they here?"

"I told ya! To investigate! They heard about the bodies and want to cover the story for their podcast. They're great at what they do. Solved the mystery of those girls who went missin' on the Colorado River twenty years ago. The police had let the case go cold but The Murderoonies wouldn't stop until justice was served. After that, they started coverin' cases happenin' in real time. Lots of people wanna engage, investigate, and solve crimes."

"They have a podcast?" I asked, still dumbfounded.

"Where've you been, Katie?" Ella asked, pushing her brows together. "Everyone listens to true crime podcasts now. How do you even talk to anyone in social situations?"

I gave her a look. "I didn't realize my lack of podcast knowledge was making me a leper."

"Well," she said, thoughtfully, "it's probably also your lack of attendance at church, but still."

I shook my head. I liked true crime, but had enough of that investigating for my job that I didn't listen to many podcasts about it. When I got free time, I wanted to relax with something escapist, not marinate on all the ways someone could kill me.

Suddenly, I remembered the parade of mom-cars I'd seen on my way back to the office earlier. There was something about murder painted on the side of the car. I hadn't been able to make out the words as they zipped by. At least that mystery was solved.

"So, these Murderoonies are here now? Investigating. Because they heard about three random dead bodies?"

"All on the same property! In a known Jeff Zundy potential

victim zone!" Ella argued, like I wasn't taking the discovery of the bodies seriously. "I'm sure you'll meet 'em all. They'll be around until the case is solved."

That sounded unpleasant. "Who are these people? How can they get up and leave their day jobs for an extended period of time for something like this?"

"This is their day job, Katie! Lotsa money in podcasts. They've got advertisers, merch…it's a whole business! I have one of their shirts, a mug, and some stickers."

I was going to have to learn more about this group, especially since I would surely run into them.

"Where are they staying?"

"The hotel. The new one, because they're fancy and you need the best tech and Wi-Fi when you're solvin' murders."

There were only two hotels in town, the old one—which I was certain had been around since the days of horses and carriages—and the new one, with recently installed electric car chargers, so I knew exactly what she was talking about.

"I can't wait to meet 'em!" Ella said as she clapped. "They're celebrities! I'm gonna get a pic with Edith, and see if she'll sign my mug."

I winced. "Celebrity" seemed like an overstatement, but I didn't know much about the true crime fandom, so maybe she was right. Ella grabbed a glass of water to help wash down all the sugar, and her Sweet Berry Pie, and went back to the archive room.

I immediately picked up my phone and called Bobby.

"Heya, Kate," Bobby said.

I didn't even say hello and instead opted to start with, "There were *three* bodies found?" It was part question and part accusation. A podcast had more information about the case I was reporting on than I did, and I was the town's freaking newspaper editor!

"Dagnabbit!" Bobby said. "How in the heck did you find out?"

"From Ella!" My voice was louder than usual, and rising. "Who heard it from a freaking podcast! How did they know before I did?"

Bobby sighed. "I thought we had things sealed up pretty tight, but people talk and things get out, especially in a small town like Branson."

"I'm the damn newspaper editor and I didn't know."

"Yeah," he said, not sounding sorry at all. "I thought one, or both of your boyfriends would tell ya for sure."

My pulse picked up speed and my temper went right along for the ride. There was an excellent chance that I'd be meeting the Murderoonies soon since I was going to kill Hawke and Drake the next time I saw them. "I don't have any boyfriends, but they're both in as deep of shit as you are for not keeping me informed." I glared at the phone as I growled, "No more cookies for any of you!"

There was a long pause before Bobby's tone came out solemn. "That's a real tragedy right there, Kate."

"Well, actions have consequences, Bobby Burns." I took a deep breath to try and wrangle my nervous system and then picked up my pen and grabbed my notepad. "Since I already know about body number three, you might as well tell me the details."

Bobby let loose a long breath. "The third body was found underneath the second one."

I paused in the middle of writing my notes. "Hold on. They were buried on top of each other?"

"Yep."

"Like in a cemetery where they sometimes bury couples together in the same plot?"

"Seems like it, but no caskets were involved."

"Were they killed at the same time?"

"Not sure yet."

"What was the state of decomposition for both of the bodies?"

"Similar, but we're gonna have to wait and see what the investigators find when they do the autopsy."

I was frantically scribbling down notes, and my own questions with it. "Do you know if they're male or female?"

"Not sure on that either."

That seemed odd since they'd had no problem getting information yesterday. "They got the gender for the first body back to you quick. Are they going to have information about the other two soon?"

"I sure hope so."

I furrowed my brow, thinking. "What does this do to the timeline for the development?"

"Puts everythin' on hold. The bodies were found in different areas of the development and since we've found three, we have to assume there could be more. The state's forensic team is involved now, and we've got another cadaver dog helpin' to search the property. If the dogs get hits anywhere else, we'll dig more."

I leaned back in my chair. "I bet that doesn't make Grant Kimball, his partners, or his investors too happy."

"Probably not. But we have to make sure we've found everythin'."

"Will you call me when you know more for real this time, Bobby?"

He paused and the pause did him no favors. Finally, he said, "Yep."

"And you'll call if you find any more bodies?"

"Yep."

I slitted my eyes and hoped the threat came through in my tone. "Seriously, Bobby. If I'm scooped by true crime podcasts or social media groups again, my mom's cookies are cut off."

He answered immediately this time. "I'll call."

"Thanks. Talk to you soon."

As soon as I hung up, I texted both Hawke and Drake the exact same thing on different threads.

> THREE?! There are THREE bodies???!!! And you didn't tell me??? When I decide to talk to you again, we're going to have words.

I finished working on a couple of articles and then left to pick up Gandalf. I had a date with Phyllis and Annie to watch the HOTBS disaster.

"This is *amazing*," Annie said, emphasizing the word. The show was thirty minutes in and there had already been two fights. One over a housewife lying about her nose job, and another over whether someone was breaking the Word of Wisdom by owning a distillery. It was hard to make an argument against distillery ownership considering Brigham Young, the second prophet of the LDS Church, had built one when Utah was settled, and good old Brigham owned the state's first saloon.

I grabbed a brownie from the plate Annie had brought. They tasted like chocolate sunshine. So far, HOTBS was exactly the train wreck I'd predicted. Influencers and homemakers, of varying degrees of religious piousness, were attempting to out-perfect each other and prove their worth via their bank account, house size, car model, and boob job.

The show cut to commercials and a teaser for the nightly news came on. A bright red banner, designed to invoke people's fear and get their attention, flashed across the screen. "Oooo! Wonder what this is?" Phyllis said, putting her popcorn down and leaning forward on the table to give the news anchor all her focus. "Must be big to interrupt the most anticipated reality show premiere in the state!"

It was the only reality show premiere in the state, but I didn't point that out.

The familiar deep and enunciated tone of "news anchor" came over the airwaves. It wasn't a reporter I knew. "We have breaking news coming from the small community of Branson Falls." Annie and Phyllis both turned to look at me. I had a pretty good idea of what that breaking news was going to be. "Three bodies have been found on an area of land being developed for a new housing community. Police are still investigating, but a source tells us the deaths are suspicious. We've received no confirmation yet from police about whether the deaths could be related." The anchor said that last part in a way that indicated the deaths could absolutely be related, probably were, and if you weren't watching the upcoming news report, you'd likely be next to die. This manipulation would guarantee people tuned in. It was part of the problem with the media in today's current environment. They were competing with a lot of other entertainment sources for people's attention, and the most interesting story package is what got viewers, even if it wasn't necessarily truthful, or even factual. "More on this story at ten."

Annie and Phyllis both gaped at me.

"You knew about this?" Annie asked.

"Yeah," Phyllis put her hands on her hips, her tone indignant. "Why didn't you tell us?"

I winced. "Because Bobby told me not to."

"That's not an excuse," Phyllis said, sounding hurt. "We're your people."

I bit my lip and tried to tamp down the guilt washing over me. "You are my people, but you don't pay my bills. I have to follow protocol and make sure I keep getting information from my sources." Not that Bobby had been particularly forthcoming earlier in the day, and Hawke and Drake hadn't either so maybe I needed new sources.

"Three bodies were found?" Annie asked, her forehead wrinkling. "I thought it was only one."

Phyllis shook her head. "You're behind on the news cycle, Annie. The first body was found Monday mornin', but then another was found late in the afternoon." She turned to me. "Where did body number three come from?"

I grabbed another brownie from the table. I was going to need it. "The same area as body number two. It was buried deeper than the first set of bones they found."

"Like, on top of each other?" Phyllis asked, sounding a little scandalized.

"Yeah."

She took a drink, her throat working before she asked the next question. "Were they married?"

"You mean like they sometimes bury couples in cemeteries?" Annie asked.

I took a sip of my hot chocolate—homemade by Phyllis, with real milk and chocolate. It was delightful. "I asked the same question and they don't know because they haven't identified the remains or genders yet."

"What *do* they know about the bodies?" Annie asked.

"Nothing they're telling me, yet. The bodies are at the medical examiners and they're expediting results so I should know more in the next few days."

"You better keep us informed this time!" Phyllis said.

I understood how she felt because I'd said the same thing to Bobby, and texted it to Drake, and Hawke.

The TV flashed back to HOTBS, and I promised them both I'd tell them as soon as I knew more. Then we continued watching the entertainment version of a dumpster fire.

Chapter Eight

I was getting out of the shower when I heard a knock on the door. And just in case I hadn't heard the knock, Gandalf helpfully amplified it.

I threw on my robe, shushed Gandalf, and opened the door to find Drake on the other side wearing a wide smile, navy dress shirt and grey slacks with a grey sports coat. He was holding a brown bag that smelled like heaven. I couldn't resist, for a lot of reasons.

"Good morning," he said, flashing his sparkling white teeth like he hadn't done anything wrong.

I put a hand on my hip and leaned against the door frame. "Good morning to everyone who told me about the third body that was found yesterday before I was scooped by a true crime podcast. So…not you."

He winced. "I'm sorry. We were trying to keep the information private for as long as possible."

"You could have told me about it and asked me not to report on it yet."

He lifted a shoulder and tilted his head in concession.

"You're right." He held up the bag. "I brought you apology breakfast sandwiches."

I took the bag from him. "I accept, but only if you promise to tell me as soon as you find out anything else in the future."

He sliced his head down once in agreement.

I stepped out of the doorway, allowing him in, and he brushed against my chest as he walked inside. He caught my gaze, his eyes full of heat, and we both stopped breathing for several beats. I was in my pajamas and the door was open so I was sure The Ladies were watching somehow. I broke our gaze and stepped back, closing the door before he followed me to the kitchen.

I thought a visit to apologize was very nice of him, but then I remembered our group discussion at the old Barret property, and Hawke's comment about seeing me.

"Did you come to apologize, or are you here because you thought I was with Hawke?" I asked, turning the coffee maker on, and taking some glasses and orange juice out of the fridge. I would most certainly be having coffee, but juice was never a bad idea. Drake probably wouldn't break the coffee rule, but judging by the way his eyes landed on my black robe plunging down around my cleavage, and the things he'd whispered in my ear at the Halloween dance, chastity was more of a religious grey area for him—at least in theory. I wasn't sure how far he'd actually be comfortable taking things in the heat of the moment.

Drake pursed his lips. "I don't like thinking about that at all, to be honest. Not only because I have feelings for you, but also because I think he's dangerous and puts his own wants and needs before anyone else. You shouldn't trust him."

I wasn't interested in arguing with him about Hawke so I

ignored that comment and focused on another part of his statement as I made my coffee. "You have feelings for me?"

He gave me a long look that said all sorts of things. "I thought that was obvious."

I lifted a shoulder. "I don't think you've ever stated that specifically, so it's nice to hear confirmation. It's rare to find a man who knows how to use his words."

"Words are kind of my thing," he said. I knew that, and it was one of the reasons it was hard for me to trust him. I'd never be able to have a relationship with an actor either. If they were decent at their job, I'd always be suspicious of them, and wonder if they were playing a role in our relationship. Knowing who people really are isn't easy.

"What are you doing this weekend?" Drake asked as I put my coffee on the table and sat. Drake took the chair across from me and his massive frame made my table look like it was built to function as the kids' table at family parties.

I had a date with Hawke on Friday. I had no idea what we were doing, but hoped it would last a while.

We both unwrapped our breakfast sandwiches and started to eat. "I'm free on Saturday," I said, not detailing where I'd be on Friday since he'd already established that he didn't like thinking about that.

"Good, I'll pick you up at six."

"Pick me up for what?" I asked. He'd done this before and every time, he'd shown up in his giant yellow Hummer that could double as a school bus on steroids. The vehicle was made to get attention, so the entire town had been notified of his arrival at my house via social media thanks to The Ladies. I wanted to know what I was getting into this time around.

"The full moon lift ride at the ski resort. Wear something warm, and I'll bring a blanket."

I raised a brow. "That sounds scandalous. I'm sure The Ladies will be around to document it for the Facebook group."

"Let's hope not," he said, a twinkle in his eye. "I have plans for that blanket."

A flush came over my chest and started working its way up. I tried to control it before it became a full-on fire. I did that by changing the subject to something that wouldn't make me think of where Drake's hands could be on Saturday, and if he really would do something sinful. "We've already established that you got my text."

He lifted his glass and took a long drink, clearly buying himself some time, before answering, "I did."

"So, what do you know about the third body that was found?"

Drake pressed his lips together. "Grant called me about it. I couldn't tell you because no one knew at that point, and like I said, we were trying to keep the information out of the public for as long as possible."

My eyes widened. "Obviously some people knew because Ella had the info before I did, and she got it from a freaking podcast!"

He frowned at that. "We're aware, and not sure how they got the information. There were a lot of people working on the property yesterday. It could have been anyone."

"Right, but you were right there, knew about it, and didn't tell me."

"I couldn't break client/attorney privilege."

I tilted my head to the side and looked straight at him.

"Well, that's good to know. What other things do you plan on keeping from me in the future?"

He sighed and reached up to tug on his ear like he was uneasy. "I tell you what I can, Katie. Our jobs make things difficult. There will be times when you have questions that I can't answer. You're going to have to trust me."

That didn't bode well for a possible future relationship between us because I always had questions. Hundreds of them. I needed a partner I could trust and be completely open and honest with. I'd thought that was a point in Drake's column, but he and Hawke might line up pretty equally on the honesty scale. "Alright, what can you tell me then?"

Drake leaned back in his chair. "It's not good for Grant and his partners."

"What's the history with this project for Grant? He's been in this business a long time and understands due diligence. I have a hard time believing he knew nothing about the bodies."

Drake's eyebrows shot up. "I guarantee you that if he'd known, GCR wouldn't have bought the property. It's been nothing but a headache for him and it's costing him, his partners, and his investors, thousands of dollars a day. There are contracts in place and the delay is literally throwing money in the trash."

"Maybe he knew the risk he was taking."

Drake shook his head. "If he'd known, he would have told them to be more careful where they dug so that the bodies wouldn't have been unearthed."

That was a good point. But also, eww. "That sounds smarmy, illegal, and like something straight out of the mob."

Drake shrugged. "Real estate disclosure laws vary by state

but in Utah, they aren't strict, and it's easy to get around them. These things happen. Probably more than most people realize."

"Because it gets swept under the rug by lawyers and politicians," I pointed out, eying him in a way that reminded Drake he was both.

Drake shook his head. "We're not all bad, but corruption does occur. The lobbyists are powerful. But as his legal counsel, I will tell you that Grant knew nothing about the bodies on the property."

"Is this one of those times I'm going to have to trust you while you omit important details?"

He pressed his full lips into a line that I would have been distracted by if I wasn't irritated. Okay, so I was distracted despite the irritation. "You're going to have to trust me."

My reporter's intuition was still pinging. "It feels fishy."

Drake shook his head. "This project has turned into a nightmare because of the human remains. Not only does it delay the development, but now everyone knows about the bodies, the media is becoming more interested by the day, and the property has a bad reputation. People think of homes built on a place where bodies are found and immediately conjure up visions of *Poltergeist*. Grant's going to have a hard time selling the homes now."

I raised a brow. "Have you seen what's happening with the real estate market? We have a massive home shortage in Utah and builders across the state, and especially in Branson, are building as fast as possible. I really don't think people are going to care."

"Would you want to build a house on a haunted lot?"

I wrinkled my nose. "No, I wouldn't. But I watch a lot of paranormal shows and read a lot of paranormal romance, so I know better."

He lifted his hand and gestured as if to say he'd made his point.

"Other people might be fine with it. Maybe they'll find their undead soul mate."

Drake's eyes sparked and his lips curved wickedly. "Is that what you're looking for? Someone to bite you?"

I licked my lips. "Maybe."

"That can be arranged."

Given my lack of attire and easily discarded jammies, this conversation and subject needed to change because I had a lot to get done and not nearly enough time for Drake to be one of those things. "I'm going to try and get a meeting with Grant today."

"They have a temporary office on the property. I'm sure he'll be there monitoring the situation."

"Good to know," I said, finishing my breakfast and coffee. Gandalf had been hovering under the table for a significant amount of time. I suspected Drake had been giving him pieces of bacon. I eyed Drake as I saw him reach down under the guise of petting, but he was really letting Gandalf lick his fingers. "You're bribing him, and feeding him from the table, which is a bad habit."

Drake's lips lifted slyly. "He's not my dog so I don't have to deal with the consequences. Yet."

My eyes widened. "That's pretty presumptuous."

"I don't play to lose," he said with total confidence.

Drake reached down to give Gandalf a little pet and

Gandalf leaned into it, clearly in love. And the next time Hawke came over, Gandalf would treat him the exact same way. I had a sudden and unsettling realization that my dog and I weren't that different.

"I have to get to work, but wish I could stay," he said, his eyes lingering on my robe again.

"If this robe does it for you, you need to get out more, and maybe look at some porn. Also, stop your compatriots at the capitol from passing stupid laws that try to control peoples' choices and make it difficult for them to have a healthy relationship with their own body." The state legislature had passed a law making it illegal to view sexually explicit material without uploading your ID to prove your age first. Since looking at sexually explicit material was against the teachings of the church, members were wary about uploading identifying information, and most people didn't think it was anyone's business what they were looking at. Utah liked to tout its support for keeping the government out of people's personal lives—unless it involved sex or controlling women, then the government was all-in on restrictions.

Drake leaned forward, closing the gap between us. "*You* do it for me." His mouth closed over mine, his tongue tracing my lips. He held the kiss for a long moment and then left me standing there, lips stinging pleasantly, and my mind racing with thoughts of Drake, kisses, and what might have happened if we'd walked down the hall instead.

I dropped Gandalf off with my mom and dad before meeting Bethany at the assisted living center. Bethany was waiting for me on a bench in the lobby when I arrived. "Thanks for meeting me, and letting me see your mom," I said, after she motioned for me to sit next to her.

"I'm happy to help. The police have been by as well, and I've told them what I can. My mom's information is a little less reliable. There's a lot she doesn't remember, and some of the things she does remember aren't accurate."

I nodded in understanding. Memory loss was a heartbreaking thing to have to deal with—for the person going through it, and the family members trying to support them.

"Can you tell me the history of the property?" I asked.

She took a breath and nodded. "It's been in my family for generations. All farmers. When my dad died, my mom leased some of the land out to another farmer in the area, Wayne Post."

"What was Wayne using it for?"

"Grazing for his cattle."

Leasing made sense, especially if Georgia and her family weren't using the land for their own cattle. There was no reason for the land to sit there when the Barret family could make money off of it. "How did Wayne handle it when your family decided to sell?"

She sighed and briefly closed her eyes. "He wasn't thrilled. It's easier to keep cattle close, and land like ours has fewer predators than property higher in the mountains. The higher ground is where he's had to move his cows now."

"Why did you decide to sell?"

She lifted one shoulder. "It seemed like the right time. We wanted to get it sold before my mom passed away. She has an estate plan, but settling an estate can take years. None of us know what property values will look like in the future. We wanted to sell while the value was high. Land is at a premium in Utah and people are moving out of the city and trying to find bigger pieces of property to build homes on. Grant made us a good offer."

"I understand the property was in a trust. Did the whole family agree to the sale?"

Her hands were clasped in her lap and she started rubbing her thumb over her other hand in a soothing gesture. "Everyone had strong opinions, but there just needed to be a majority. My mom's still alive and still has a say. She liked Grant."

So, Jordan must not have wanted to sell. I needed to talk to him, and hoped he'd call me back soon. If not, I'd follow up again.

"Your mom met Grant?" I asked.

"She did." Bethany glanced at her watch. "She's done with breakfast now and should be ready for us if you want to meet her."

"I'd love to."

I followed Bethany and we went down the hall. A woman with short gray hair and a kind smile came out of the room wearing a lavender knit sweater, and white linen pants.

"Well, hello, sweetheart!" the woman said to Bethany.

"Hi, Grace," Bethany said with a warm smile. They gave each other a quick hug, the mutual admiration clear.

"I was checking in on your mom. I was worried about her, especially with everything going on at the property."

"It's a little crazy," Bethany agreed. "Thanks for looking after her and being a good friend."

Grace smiled and got a distant look on her face like she was remembering the past. "She's always been an incredible friend to me. There's not a more loyal person on the planet."

Bethany nodded. "I know she loves your visits."

Grace touched Bethany on the forearm. "I'll be back to visit again soon." She gave us both a soft smile and walked away.

"Who was that?" I asked.

"Grace Caldwell. She and my mom have been friends for longer than I can remember. She comes to visit sometimes, and it's good for my mom."

I followed Bethany into the room her mom was staying in. Pale pink curtains covered a large window. She had a seating area, a dresser, closet, and her own bathroom. A chair in the corner had a multi-colored crocheted granny square blanket covering it. The hospital bed took up most of the room, but the space had a surprisingly homey feel to it.

Georgia had light brown hair with streaks of grey, curled to perfection. She was wearing earrings and a necklace, and a gold diamond wedding ring on her left hand. She offered Bethany a wide smile when we walked in. "There you are," she said, her eyes twinkling.

Bethany smiled back, her eyes bright. "Hi, Mom. How was your morning?"

"Well, it would be much better if they'd stop bringing me oatmeal with raisins every morning for breakfast." She pointed to the tray sitting next to the bed. "Why don't you sneak out and get me some cereal. Or better yet, some ice cream!"

Bethany's expression softened, lines forming at the

corners of her eyes. "Are you trying to get me in trouble, Mom?"

She gave Bethany a sly smile. "You could be sneaky. I know it."

Bethany shook her head and laughed. "I'd like you to meet a friend of mine, Mom. Her name is Kate, and she's the editor for *The Branson Tribune*."

"Oh!" She clasped her hands together in excitement. "I know your name, Kate! The kids come in and read me articles from the *Tribune*."

A warm feeling bubbled up in my chest. I was surprised she knew my name, or remembered any of my articles, but I felt honored and humbled at the same time. "Hi, Mrs. Barret. I've heard a lot about you. It's nice to finally meet you."

"What brings a reporter to my room? Heavens, I didn't even get my hair done!" She looked to Bethany. "We need to get Greta over here right away to make me presentable!"

"I'll see what I can do," Bethany said, patting her hand. "Kate's doing a story about our old farm that we sold."

"Really?" Georgia said, her eyes popping open more with interest. "That man we sold it to. I liked him a lot."

"Grant?" I offered.

"Yes," she answered with a sweet smile. "He was so kind and said he'd take good care of everything."

"The property was in your family for a long time," I said. "It's no wonder you wanted to sell it to the right person."

"It was," she agreed, nodding her head. "Generations. We even had a cemetery on it."

My eyes swung to Bethany.

She closed her eyes and shook her head slightly, indicating

it wasn't what I thought. "It was a family cemetery from pioneer days, in an area that was marked off. Grant knew about it, and it had been separated from the lots that were being developed for housing so it could be turned into open space."

Still, it made me wonder if the cemetery location was bigger than they realized and maybe the remains found were from the family plots.

"And cows," Georgia offered. "We kept cows on the land."

I nodded. "I heard you leased the property to a neighboring farmer."

She shook her head and frowned. "I never agreed to that."

I glanced at Bethany again. "My dad had the agreement. We kept it in place after my dad died because it brought in extra money for mom."

"Your dad," Georgia said, shaking her head. "That man thought he knew it all and never listened to me. He wasn't nice."

Bethany leaned down. "We're here, and we hear you," she said, rubbing Georgia's hand. "And you're not alone."

"I took care of everything," Georgia said in a sing-song voice. "Everything." She paused. "Now where do you think my breakfast is, sweet little Beth? Do you think they'll bring me that nasty oatmeal with raisins again today?"

Bethany, glanced at me and I knew it was probably time to go. "I'll be back in a few minutes," she said to Georgia. She squeezed her mom's hand and kissed her forehead before standing.

"It was nice to meet you," I said to Georgia.

Georgia smiled at me as I followed Bethany out of the room.

"She seems to be doing fairly well," I said, noting that she was able to respond and still seemed to have pieces of information. She forgot she'd already eaten breakfast, but her answers were clear.

"Greta was her hairstylist twenty years ago," Bethany explained. "She's on some new medications that have helped, but her memory gets worse as the day goes on."

"I can't imagine having to watch that kind of deterioration in someone you love. I'm sorry you're going through that."

"It's okay." Bethany said, wrapping her arms around herself. "I have a supportive fiancé and that helps."

"I'm glad. Thank you for talking to me and for taking me to meet your mom."

"You're welcome."

As we walked outside, I asked, "Does anyone in your family know anything about the bodies that have been found? Your brother, Jordan? Or any extended family members?"

She shook her head. "We have no idea what happened, or how the bodies got there. Our family is as eager as everyone else to find out more."

"Have you tried asking your mom about it?"

Bethany put her hands in her pockets and nodded. "I have, but she hasn't told me anything. If she knows something, she's guarding it well. Even if she mentioned something, we'd have no real idea of what was or wasn't true."

I nodded. Dementia was a horrible disease and even if Georgia could remember something, there was a good chance it wouldn't be accurate. "Thanks for all of your help," I said, stopping by my Jeep.

"You're welcome. Let me know if you have any other questions."

"I will."

I watched as Bethany went back into the building to spend time with her mom.

Meeting with Grant was next on my list. When I arrived at the Barret property, police cars and vehicles from various agencies were scattered around the development, and there were teams all over. Grant's temporary office for the development was on the other side of the crime scene. I pulled up and found a dark blue BMW eight series parked outside a metal bin that strongly resembled an enlarged porta potty, or one of those portable storage containers, only bigger.

I knocked on the door and a male voice told me to come in.

Grant was sitting behind a desk, his laptop open and his phone next to it. There were two other desks in the room, probably for his partners, Chris, and Ryan. Grant's sleeves were rolled up and he looked haggard, like he hadn't slept well. He glanced up from his computer.

"Hi, Grant," I said. "I was hoping to ask you some questions about the property if you have time."

"Sure, Kate." He let out a long breath, and ran his hand through his hair. "I'm happy to help with anything I can."

I took a seat in one of the chairs across from him and placed a recorder on the desk. "Can you tell me about how you heard the property was available, and your acquisition of it?"

"Sure. GCR Development is well-known in the Salt Lake City area, but we noticed a demand for larger lots and more rural locations, so we started looking outside of the metro area. Branson Falls was one of the cities gaining a lot of traction. This piece of property was large, in the mountains, and perfect for estate lots. Our research shows that a lot of people want to move out of the city and have more space so their neighbors aren't right on top of them. This piece could offer that, and we could charge a high premium for the lots, especially the lots with a view."

I took notes as he talked. "Was this the only piece of land you were looking at?"

"No, our broker found several pieces. There are other properties we're still interested in, and we're planning to expand if this development does well. But the Barret family was highly motivated to sell, and the location was great. We had investor interest, so we picked this one up first."

That piqued my interest. "Why were they motivated to sell?"

"The family matriarch's health is in decline, and her kids wanted the land sold before she passes away."

Bethany had said the same thing, but it seemed like she was the only kid who wanted it sold. "How did you find out it was for sale? Was it listed with a realtor or broker?"

"We got it before it was listed. One of the brokers we work with, Trent Aslow, knew we were looking in the area and tipped us off that it would be going up for sale. We got it pretty quickly, for a price the Barret family wanted, and one we knew we could turn a profit with."

"Did you have any inspections or reports done before you bought it?"

"We did basic inspections, and had an engineering firm look at the topography and soil composition—standard things. It was a good deal in a great location, and we knew we'd be able to make a substantial profit once the homes started to sell. Our investors were eager to get the property and start building."

It seemed strange that they did basic inspections, but I didn't know much about buying land, so maybe that was normal.

A knock sounded on the door with a perky feminine, "Yoo-hoo!" coming from the other side. About five seconds passed before the door swung open revealing a short woman with shoulder length dark brown, straight hair, a heart shaped face, and a smile that was as overly enthusiastic as her voice. She looked like she was probably in her sixties.

"Grant," she said with a blinding smile. "I'm Edith Coon, with the Murderoonies podcast. It's so lovely to meet you. I was wondering if I could ask you some questions?"

Grant took a deep breath. I wasn't sure if he knew the Murderoonies were in town covering the case of multiplying bodies on his property development, but the extra notoriety probably wasn't going to help his business. "Sure," Grant said with a tight smile. "I was answering some questions for Kate Saxee, the editor of the town newspaper, *The Branson Tribune*." He gestured toward me and while I appreciated the introduction, it kind of felt like a way to distract from himself.

Edith's eyes went over me with part interest, part assessment. Almost like she saw me as her competition. The corners of my lips lifted in amusement. I'd been a reporter for years, and had won awards for my work. I hadn't looked into the Murderoonies yet so I didn't know Edith's professional experience, but I didn't see her as a threat. She might even be a resource at some point. She obviously had news about the third body before I did. Maybe we could each be assets to one another.

"It's nice to meet you, Kate. I'm sure we'll be able to help your investigation. I heard we even broke news before you did yesterday." She said it with a too sweet smile that was full of teeth. If this was her way of making a first impression, she'd certainly done so by implying I wasn't good at my job. I amended my earlier thought because I didn't think the Murderoonies and I were going to be assets to each other. And based on the competitive energy she was throwing my way, I didn't think we were even going to be friends.

"Do you mind if I record this?" Edith's eyes went from Grant, to me.

"That's fine," Grant answered.

I lifted a shoulder, but was a little uneasy. "I'm already recording it." The difference was that I was recording it so I had the interview on file and could go back and check my facts while I was writing news articles about the case. Edith was recording it so she could use it on her podcast, and I wasn't sure how I felt about being an unintentional featured guest.

Edith gave a satisfied smile and put a high-tech recorder down on the desk between the three of us so it could pick up all of our voices. "Excellent," she said. "Why don't you start with giving me a history of the how you came to be in possession of the Barret property."

"I actually just went over that with him," I said.

Grant nodded. "It's fine." Then he repeated the same information he'd already given me.

"How long will the delay be now that they've found three bodies?" Edith asked, sliding her eyes to me when she said *three*. I wondered how she found out that her podcast broke the story before the *Tribune*.

Grant shrugged. "Drake said the police told him they would try to get us back to work as soon as possible, but it depends on what else they find. They brought cadaver dogs in and that should help speed things up. If there are more remains on the property, the dogs will know and the remains can be excavated. If there aren't more remains, we should be able to get back to work as soon as they clear the scene."

"I'm sorry," Edith said, her brows pushed together. "Who exactly is Drake?"

"Dylan Drake," I answered.

"My attorney," Grant said.

Edith's eyes went very wide. "Dylan Drake, the politician and *extremely* eligible bachelor?"

"Yes," Grant said, matter-of-factly.

"Well," she replied, her tone almost as flushed as her cheeks, "this case just got even more interesting."

I couldn't tell if I was annoyed, jealous, or amused. Maybe all three. Drake had charisma and charm, and women everywhere knew it. I'd just started to think of that charisma and charm being directed mostly at me. But it wasn't, and we weren't in a committed relationship, so my emotions needed to settle down.

Edith got control of herself and asked another question. "What do you think about the rumors that the bodies might be victims of a serial killer?"

Grant kept his expression impressively neutral. "I think we'll have to wait and see what the medical examiner finds out." It was like Drake had tutored him on how to give the bare minimum information, and answer questions without answering questions.

"Do you have any enemies?" I asked, a theory forming in my mind. "Someone who might have planted the bodies there?" It was a long shot, but all theories start out that way. We had information on the first body, but not the second and third yet. Maybe the first body was a natural death, like a hiker, and the others had been buried later.

"Oh!" Edith jumped in her seat with excitement. "Excellent question, Kate. Do you have any enemies, Grant?"

I stared at the woman and tried hard not to open my mouth because if I had, a whole slew of admonishment would have come out, including the fact that this was my interview, I didn't need her validation, and she was stealing my questions and trying to pass them off as her own. I wanted to tell her she was welcome to come back and conduct her own interview on her own time instead of taking up mine.

Grant looked like that was a question he hadn't even considered, and didn't know what to do with. "Not that I know of. I'd never even thought of that. Do you think someone could have put the bodies there on purpose?"

I was about to answer but Edith immediately cut in.

"Oh," Edith said assuredly, "someone definitely put the bodies there on purpose. We just don't know what the purpose was, or who did it."

I tilted my head and my attention went between Edith and Grant. "I asked the question because I'm trying to investigate all avenues and develop theories," I said, explaining, "but we actually don't know if the bodies were put there on purpose, yet. The police haven't released the information."

Edith gave me a look that was almost condescending. "Why else would bodies be found on the property?"

I cocked my head toward her. "The is the Rocky Mountains, in rural Utah. People hike and recreate here, and go missing all the time because of it. It could have been an accident."

She tilted her head and gave me a sideways glance. "Three bodies in the same place would be quite a coincidence. I suppose there's an extremely small chance it could have been an accident, but there's a much bigger chance that it was murder."

That's the funny thing about belief. People tend to gravitate towards things that confirm the biases they already have instead of staying objective, looking at all sides, and seeking out new information.

Grant interrupted. "No one's more interested than I am in finding out what happened and why the bodies ended up on the property I'm developing, but I don't think we're going to get much information until the police know more."

"I agree," I said, standing up. It seemed like the interview was winding down, and it was difficult to ask questions with Edith there interjecting. I decided I'd leave to pursue some of the leads I'd gotten talking to Grant, before Edith arrived. If I had more questions for Grant later, I knew where to find him.

Edith stood as well and put her hand out. "It was *so* nice to meet you, Kate!" Her tone, gestures, and everything about her rubbed me the wrong way. I was trying to be open-minded, but my initial interaction with her had not gone well. She seemed like the type of person who was used to being adored and was desperate to get that constant validation.

"It was nice to meet you as well," I said, still trying to decide how I was going to handle her going forward.

"We'll talk again soon." Edith handed me her business card, gave me a saccharine sweet smile, picked up her recorder, and walked out the door. I was surprised she didn't stick around to wait for me to leave first so she could talk more with Grant.

"I'm not sure if I'm happy about that podcast being here and covering the case," Grant confided once Edith was gone.

I didn't blame him. And based on this first interaction with Edith, I was a bit worried they were going to make my job more difficult as well. "I can understand that. It will definitely bring more publicity to the case, and your development." Probably not in a good way, but I kept that part to myself since I was pretty sure Grant was thinking the same thing. "Have you spoken to the Barret family since this all happened?"

He took a breath. "I have. They've denied any knowledge of the bodies."

"Exactly how good of a deal did you get on the property?" I asked. Maybe the family really did know about the bodies and they were trying to sell the land before anyone found out. I could probably find the sales price in public records, but it would be easier if he told me.

"It was a good investment, and they settled for a bit under market value, but nothing that would have made me suspicious of the property. If they would have listed it for sale, they would have had multiple offers from other developers, for more than we paid. My understanding was that they wanted the land sold while Georgia Barret was still alive, and they wanted it sold to someone Georgia approved of. The market is on fire right now and they wanted to take advantage of that. We had investors and were capable of closing on the project quickly. I wouldn't have bought the property had I known about this."

Drake had said the same thing about Grant and the land purchase.

"I'll reach out to the Barret family and let you know if I find out any additional details."

"I appreciate that," he said.

I left and went back to the office to make some calls.

Chapter Nine

"I met the Murderoonies this morning." I put my bag down on my desk and grabbed a doughnut from the treat table. After my introduction to Edith, I needed the sugar pick-me-up.

Spence's brows went up.

Ella was practically bouncing, her excitement boiling over. "Which one," she asked, breathless.

"Edith."

"O. M. G! She's the OG!" Ella said, clapping and jumping. "She started it all! Everyone loves her!"

"Not everyone," I said, leaning against the treat table and eating my doughnut.

Ella narrowed her eyes. "Who doesn't like her?"

"Grant Kimball, for one. She's bringing a lot more attention to the bodies on his property than he would like. She also barged in on my interview with Grant and tried to take over."

"She's tryin' to get info for the podcast," Ella defended.

I gave Ella a look. "She also insinuated I wasn't good at my job."

Ella was nice enough to wrinkle her nose at that.

"Will they be a problem," Spence asked.

I grabbed a glass of water from the dispenser and took a drink. "I'll handle it." It wasn't the first time I'd had to deal with other people trying to hone in on a story I was covering. But usually those people were other journalists, and we all had some level of professionalism toward one another. I hadn't gotten that feeling from Edith. She seemed intent on the story she wanted to tell, and unapologetic about it.

"What's her background?" I asked Ella. "Does she have training in investigations?"

"She liked true crime and started lookin' into cold cases with her friend, Margie. The Murderoonies really took off when they solved the case of the two missin' women on the Colorado River. After that, the Murderoonies kept coverin' cold cases, but also realized people loved to follow cases happenin' right now, so that's what they do the most of."

I'd have to listen to some of their old podcasts. "So, she has no training in journalism, investigating crimes, interviewing, or anything related?"

Ella folded her arms over her chest. "Not that I know of, but it doesn't seem like she really needs it, does it."

Ella was being rather defensive of someone she didn't even know. "What about other people who work for the podcast? You said there's more than Edith?"

"She has a friend who's her co-host. Margie Fay. They've been podcastin' together since the beginnin' of the Murderoonies. Edith's daughter also helps, and they have a producer who runs the business."

"Does Margie have any special training?"

"Don't know, but the two of them together are a great team!"

I needed to meet them both and find out more, especially if they were going to be in my realm for a while. The whole "keep your friends close and enemies closer" thing.

"It's so excitin' they're here," Ella said, clasping her hands in front of her, a dreamy look on her face. She was still unable to contain her glee. "They're havin' a get-together tonight at the hotel, and *everyone's* gonna be there. You should come."

"You should," Spence piped up. "And write something on it."

Ugh. It had already been a long day and I wasn't sure I had the capacity for a room full of people obsessed with The Murderoonies. "Can we get one of the part-time staff members to do it?"

Spence leaned against the desk and crossed his feet at the ankles. "Yeah, but they're not you. You'll get more information if you go. And it would be smart to see who else is there and interested in the podcast, and what the Murderoonies are saying."

He wasn't wrong, and that made it even more irritating. Law enforcement officers did that all the time when they were investigating something like a murder. They'd show up at vigils and celebrations of life to see who was there, and who might be acting suspicious. Especially if they had a suspect in mind. Officers might even show up at the Murderoonies event tonight because if someone had killed three people and buried the bodies on the Barret property, the killer might be intrigued by all the interest the story was getting and want to be involved. Psychopaths were going to psychopath.

"What time is the event?" I asked Ella.

"Starts at seven. But I'm sure people will show up early to talk to the gang."

"They're a gang now?"

"In the best way!" she said, slapping her hand on her thigh. "I'm gonna wear my Murderoonie tee!"

"I guess I'll see you there," I said, relenting. Not only would it be good to see who attended and get more information on the story and hear rumors about the bodies, but now it was also a full-fledged town event, and it would need to be covered for the *Tribune*. Like Spence said, I was the best person to do it.

I had more research to do on Grant Kimball, and the Barret property, but first, I was going to get some lunch.

I texted my mom to ask if she could keep Gandalf a little longer tonight. She said she could, so I texted her back the little poop with hearts. She'd texted it to multiple people by accident recently, and now it was my fun little way of letting her know I loved her. I wasn't sure she appreciated the gesture.

I walked across the street to Fry Guy. I ordered a chicken sandwich with fries, and an Oreo shake with extra Oreos, then turned around to find a table. Hawke was sitting in a booth. He grinned at me widely and the smile was more than an invitation.

I sat across from him.

"Not going to sit next to me?" he asked.

"I'm not sure that's wise," I said, gesturing around the booth. "This feels familiar."

His lips curved up slowly. "Last time we were in this booth sitting across from each other, you had a milkshake that I got to taste."

"Oh, I remember," I said. "It was recorded, and the whole town, my mom included, accused us of having sex on the tabletop and being porn stars."

He gave a very male, wicked grin. "I wouldn't mind making a video or two with you."

I raised a brow. "Maybe not at a fast-food restaurant."

"Fast food restaurant, car, the city park, I'm flexible," he said with a wink.

Hawke's order was called, and mine was called right after. Hawke got up to get them both and I grabbed some extra fry sauce. The fry sauce was the best part of eating at Fry Guy.

"I see you got the Oreo shake again," Hawke pointed out.

I took a bite of said shake. "I always get the Oreo shake. With lots and lots of extra Oreos. Especially when I need to eat my feelings."

His eyes shifted over me, assessing. "Long day, Kitty Kate?"

I took a deep breath. "I had an interview hi-jacked this morning by the most perky woman on the planet, who insulted me with a smile. So that's how it's going." I decided to leave out the part about it starting with breakfast in a robe, and Drake at my kitchen table.

"More infuriating than Mrs. Olsen?"

I had to think hard about that. "It remains to be seen, but this woman is right up there with The Ladies and Mormon Relief Society on the perky meter. I got the impression that she thinks she's better than everyone else, especially me. Most people probably think she's charming and friendly AF, but I'm not one of them."

He nodded in understanding. "I have some info for you."

I perked up. "That sounds like a bit of good news that I

could definitely use. What do you know? And you better not hold anything back this time."

"I got your text and know that you're aware they found three bodies on the Barret property, not two."

"Yeah, and I didn't find that out from Bobby, or *you*." I didn't try to hide the annoyance in my tone because I was certain Hawke found out about that third body right around the same time Bobby did…maybe even before. Hawke was helping them at the scene and he still hadn't informed me of the breaking news.

"Who told you?" Hawke asked.

I picked up my spoon and took a bite of my Oreo shake. Hawke's eyes followed the movement. "Ella. Who heard it from the freaking Murderoonies podcast. I was scooped by people who aren't even from here, and definitely are not editors of the town newspaper."

He winced. "I should have told you, but we were asked not to share the information so I tried to respect that."

"Well, someone clearly didn't follow those instructions. You could have told me and asked me not to tell anyone. Then I at least would have had the information and wouldn't have been blindsided. You're lucky I'm even here with you right now. Yesterday, I was mad enough to revoke your milkshake privileges."

Hawke picked up my shake spoon and slowly ran his tongue over the ice cream, licking it clean. "That would have been a tragedy for us both."

I pointed a fry at him. "Touché."

He pressed his lips together. "I'll try to keep you more informed in the future."

"That's not an agreement to keep me in the loop."

"I'll be more aware and tell you as much as I can."

"Still not an agreement." But it was the best I was going to get. "I'm going to their Murderoonie welcome event tonight at the new hotel."

He nodded. "I saw their vans. I'm not surprised they're here. If anything, I'm surprised they didn't get here faster."

"Really?"

He swallowed a bite of his burger before answering. "They're based in the suburbs of Salt Lake City. This case fits their target demographic perfectly, and it's close to home for them."

"What do you know about them?"

"That they're one of the top-rated true crime podcasts, and they've won awards for their work. They solved a cold case that put them on the true crime podcast map years ago, and they've been attracting more and more listeners ever since."

"Ella's obsessed with them. Do you know their background?" If he did, that would save me some time.

He popped a fry in his mouth, sans fry sauce, and I tried not to let the horror of his naked potato show on my face. The fry sauce was what *made* Fry Guy. "Edith was a school teacher and Margie was a stay-at-home mom. Now they're both in their late sixties. So, they don't have professional experience; but they're amateur investigators who hit it big after solving a case that had a lot of interest at the time and seemed like it couldn't be solved."

I took another bite of my shake. "I'm worried about the damage they might be able to do by covering this case. As a journalist, I have rules around obtaining and releasing information. A podcast doesn't have that, and I'm worried they won't be selective about disseminating what they find out, or even verifying their sources." When I had ideas or theories, I investigated them. From what I'd seen of Edith and the Murderoonies so far, they reported their knowledge as soon as they had it whether it had been vetted or not. The third body situation was a perfect example.

Hawke gave me a look. "Grant should also be worried."

"He is. I talked to him this morning and then Edith showed up in the middle of my interview."

"I take it she's the most perky woman on the planet you mentioned earlier?"

I tipped a fry sauce covered fry at him. "Bingo."

"They'll be annoying, but hopefully they won't get in your way."

"They already have, and I'm going to try very hard not to murder them myself."

One of Hawke's brows ticked up. "Let me know if you need me to do something about it."

"Something like murder?"

He lifted a shoulder. "We can explore options."

"You can't," I said, ignoring the fact that he was basically offering me a menu of how to get rid of people I didn't want to deal with. His skills would have been super helpful for me in high school. "They investigate murders and have a podcast about it. You'd be caught."

Hawke gave a slow and deliberate smile. "I'm never caught, Kitty Kate."

I pressed my lips together and looked at him long and hard. "That's not as reassuring as you probably think it is."

"You always know who to call to help you hide the bodies."

I lifted a finger in the air like I was making a point. "Again, not as reassuring as you might think." I paused. "On second thought, it actually is because I'm certain that unlike the dead bodies on the Barret property, your bodies would never be found."

"That's actually part of the info I have for you."

I urged him on with my hand, which was holding a spoonful of the Oreo shake I'd licked.

"That's not helping me think, Kitty Kate."

I licked the spoon very carefully with my tongue. He deserved a bit of torture, especially after leaving me with blue ovaries on Halloween, *and* not telling me about the third body. "Go on," I said. "What do you know?"

He held my eyes, a dangerous look that promised all sorts of sins playing out across his gaze. "I know you'll be paying for that later." He slowly licked his lips. "Did you ask Bobby how far down in the ground the remains of the bodies were?"

I wrinkled my forehead. "No."

"The first body that was found on the property was a couple of feet under ground-level. It's probably why they suspected it was a hiker—it wasn't well buried. But the second body was found four feet below ground level, and the third was almost six feet down—in the same hole."

I knew about the second and third bodies being buried on top of each other. "So, the second and third bodies were put there on purpose, and maybe the first one too. The hole was deep enough to show that someone actually dug graves—for bodies two and three at least."

"Seems like it."

"Do you know if the second and third bodies were buried at the same time? Like, did they dig down six feet, throw a body in, shovel two feet of dirt on top, then throw the other body in?"

"I'm not sure yet. Once we get info back from forensics, we'll have a better idea about when they died and if they were buried at the same time. The teams removing the bones think they're all male."

My jaw fell open. "I didn't know that."

"I wanted to tell you first before you threatened to take my milkshake away again."

I tried not to smile but the corners of my lips twitched and he saw it. "If the bodies are all male, that doesn't fit Zundy's victim profile."

"No, it doesn't. I don't think it was Zundy."

I didn't think so either, so did that mean it was another serial killer, or something else entirely?

"But that's not all," Hawke said.

It was like the infomercials where the salesperson kept saying, "But wait! There's More!"

I gestured for him to go on. "Don't leave me hanging."

"There was a card found in the same area as the first human remains."

"Like an ID?" Bobby had said something was found with the first body that helped them figure out an age range.

"No, but it's something. It's pretty faded, but some things were visible and I have a good idea of what the card was for."

I wondered if it would help identify who the person had been.

"So, three bodies—"

"—So far," Hawke amended.

"Three bodies so far, all on the same property. What are the chances that the Barret family didn't know about this?" I'd wondered the same thing when I'd talked to Grant earlier and hadn't been able to shake the thought.

Hawke shook his head. "It would be shocking if someone in the family didn't know, but I've heard stranger things. Maybe that's the exact reason why they sold the property."

"You think they were trying to get rid of it because they knew bodies were buried there?"

"Maybe not everyone knew about it. Maybe only select family members were aware."

Hmmm, that was an interesting thought. "I talked to Georgia Barret and her daughter, Bethany."

"You know Bethany's fiancé, Eddie Prestman, was the Barret family realtor, right?"

I almost dropped my ice cream filled spoon. "I didn't know that. Do you think that caused some issues with the family."

Hawke bit his bottom lip like he was trying to decide how much to say. "I don't think it helped. I've heard Bethany and Jordan aren't on good terms."

"I haven't talked to Jordan yet. I've left messages, but he hasn't returned my calls. I need to get a meeting with him."

Hawke leaned back in his seat and smiled in a way that indicated he knew something I didn't. "Good luck."

"What's that smile for?"

"Have you met Jordan Barret?"

I thought back to my time growing up in Branson. I knew of the family, but hadn't spent time with Jordan. He was older than I was. "I don't know him well."

"He's not a fan of people, so you might have a hard time getting a meeting."

"I'm a journalist. I'm good at asking for things, not feeling rejected if people say no, and then asking again until I get what I want."

Hawke chuckled. "I don't imagine many people say no to you. I wouldn't."

"I'm not sure if that's a compliment, an innuendo, or both."

"Always both, Kitty Kate." He took my spoon from my shake and licked it again in a way that got me in a lot of trouble back when we first met, and could only be described as obscene. "Why don't we take this Oreo shake somewhere more private?"

I looked at my watch and had a silent debate with myself about whether I wanted my first real sexual experience with Hawke to be quick and dirty, or long and uninterrupted. Given my schedule for the rest of the night, I only had time for quick and dirty at the moment.

"Kate!" The voice was one I recognized and wished that I didn't. Quick and dirty had just been crossed of my option list. Edith came over, waving her arms in case I'd managed to lose my hearing and hadn't heard her yelling my name across the three hundred square feet of dining room space.

"Hi, Edith."

She came to a stop in front of our table, cocked her hip out, and rested her hand on top of it. "What a coincidence finding you here!"

"Small town," I reminded her.

"That's true, I forget that about towns where everyone knows everyone. Speaking of that, I haven't met your friend yet." She turned toward Hawke, flashing so many bright teeth that I wondered if she'd stopped in for a whitening session between interrupting my meeting with Grant and now interrupting my lunch with Hawke. It's like she'd made interrupting me her personal mission. "I'm Edith Coon, the creator of The Murderoonies podcast. We're here covering the recovery of the bodies on the Barret Property, and the potential victims of serial killer, Jeff Zundy."

She'd thrown Jeff Zundy into her pitch pretty fast. I hadn't heard that part of her intro with Grant this morning.

"It's nice to meet you," Hawke said. "I've listened to your podcast."

I lifted my brows at that revelation.

Edith looked like she might flat out faint. She put her hand to her chest and gushed, "Well, that's the most flattering thing I've heard all day, Mr.—" she let the salutation drag out, waiting for Hawke to fill in the blank.

"Hawke," he answered.

"That's an unusual and oddly appealing name," she said with a tilt of her head. "Is it your first, or your last?"

The fact that she was trying to get his personal information so she could dig up more personal information was painfully obvious. Hawke practically had a doctorate degree in information, so I knew he was aware of her tactics, and could take care of himself. "Neither," he told Edith with an unapologetic smile.

She looked at him like he was a mystery all by himself and she couldn't wait to unravel him…which was unsettling and if I were Hawke, I might be concerned. Then again, Hawke was basically an Apex predator and probably didn't have much to worry about. I investigated people and things for a living and even *I* couldn't get information about Hawke, and I knew his full name…and what he tasted like, and how magic his hands were.

"Well, it's very nice to meet you, not-my-first-name-or-last-Hawke." She gave him a little shrug that was probably meant to be adorable and might have worked if she'd been four. "It was *so* good to see you again, Kate. I suppose we'll be running into each other a lot."

"Undoubtedly," I agreed with the nicest smile I could conjure up. "Have a good lunch, Edith."

We both watched her walk to the front of the restaurant and pick up her order.

"You deflected her well," I said after Edith had left.

"I have some experience in that arena."

"In knocking down unwanted attention from women?"

"That too." He grinned and his eyes danced with mischief. "I suppose we won't have time for the Oreo shake if you're going to the Murderoonies event tonight."

I frowned. "Probably not."

"That's disappointing."

"I couldn't agree more. An orgasm would really take the edge off."

"Hopefully we can remedy that this weekend. Will I see you on Friday?"

That was two days away and it seemed like far too long, but I'd survive. "Yeah. What are we doing?"

"I'm sure I'll think of something," he said, biting his lip and pulling it back with his teeth.

I took another spoonful of my shake and licked it clean. His eyes didn't leave my mouth until I was done. "I can too. See you then."

I got back to the office and settled in at my desk and placed another call to Jordan Barret. Once again, it went straight to voice mail. I left another message telling him I'd like to talk to him and I'd already spoken with his sister and mom. If this continued, I was going to have to show up at Jordan's house and hope he was better at answering the door than answering his phone.

When I finished that, I looked up how much GCR Development paid for the Barret property. It was in the millions, but still less than what I would have expected. Maybe the family wanted to sell before Georgia passed away, like they'd said. Or maybe some of them wanted to keep the property because of the secrets buried there.

Chapter Ten

Ella wasn't kidding when she said everyone would be at the Murderoonies event. I had to park down the street because all the parking spots at the new hotel were full. They should have used one of the Mormon churches with their giant cultural halls—also known to the rest of the world as gyms, but with a built-in stage on one end in case anyone decided they wanted to perform an impromptu monologue after attempting to dunk a basketball and fracturing their arm.

I walked into the building and was greeted by a giant sign with a white background and black font that said *Meet the Murderoonies*! Bright red blood splatter dotted the corner of the banner. The two "O's" in Murderoonies looked like eyes spying on people walking by, and reminded me of those paintings where the figure's gaze follows you regardless of what position you're standing in. The "I" in 'Murderoonies' was cleverly disguised as a knife that was dripping blood.

It was a creative logo, and not one I would have guessed the Murderoonies would use. Their demographic seemed to be women who liked solving mysteries but not graphic, bloody crime scenes. The knife was also an interesting choice since most murders in America happened via firearm, not kitchen chopping implement. So based entirely on their banner and logo alone, I was already suspicious of this podcast that was supposed to be one of the best ever.

I saw Ella standing with some of The Ladies. Ella was wearing jeans with a black t-shirt that said *I'm a Murderoonie*. Several other people were wearing similar shirts, and I wondered exactly how much this podcast was bringing in a year. Ella had mentioned advertising and merch, but the merchandise was prominently displayed as soon as I walked into the hotel's conference room, and there was even a booth set up selling more with a line of people waiting to buy. So, I guessed they were making a decent profit.

Ella came up to me. "Isn't this excitin'?" she asked, bouncing from foot to foot.

My eyes trailed past the merchandise booth to the front of the room where people were setting things up for whatever the Murderoonies had planned next. "It's definitely something." And it was. This was quite an event for a small town like Branson Falls, and there were far more people crammed inside the room than I expected would attend. Usually I recognized most people at events in town, but there were a lot of new faces in this crowd.

"As soon as the Roonies announced they were comin' to Branson, the social pages were all abuzz," Ella said. "People are here from all over and the hotels are full! Both of 'em!"

"Roonies?"

She nodded several times in quick succession. "It's a nickname!"

"When did they announce they were coming?" I asked.

"Yesterday."

That was fast. "The bodies were found two days ago."

"They monitor police channels for stories that might be interestin', and they also take tips from listeners. So, they either heard it, or someone called it in."

Huh. I wondered which it was. If someone called in the tip, it must have been a person with knowledge about the bodies, and if that was the case, I wanted to know who it was.

I felt the energy in the room shift, kind of like when the hair on the back of your neck stands up and you get a feeling something bad is about to happen. I turned around and came face-to-face with a whole herd of The Ladies, so my intuition had been right.

I smiled without showing my teeth. "Hi, Jackie." I nodded toward the others. "Ladies."

Jackie gave me a too sweet smile right back that was fake AF—and that AF didn't stand for *And Fantastic*. "Hello, Kate. I heard you and Drake spent some time together this morning and were practically having sex with the door wide open." She jumped right on that tidbit of info. I was sure she was reveling in the knowledge since I'd caught her spending the night at Grant Kimball's. They were most definitely not married, so that was most definitely Mormon illegal, and if the information became public, would probably become a Mormon true crime.

"Where did you hear that?" I asked, always curious to find out where the gossip about me was coming from this time around. It was like when marketing companies asked for details about where you heard about their product so they would know what efforts were lucrative. I wanted to know so

I'd have information about what, and who, to avoid in the future. My privacy mattered a great deal to me, and so did loyalty.

Jackie thrust her nose in the air. "When you entertain a man in the wee hours of the mornin' wearin' nothin' but a tiny robe, word gets around."

I held up my hand to tick off numbers on my fingers like I was making a bulleted list. "One, it was seven-thirty AM, not the wee hours of the morning. Two, I was wearing pajamas *and* a robe. Three, Drake was dropping off breakfast for me because he's nice." Jackie wrinkled her forehead at that and I knew a response was on the tip of her tongue so I continued, "And weren't you up long before that the other morning *baking?*" I asked, making sure to put the emphasis on "baking" since that had been her excuse for staying at Grant Kimball's overnight and not changing clothes after getting flour-attacked for shopping on Sunday. I wanted to give her a reminder that I hadn't forgotten about her oversight, and if she wanted to push me, I was happy to push back. And I had better ammunition, and a whole damn newspaper at my disposal.

She folded her arms tightly across her chest and glared at me in warning, so I knew my threat had been received. I smiled widely at her, waiting to see what she'd do next.

Jackie's sidekick, and my other nemesis, Amber Kane, stepped up to the plate. "I also heard you were at lunch with Hawke and eating another Oreo shake."

"I was, and it was delicious," I said without apology.

Amber's chin jutted out and her nose turned up. "You'd think that you'd have learned somethin' from last time."

Jackie subbed back in and made a tsk tsk tsk noise. "Sinners never prosper," she said.

I considered offering Jackie and her Sunday shopping and flour covered shirt the same advice back.

I glanced at Ella. She usually warned me about rumors circulating, especially if the rumors had to do with The Ladies. Her lips parted in a toothy expression that looked a lot like the grimace emoji, then she pulled out her phone. My phone buzzed with a text and Ella looked up at the ceiling, trying to pretend she hadn't just sent it to me and she'd been on her phone for a totally different reason. I looked at the text.

> Sorry, I was so excited about the Murderoonies that I forgot to tell you they were talking about you having breakfast with Drake and lunch with Hawke today.

I texted her back.

> It's fine. You know this stuff happens to me every day.

I turned back to The Ladies. "It's so strange you all keep such a detailed account of what you think I'm up to." I tilted my head, thinking. "It's almost like you don't have anything better to do because nothing is happening in your own lives."

Jackie looked me up and down with clear distaste. "We're tryin' to make sure the town stays safe." She said it like she meant "safe from my vagina," which really had nothing to do with her, or the town, and was definitely no one's business but my own.

I'd learned a long time ago that directing attention away

from myself was a great way to get out of the hot seat, as well as get some additional information. Offense is the best defense. "I'm surprised you're at this event, Jackie."

She shifted her head and watched me, waiting to see where I was going with my statement.

"Considering the Murderoonies are in town to investigate your boyfriend," I finished.

Jackie's eyes flashed with anger. "They're not investigatin' Grant," she huffed. "They're investigatin' what happened on the property."

I nodded. "Which Grant owns. I've talked to sources who say the human remains won't be a good thing for him, and could threaten his development. The added exposure from the podcast won't help that."

She pursed her lips. "Grant's certain the police will figure out who the bodies belonged to, and what happened to them, and it won't be a problem at all. I'm sure that's the angle the Murderoonies will take as well."

I'd spent less than thirty minutes with Edith when she crashed my interview with Grant this morning, and then crashed my lunch with Hawke, and I got the distinct impression that wasn't the direction they were going with the story at all. When I got back to the office after lunch, I'd listened to one of their podcasts. It seemed that when it came to choosing cases to cover, the more scandalous, the better.

I was certain Jackie had also listened to the Murderoonies, and had come to a similar conclusion. While Jackie wasn't the brightest, she had been "head mean girl" in high school and that had absolutely carried over into her adult life. She knew how to control and manipulate a situation. I eyed her speculatively. "So, you're here to socialize and try to convince the

Murderoonies to paint Grant and his development in a positive light." She'd tried to do the same manipulation to me, only she'd used threats.

"No!" She said it a *little* too fast.

I gave her a slow smile and was about to tell her good luck when Edith walked up. "Well, Kate! I've seen you today almost as much as I've seen myself!" I doubted that since she struck me as the type of person who spent a lot of time in front of a mirror.

"Hi, Edith. We're definitely running into each other a lot." I managed to keep my tone neutral.

"Let me introduce you to my podcast host partner, Margie Fay; our producer, Vera Larson; and my daughter, Chloe. Vera manages the business side of our show, and Chloe helps run our website and social media." Margie had brown hair, a warm smile, and reminded me of my grandma. Chloe was a bit shorter than me, around 5'5, with an average build, high cheekbones, green eyes, and long, straight, platinum blonde hair with bangs. I guessed that she was probably in her thirties. Vera was tall with honey-hued highlights in her blonde hair that hit about shoulder length, and she looked like the definition of a Boss Babe. She was wearing a tailored black pant suit and jacket, carrying two phones, and it wouldn't surprise me if she had plans for taking over the world in her pocket. I could respect that—the world needed more women like her.

"It's nice to meet you, all," I said. "Are you also interested in true crime, Chloe?" I wondered if she enjoyed investigations, or if she'd been dragged into it because it was the family business.

She gave me a kind smile. "I am. I used to be obsessed with

investigative shows on TV, and the investigation channel. I loved trying to solve the mysteries."

"It's always interesting to follow a story and try to solve a crime," I said.

She nodded and her smile brightened. "It's what we do."

Me, too.

"How many Murderoonies hosts are there?" I asked, already knowing the answer.

"I host the podcast with Margie," Edith said, jumping in to ensure I knew exactly who the star was. "But we have a roundtable of women and guests who come on to discuss things."

Chloe leaned over and touched her mom on the arm. "Mom and Margie are the most popular though."

Edith had the grace to look embarrassed. "You're supposed to keep me humble." She turned back to me. "We're good at what we do because we love doing it."

"You arrived in Branson Falls surprisingly fast," I pointed out. It was Wednesday. The bodies had been found on Monday. "How did you hear about the bodies, and what made you connect them to a possible Jeff Zundy murder?"

Edith gave me a too sweet smile, but Vera stepped in to answer my question, "We have an anonymous tip line. Someone left a message saying human remains had been found on Monday, and then the remains of two more bodies were found. Considering Zundy's history in the area, we felt like it warranted us being on the scene. Who knows, they could find nine bodies! And covering an active investigation is what we're known for, and best at."

I cocked my head with interest. No one knew about the third body that was found on Monday except law enforcement. Bobby had said someone must have leaked the info, so maybe the tipster was that person, but it still caught my attention and made me curious. I shifted my stance so I could better see all of the Murderoonies. "That's right, I heard you helped solve a cold case and that's what put you on the map."

"It was," Margie agreed, speaking up for the first time. "I'm so glad we were able to help the families of those girls get some peace."

I'd read a general overview of the Murderoonies, but I needed to find out more about that specific case, and how the Murderoonies had gotten involved.

"We couldn't pass up an investigation like this, especially not with Zundy's history," Edith said. "Plus, it's close to home, and investigating in real time is always fun."

Fun and lucrative. There had been several cases of missing women and kids that had been followed by people on social media. One high profile case had even been solved because of amateur investigators who used the information being reported online to help them find a missing woman's vehicle. Those people had become overnight influencers, and there was a lot of money in that.

Chloe's watch chimed. "You'll have to excuse us, Kate. It's time to address the crowd. We're going Live, so we're on a schedule. It was nice to meet you, and I'm sure I'll see you again."

I liked Chloe far more than I liked her mom. "It was nice to meet you, too," I said, and watched as all four of them walked toward the front of the room.

The crowd quieted as Edith took the stage, but the excited energy in the room didn't dissipate. "Thank you so much for coming, everyone! We're beyond thrilled to be here in Branson Falls covering this case and the potential victims!"

The crowd broke out into enthusiastic cheers.

"We'll be staying at the hotel for the foreseeable future, and this will be our homebase. If you have tips to call in, or know of things that you aren't seeing reported anywhere else," Edith looked directly at me when she said it, "the tip line number is on all of our social media. You know we love tips!"

I loved tips too, but wasn't a fan of sifting through them all. I wondered who they paid to do that.

"I think it's a serial killer," a woman next to me stage-whispered to a friend. Her friend nodded repeatedly in agreement.

"We know Jeff Zundy used to visit here," Edith said, her tone conspiratorial. "We think these bodies *might* be some of his victims. We talked about it on the first episode of the podcast for this case, so if you haven't caught up yet, now's your chance!"

They'd already released a podcast about it? It must have been a pretty short episode considering not even the police knew much about the bodies yet, and they had far more information than the Murderoonies.

"We'll also be adding some new merchandise to the store soon, and some of it *might* be serial killer related."

The crowd gasped with excitement.

"Keep in touch on our podcast, YouTube channel, and all of our socials! We love to hear from fans, and we even plan to have some residents on our show!"

Another excited rumble went through the group.

"Make sure you grab some free swag from the table at the front. We love seeing our Murderoonie stickers all over! And don't forget to get some treats. We have fresh cookies brought from the most popular cookie chain in Salt Lake City! You can also get a drink with pebbled ice at the soda bar in the corner. We love *all* of our Murder-y friends, and appreciate your warm welcome so much!"

Edith finished her speech and people splintered back into their smaller socializing groups. I was still standing with Ella and some of The Ladies, mostly because I hadn't excused myself—and by excuse, I mean escape.

"Zundy used to visit here?" one of The Ladies asked.

Cami Dews nodded forcefully, like the harder her head moved, the more she would be able to make her point. "My aunt's roommate's cousin was one of the girls he tried to abduct in Salt Lake, but she'd been trained in martial arts and she fought him off."

"Really?" I asked.

Cami nodded again, slower this time. "She was so lucky. Thank heaven she'd prayed for safety before she left the house."

The other women around her nodded, like they agreed the prayer had saved her life. Maybe it had helped, but I gave more weight to her athletic training and willingness to fight back.

Brinley Dart spoke up, "My dad dated a girl who Jeff asked out on a date. She was getting ready to go out with him, but got a bad feeling and knew it was The Holy Ghost telling her not to go." The Holy Ghost was a "gift" that Mormon kids were "given" when they turned eight years old, got baptized and confirmed, and were now completely responsible for their own sins. They also carried the weight of making sure their families stayed together for eternity—as long as they all practiced the teachings of the church. No pressure, second graders. They were told they had to be righteous and follow all church rules to be able to hear the Holy Ghost and if they couldn't hear him, they weren't safe. It was a blatant means of control.

"What kind of a bad feeling?" I asked, genuinely curious to see how the Holy Ghost had manifested this time—the stories were endless.

"Stomach ache."

I nodded. "So, she was saved from certain murder by the flu or some bad Mexican food?"

Brinley gave me a solid glare and then in a tone the brooked no argument said, "She was saved by the Holy Ghost because she listened to her promptings."

"What about Cami's aunt's roommate's cousin?" I asked. "The spirit didn't deem her worthy of a warning?"

Brinley turned her nose up. "Maybe she wasn't listening as hard. Or maybe she wasn't righteous enough."

Yes. I was sure that was it. Maybes were another constant in Mormonism and something that kept people in the Church because they constantly questioned their decisions by "Maybe-ing" themselves to death. "Maybe I was supposed to turn down that road to avoid an accident?" "Maybe I was supposed to miss the flight because something was going to go wrong." "Maybe I should circle back around the corner because I felt prompted to help that person and it could be my eternal companion." The list was endless, and the constant outsourcing of their intuition taught people not to trust themselves.

"My dad met him," Robin Gorse, who was probably ten years older than me, said. "Jeff liked my dad's Firebird and my dad gave him a ride."

My eyes widened. Now that was interesting. An actual encounter with the killer by someone in town, not a story with a warning by an entity. "Did your dad say anything about Jeff, or what his personality was like?" I asked.

Robin shook her head. "My dad passed away years ago, but I never asked him about that. Jeff liked muscle cars. He was in Branson and visited my dad's Mormon Ward a lot. My dad gave him a ride after church one day."

"Jeff was a member of the Mormon Church?" Farah Smalls asked, eyes wide.

I was surprised she didn't know that, then again, I always got the impression that while Mormons loved claiming famous people who were members, they tended to shy away from the infamous, and especially the serial killers…unless they were named Porter Rockwell and murdering for God. "Zundy joined the Mormon Church when he came to Utah because it was an easy way to make friends and find community." And victims, I thought, but I didn't say that part out loud.

"What?" The woman seemed very alarmed. I couldn't blame her; I'd been concerned the first time I'd heard the story as well.

"It's true," Ella said while nonchalantly scrolling through her phone. "I met him."

My head swung to Ella faster than I realized my head could move. "You *met* him?" She hadn't told me that. Hadn't even hinted at it. "You didn't tell me that when we talked before!"

She nodded. "Yup. Charmin' as all get out, and easy on the eyes. Like some other men we know," she said, looking right at me and implying I was dating two murderers. She was wrong though, only one of them had maybe probably killed people—well, only one of them had admitted to it at least.

Ella continued, "I probably would've followed him home without much convincin' if I hadn't been married at the time."

I couldn't stop the shock from registering on my face. "He was a serial killer!"

She lifted her shoulders, unconcerned. "I didn't know that then."

"You could have been killed!"

"If I had a dollar for every time someone in my life said that..." she trailed off.

That was a whole other can of worms I didn't have time to open at the moment. "How did you meet him?" I asked, still stunned.

"The Gable family had a son who was his roommate at college in Salt Lake. Zundy used to come visit on weekends every once in a while with the Gable boy. We had back yard parties with the Gables, and Jeff was there sometimes. Mostly I think he came for the dinner. And the girls. He sure met a lot of 'em at church!"

Chills ran up my spine at that.

"Were there ever any girls who went missing around that time?" I asked. It would have been well before I was even born.

"Course there were," Ella said. "You know what it's like around here. Girls go missin' all the time, the question is why. Usually because their parents are tryin' to hide somethin'." That was unfortunately true, and had been the subject of the first big story I'd covered when I'd moved back to Branson Falls.

I'd known Zundy had spent time in Utah and had

converted to Mormonism, but wasn't aware of a Zundy connection in Branson Falls until the bodies were found on the Barret property. I thought Zundy had mostly stayed in the city, where he went to school. But if he was stalking other rural areas, like Branson, where women frequently left town and no one questioned why to any authorities, there was no telling how many women he'd killed. I knew Zundy had admitted to murdering around forty-five victims, but authorities suspected the number was actually much higher.

"I met him too," Ella's friend, Carol Weeks, said.

I blinked. Had the entire town over the age of sixty interacted with a serial killer and not told anyone about it? "Where?" I asked.

"Tres Tacos. I grabbed a quick lunch there one afternoon. He was driving through and stopped for lunch. We were both eating alone and when he saw me, he gave me a huge smile and told me I was too pretty to eat lunch by myself. I admit, I was a bit flattered. I'd been married for a while, so a young, handsome man like him complimenting me meant a lot. I felt old."

"How old were you?" I asked.

"Twenty-five."

Only in Utah would twenty-five be considered old. Most women were married by twenty or twenty-two, and if a man was unmarried by twenty-five, church members considered him a menace to society because they believed men had zero control of their sexual desires, and needed a wife to stop themselves from committing the second worst sin—sex outside of marriage. That made Drake and Hawke, both over thirty, very appealing menaces.

Carol Weeks continued, "I invited him to sit down. He did,

and we had a great conversation. He told me about how he used to live in California, but he was moving to Utah for med school. He seemed like a great catch, what with his good looks and career path. Doctors make enough to let a women stay home where she should be, raising a family." She said that last part with an air of judgment that I was not unfamiliar with in Utah.

I had not chosen the "find a rich husband, get married young, and have a herd of children" path that was espoused by the leaders of the LDS Church, and it wasn't one I understood, or ever strived for. The pressure and focus on women to dedicate their whole lives to their husband and kids instead of their own goals, was one of the many reasons I'd left the church. I was far too independent, opinionated, and goal-oriented to fit in the Mormon Church's carefully constructed and controlled boxes.

"He even tried to ask me out on a real date, but I had to tell him I was married." Carol paused for a minute, like she was remembering and reliving her glory days of 'murderer lunch.' "I was a bit sad about being married, to be honest. He was a hottie!" She basically echoed the same thing Ella had said, like being attractive or charming gave him a murder out.

"He was a serial killer!" I reminded everyone again.

"Doesn't change anythin' about how he looked. It's not like he was wearin' some 'I murder people' t-shirt," Ella said.

Even if he had been, I wasn't sure Ella would have believed it. People like Carol and Ella were the reason so many women had been obsessed with Zundy. They were probably why Zundy had decided to stay in the state for so long instead of moving on. He likely realized what easy marks Utah women could be because they were so trusting, especially of men.

People started talking among themselves. I was still trying to wrap my head around Ella's potential abduction by one of the most notorious serial killers of our time when Bethany Barret, walked up. "I didn't know you'd be here tonight," I said as she got a drink from the table behind me.

"Hottest ticket in town," Bethany replied. "Honestly, I was hoping to hear some new information about the property. Do you know if they've found out more?"

"They're waiting on forensics, but a lot of people are trying to figure it out, clearly," I said, gesturing to the room full of murder fans.

Bethany nodded and took a drink from her glass.

"There are people of all age ranges with a lot of stories to tell," I said. "It's a good place to gather information." And I'd gotten some leads, especially with the Zundy stories. I'd follow up on that angle for sure.

"I heard that the real estate broker for the property was your fiancé, Eddie Prestman. Is that correct?"

Slight lines formed at the corners of her eyes and she took a breath before answering. "He was. He did a great job, but his involvement caused some issues with my other family members."

"Why is that?"

She took a deep breath. "Because he charged for his services."

"That seems fair. He was doing a job."

"Some family members didn't see it that way."

So, Jordan.

"Did you interview other real estate brokers?" I asked.

She shifted her weight from one leg to the other like she was uncomfortable. "Yes. But Eddie was willing to do it for half the price, which should have made everyone happy. It really comes down to the fact that my brother thinks I'm going to get extra money from the deal in the long run because Eddie and I are engaged. But that money is for Eddie's business because he did a service, and it stays in Eddie's business. I'm not getting anything from it, and wouldn't ask for it. Jordan is being unreasonable."

"Was Jordan the only one who had a problem with Eddie as the broker?"

She rubbed the side of her cup, almost in a soothing gesture. "As far as I know. Things between us are tense right now because of the deal, and the human remains being found hasn't helped. It brings up a lot of stuff from our childhood. I'm also worried selling questionable property to one of the most well-known developers in the state will affect Eddie's reputation as a broker."

The childhood comment caught my attention. "Stuff like what from your childhood?"

She pressed her lips together like she'd said too much. "I shouldn't have said that. My dad wasn't the nicest person, and he was domineering. I think Jordan feels like the decision to sell the land is another way he's being controlled."

"I'm sorry. It sounds like things are hard in general."

She nodded.

"How's your mom doing?" I asked, trying to change the subject and give her a reprieve.

She shrugged. "It's like watching someone age in reverse. Some days are better than others, but her health has been failing for a long time and the dementia exacerbates the problem. Aging isn't for the weak."

I couldn't argue with that.

Another woman came up and started talking to Bethany. I stepped away to get some photos and mingle. I noticed Vera and Chloe standing in the group of women I'd been talking to about Zundy. They were watching me closely, and I wondered how much of my conversation with Bethany they'd overheard.

Chapter Eleven

I'd done some research on GCR Development yesterday, and found out more about their investors. The development company was composed of Grant, Ryan, and Chris. But they frequently had other investment companies contribute money for specific developments and not all of the information was public. Those investment companies could be one person, or hundreds, and they were all under the umbrella of their individual company name. Depending on how, and where the investment company was registered, as well as their company articles, I could probably find out some information about the actual people in each company, but I didn't have the resources to spend on that kind of research. I knew someone who did though, and I'd called Hawke and explained the situation as soon as I'd started my morning coffee.

"So, can you help me figure out who the investors are in Grant's development?"

"I can. It will take some time though. And I might not be able to get all of the info. People often use companies to conceal things."

I knew that, and knew Hawke was one of those people. "Something you have some experience with."

I could hear his smile on the other end of the line. "I know a little about a lot of things."

I scoffed. "You know a lot about a lot of things."

"You're going to give me an ego."

I laughed as I put the lid on my coffee thermos. "I don't think I'm really going to affect that in any way."

"You're wrong. I don't care about what many people think, but you're one of them."

He'd said something like that before and it had taken me aback then almost as much as it did now. "I'm flattered. And thanks for your help. I don't have the resources to spend sifting through the red tape it would take for me to get the names."

"I go around the tape."

"I know. That's why I asked." My situational ethics weren't as developed as Hawke's, but they were getting there.

"Are we still on for our date?" he asked.

"Barring a disaster, some other story, or your work getting in the way." I wondered how often we were going to have to worry about each of our jobs interrupting the potential relationship we were trying to explore and build. So far, it seemed frequent.

"Let's hope things stay calm because I can't stop thinking about you wearing nothing but a Wonder Woman tiara and boots."

I was glad we weren't on a video call because I was heated in multiple places. "And I can't wait to see what the tattoo under your shirt looks like."

His voice was deep and tempting, "I have more than one. In more places than under my shirt."

That was a mystery I wanted to unravel. "I'm intrigued. Ella will be too, so get prepared for her to try and see you naked. The mystery of your tattoos might even rival her search for the possible serial killer." I'd mentioned Hawke's tattoos to Ella a while ago and she'd been very interested in them ever since.

He laughed. "I'll talk to you soon, Kitty Kate."

I hung up and finished my breakfast before throwing on jeans and a royal blue sweater. I grabbed my coffee and Gandalf, and left the house for the day.

I pulled up to my mom and dad's house to drop Gandalf off and my mom was already outside, draping something over her witches. She had several of her craft totes out and based on her smirk, I was certain she was causing trouble. Gandalf went running straight to her, and she made an entire event of his excitement. She draped him in some brightly colored beads, and he pranced around as if a parade was being held in his honor.

"What's going on?" I asked, walking up and looking at her witches. They were all wearing various outfits now. One had a lacy black cape and hot pink metallic beads hanging over her chest like a necklace; another had a thick rainbow-colored shawl; and the third had a sparkling purple belt and black and purple glitter covered scarf wrapped around her neck. I wasn't sure what my mom was up to, but I was certain it involved making a point and I wondered when it would evolve into a Catasophie—the nickname people had given my mom, merging "Catastrophe" with her name.

"I thought the witches could use some accessories," she answered innocently, but I knew her well enough to know there was nothing innocent about her tone.

"Is that what this is?" I gestured to the witches. "Accessories?"

She gave me a pert nod and continued arranging the witch outfits. I noticed Gladys, her neighbor across the street who had complained about the witches, watching from the window with a scowl. Gladys had also added several signs in her front yard that said: Stop the war on Christmas! Which seemed like strange signs to have up when it wasn't even Thanksgiving yet.

I folded my arms across my chest. "And this outfit change for your yard decor has nothing to do with your neighbor across the street, or her signs?"

My mom pursed her lips and glanced up, seeing Gladys perched in the middle of the window, watching us like a bird of prey. My mom sent her a lethal glare and Gladys quickly disappeared from the glass, so maybe she was more like a puffin than an eagle. She was probably worried about the spells my mom was surely attempting to cast in her direction. My mom added a gaudy crown full of fake jewels and so much glitter it could be seen from space, to one of the witch's heads. "Gladys is trying, and failing, to make a point. I've already won, so I'm celebrating my victory and will continue to do so."

I closed my eyes and took a breath. When I opened them, I saw Gandalf dragging some fuzzy fabric out of one of my mom's totes. "Okay. You and Gladys should try not to kill each other. We have enough bodies around here already."

I gave Gandalf a pet and a kiss on the head, and left him to play in my mom's craft bins. Hopefully he wouldn't end up covered in glitter as well.

I walked into the office and Ella was already there waiting for me. She was wearing more Murderoonie swag that I was certain she'd procured at the event last night. This time it was a scarf tied around her neck with the Murderoonie logo printed on it, and a matching button on her shirt. Just like the Murderoonies banner, the eyes in the logo kept following me regardless of what direction I moved. The eyes were currently watching me pick up a doughnut from the treat table. "Did you bring these?" I asked her.

She nodded. "I was up early. Couldn't sleep. Got the freshest ones at Frosted Paradise. Sugary goodness!"

I gave her a once over. She was bobbing from one foot to the other in the way a kid does when they're really excited about something, or they need to pee. Or like me when I have too much espresso. I raised a brow. "Have you been drinking espresso?" I asked, taking my doughnut to my desk, and putting my coffee thermos down.

She made psshh noise. "You know that's against the rules." She took another swig from the thermos she was holding and the unmistakable smell of coffee wafted into the room.

"Sure smells like coffee," I said, picking up my doughnut to take a bite. "And you're pretty jittery."

"It's hot chocolate! Chocolate can have the same effect," she responded without taking a breath.

The number of times I'd heard people lie about what was in their thermos—and claim it was chocolate that smelled exactly like coffee—since I'd moved back to Branson Falls, was high. I picked up my coffee and blew on it a little. "Why couldn't you sleep?"

"I was too excited about the Murderoonies! I called the Gables and got you an interview." She said the second part like it was an afterthought.

"You did?" I asked, taking a sip of my salted caramel flavored coffee with lots of milk.

She nodded very fast, repeatedly. "You, Edith, and Margie are meetin' with 'em tomorrow afternoon."

I almost choked on my salted caramel swallow. "Edith?" I asked, trying to pretend it was my coffee making my face screw up, not the idea of having another interview highjacked by the podcaster.

"Yeah! Chloe and Vera heard us all talkin' about Zundy last night and wanted to speak to the Gables. I said I could get you all an interview."

I wrinkled my forehead. "Did the Gables agree to be on the podcast?"

She hedged. "No. I don't think they want to be on the show. But they're willin' to tell their story, so Edith will have to tell people what she hears when she talks about it on the podcast."

"Kind of like a reporter does."

"Exactly!" she said, pointing at me and not getting that I was an actual reporter who could report on what was said without putting the Gables on camera or recording them.

THE DEVIL SHOPS ON SUNDAY

I'd been planning to call the Gables and get an interview set up today anyway, so this took something off my plate. I had a lot of writing to catch up on, as well as some other calls to make and research to do. "Thanks for setting it up. I'm interested to hear what they have to say."

Ella flashed a self-satisfied smile. "You're welcome! Happy to help the best investigators around!"

I wondered if she was including me as one of the best investigators. I tried not to take offense at my job being compared to a citizen detective podcast, and thanked her again before she went back to the archive room to be jittery while filing old documents.

I turned my computer on and while it was booting up, I called Eddie Prestman, the Barret family's real estate broker, and Bethany's fiancé.

He answered on the second ring. "Eddie Prestman here," he said, his voice upbeat and ready to sell things. "What can I do for you?"

"Hi, Eddie. This is Kate Saxee, editor of *The Branson Tribune*. I met your fiancée, Bethany, and she told me I could reach out to you with questions about the property you sold to Grant Kimball."

"Hi, Kate. Bethany told me you'd probably call. I'm happy to answer any questions I can."

"Thank you. Did the Barret family approach you to sell the land, or did you approach them?" I knew Bethany and Georgia had decided to use him because he was engaged to Bethany and it was easy, and they trusted him. But it had caused a family rift with Jordan, so I wanted to get Eddie's perspective on the whole situation as well.

"I'm engaged to Bethany, and I've known the Barret family

for a long time. I'm good at my job, and I've been watching the Utah market and Branson Falls in particular. The family had been talking off and on for years about selling the land, but when Georgia's health started to deteriorate, it became more of a priority. I felt like it was a good time to sell, and based on my network in Salt Lake, I knew some developers who would be interested in expanding to more rural areas because that's where the buyers are going. We talked, and almost everyone agreed that it should be sold before Georgia passed away to make things easier."

"Did Georgia agree as well?"

"She did. She had mixed feelings because it had been in the family so long, but she understood there was value in selling it now."

"Grant told me that the deal was made before it went on the market. So, the family could have made more if you'd listed it widely and waited six months to sell it, correct?"

He paused. "That's the thing about the real estate market, no one has a crystal ball. I knew what the land was worth, and knew Grant and his partners and investors could have the money quickly and wouldn't squabble on the asking price. Could we have gotten more money if I'd listed it publicly? Maybe. But it also could have taken a lot longer, and had more potential for the deal to fall through."

"What about Wayne Post, the farmer who was leasing and wanted to buy it. Did you talk to him?"

"I did. That was a tricky situation in general, but it came down to the fact that he didn't want to pay the price we were asking. Grant's company did."

That made sense. "Did everyone in the Barret family agree to the sale?"

Eddie sighed. "That's also hard to answer. Jordan was difficult to convince. The land was in a trust and required a majority vote to sell it. Jordan voted no, but Georgia's still alive, so she still has a vote. She voted with Bethany. The money from the sale was split evenly among the three of them."

It was another confirmation that Jordan was the holdout. I wondered why he didn't want to sell.

"Bethany was worried that selling land with human remains found on it could affect your reputation as a broker. Is that a concern for you as well?"

He blew out a breath like he was tired. "It's not a resounding recommendation, but it's not a deal breaker either. Things like this happen all the time. You have no idea how many houses are sold after someone has died in them and the new owner doesn't know it."

"Isn't that something that has to be disclosed?"

"Not unless a buyer specifically asks whether or not someone has died in the house."

Real estate laws were weird. I'd absolutely be asking about dead bodies when I eventually bought property because I didn't want to end up with a mortgage on the next Amityville.

"Have you had any contact with Grant or his investors since the human remains were found?"

"I reached out to them, but haven't heard back. Probably on the advice of their attorney."

I knew that attorney, somewhat intimately. "Do you think it could become a legal issue for you or the Barret family?"

"Anything can become a legal issue, but the property was sold and title transferred. The contract was clear and the Barret family doesn't have any legal responsibility here."

"Did you or anyone in the family know about the human remains?"

"Other than the old cemetery, which we told Grant about going into the sell, I haven't ever heard Bethany's family mention bodies on their land. We're all as eager to find out the story behind it as everyone else."

"Thanks for your time, Eddie. I'll call if I have any other questions."

"Please do." He hung up.

It's always hard to get a read on someone over the phone, but he seemed confident in his answers. I did note that some of his responses were non-answers, probably because he was trying to protect himself, and I couldn't blame him for that.

I wrote up some of my notes, and worked on articles with information about what we knew about the human remains so far. I also edited some articles from correspondents. By the time I was done with that, I was ready for a break. I walked down to Beans and Things because I needed an afternoon pick-me-up and decided I deserved it after finding out I'd be dealing with Edith in an interview again.

As I walked down the street, I noticed the sidewalks had been painted with something that looked like a mixture of paint and chalk. It was similar to the substance used every year around homecoming to decorate for the celebrations and let the whole town know football was arriving—as if people weren't aware. It was more of the strange interlocking snowman-like symbols that I'd seen around town: on one of Hyrum's buttons at the soda shop, and that I'd watched Kelcie try to wash off from the Beans and Things building.

I snapped some photos of the sidewalk with my phone before entering the coffee shop and ordering a mocha with pistachio flavoring from Kelcie. She smiled and told me my drink was taken care of. Again. I looked around the room. "Who keeps paying for my drink?"

She lifted her shoulders. "We're not allowed to say."

I leaned in like we had a secret. "I could bribe you."

Her lips curved up in a sly smile. "We're already being bribed."

It was either Hawke or Drake, I knew it. But wasn't sure why they were doing it.

She started working on my drink.

"Have you seen the symbols painted on the sidewalk?" I asked her. "They look similar to the ones that were sprayed on the coffee house."

Kelcie nodded. "I think they're the same."

"Any idea what they mean?"

Surprise flashed across her face at the fact that I didn't know. "It's a bunch of people playing around like they're in some club only they have answers for."

"What's the club?"

"CFNP. It stands for Citizens for No Progress. They basically want Branson, and the whole world, to go back to the 1950s or even earlier."

Of course they did. A lot of people in various U.S. states seemed to be pushing that narrative recently, and a lot of people were promoting the cause. I felt like the whole idea was rooted in fear and nostalgia for what seemed like an easier time. "I haven't heard of CFNP before."

"You should look them up on socials. Their videos are wild," Kelcie said.

"Are they only in Branson Falls?"

She shook her head. "Oh no, they're everywhere."

She handed me my drink and I took a sip. It was delightful. "Thanks for the info, and the drink. And please thank whoever bought it for me."

She smiled wide. "Will do."

I walked back to the office and settled in at my desk before pulling up social media and searching for Citizens for No Progress. It was video after video of people railing against the current state of America, new ideas, change, technology, rights, and life in general. It was similar to the attitudes and opinions of most Branson Falls residents, but this was farther reaching than Branson Falls. I clicked a video and paused it, recognizing the park, and one of the people yelling: Jack Pine, the flour bandit. The video was from a day ago, so clearly, he was using his time out on bail wisely. I was scrolling through more videos when my phone started belting out "Comin' to America" and I knew it was Bobby.

"Hey," I said, answering while still scrolling through videos. "What's up?"

Bobby heaved a huge sigh. "You're gonna want to get over here, Kate. We've got more bodies."

My eyes widened. "The cadaver dog found more?"

"Yep. Don't say I never told ya nothin', and I better be off the no-cookie threat list. The only other people who know right now are Grant, the forensic teams, and your boyfriends. Get here, and fast."

He didn't have to tell me a third time. I closed my laptop, grabbed my keys, and drove to the Barret property.

Chapter Twelve

When I arrived at the scene, it looked similar to the last time I was there, only a lot more white tents were pitched around the property. I saw Grant and his partners, Chris, and Ryan, dressed in suits and standing in a group that included Drake. Drake was gesturing like he was explaining something. Hawke was with Bobby, and seemed to be instructing people on a piece of equipment.

I walked to Bobby and Hawke first. "Thanks for the heads-up this time, Bobby. Your cookies are safe."

Hawke leaned into Bobby like he was telling a secret, "She tried to take milkshakes away from me."

I slitted my eyes at him. "Yeah, you were both on the sugar chopping block." Only Hawke's was sugar of a different kind. "Tell me about the bodies."

Bobby pointed to the new areas with white tents covering them. "The cadaver dogs got hits on other parts of the development. Hawke helped us with some tech, and we were able to section off the locations."

"What kind of tech?" I asked Hawke.

He crouched down next to a machine that looked very advanced. "Ground penetrating radar."

"Have you already started digging?"

Bobby shook his head and pointed toward a team of people under the tent nearest to us. "The forensics team is about to."

I looked at the additional tents and did the math. "That puts the total body count at nine—assuming there aren't multiple bodies buried together again. Do you think there are more bodies than that?"

Bobby shook his head. "Not here."

"How can you be certain?"

Bobby gestured toward Hawke. "Hawke says so."

I looked at Hawke. "I didn't realize you had that kind of authority."

"I don't, but the data does. The radar, combined with the cadaver dogs, gives us a high degree of certainty."

Another officer walked up. "We need the ground penetrating radar over here."

Bobby nodded, sliced his head toward Hawke like he should follow, and started walking away.

Hawke gave me a once over, stopping around my chest area. If eyes could sin, he'd be in the Mormon version of hell, otherwise known as Outer Darkness. "Glad I got to see you and all your assets, Kitty Kate. I hope to see more of them soon."

He walked away before I could respond.

I crossed the property to meet Grant, Chris, Ryan, and Drake next. "How are you guys holding up?"

Grant scrubbed a hand over his jaw. "I've had better days."

"All development work will be paused for even longer now," Chris said. "It's a pain in the ass."

He'd used a real swear instead of an imitation one, so I knew things were serious.

"Do you have any options legally?" I asked, looking from them to Drake.

Drake shook his head. "It's the same story as before. The police don't like to interrupt commerce so they'll get things investigated and back to status quo as quickly as possible, but this complicates things."

It seemed like a full-on disaster that they'd stumbled into simply by buying a piece of land. "Is there a chance someone was targeting any of you personally, or targeting your company?" I'd asked Grant this before, but I wanted to see what Chris and Ryan said.

Grant, Chris, and Ryan looked at each other and all shrugged. "Not that I can think of," Ryan answered.

"Let me know if anything comes to mind," I said. I walked around to the various tents, taking notes and talking to a few other officers.

I heard what sounded like a yodel coming from behind the police tape, where the public had to stay. I looked over and saw a large cat, squirrel, and raccoon. The Speedy Superheroes had arrived. They usually stuck to crimes they could try and prevent, but they'd been absent at this crime scene, and I wondered how much of that had to do with Bobby and potential threats of jail time.

The Speedy Superheroes weren't alone. Edith, Margie, Chloe, and Vera were trying to get past the police fence and failing, thanks to the officers there who were stopping them.

The Murderoonies looked like they'd shown up with half the town, and they probably had. "Yoohoo, Kate!"

I now knew the owner of the yodel.

I tried to pretend I hadn't seen her.

"KATE! YOUHOO!!!"

"Does she think that's some sort of Kate call?" Drake asked, walking up behind me.

"Probably. Everyone else gives me nicknames." I gave him a pointed look.

"Drake! Youhoo, Drake!!!"

I couldn't hold back my smile. "Now you've been enlisted, too."

He nodded. "Why don't we go over together. There's safety in numbers."

"Good point."

We moved toward the fence. Vera was on her phone, surely trying to get access past the police tape, Chloe was recording on her phone, and Edith and Margie were waving their hands and trying to get our attention. "Can you tell us what's going on?" Edith asked. "We heard rumors something was happening, and we see more tents."

"The police are continuing their investigation," Drake said. "We hope to have it wrapped up soon."

"But it seems like it's expanding," Edith pointed out, not missing a thing, that one.

"They're doing their job, and we're doing ours. Grant and his partners are eager to have things settled and get the development back on track," Drake explained, more patiently than I probably would have.

"Can I come in and talk with them?" Edith asked.

"It's an active investigation," Drake said. "You can't come in."

Lawyer Drake was certainly handy to have around. I wanted to give him a high five or something.

Edith pointed at me. "She's inside and talking to people."

"Because I'm the editor of *The Branson Tribune*," I explained, as if Edith didn't know. I got the impression she was one of those entitled people who thought they should be able to do whatever they wanted, whenever they wanted, simply because they wanted to.

Edith rolled her eyes. "You're a reporter, like me."

Drake stiffened visibly and a muscle feathered at his jaw. "Kate Saxee is an award-winning journalist who's traveled around the world investigating everything from government corruption to murder. She is *right* where she's supposed to be."

I didn't need the defense, but I appreciated it.

"Now if you'll excuse us, we have some more work to do." Drake put his hand on my lower back as we walked away from Edith and her judgment.

"Thanks for that. I didn't need validation from her, but it's nice to have someone else reminding people that this is my actual job and I have years of experience doing it."

"You're an excellent reporter, Katie. She's a podcast host who got lucky and plays at trying to be even a quarter of the person you are. She's not, but she wishes she was."

A warm, fluttery feeling spread through my chest at his words. It meant something to me to be seen, and I appreciated that he felt that way about me. Especially considering how most Mormon men felt about women working—that they shouldn't do it.

Grant called Drake's name, and he started to walk away. "I'll see you soon, Katie."

Bobby walked back over to me and nodded toward Edith and The Murderoonies beyond the police tape. "Bet ya aren't too happy about them tryin' to help you investigate."

I gave him a long-suffering look. "I wouldn't call it helping."

His gaze drifted to the Speedy Superheroes standing next to the Murderoonies. "Now ya know how we felt when the Speedy Superheroes started their mission."

I did, and it was miserable. "Why are the Murderoonies following me instead of bothering you?"

"Because I'm a police officer and I don't care about their entertainment nonsense and don't have to deal with it. Police business is private, and we don't have to tell anyone anythin'."

"You tell me things."

"Because I'm almost as scared of you as I am of your boyfriends."

I flatted my lips into a line. "I don't have any boyfriends."

Bobby pushed his chin out and nodded. "You're right. They're men. You have two scary man-friends."

"That's absurd. And I'm not scary."

"You're the town newspaper editor *and* you tried to ban me from your mom's cookies for life."

"Because the Murderoonies scooped me on a story that you and your police friends had info on! I'm the editor of the town paper and it made me look bad!" My job was really important to me, and being good at it mattered. I wouldn't say I was threatened by The Murderoonies, but I definitely wanted to be on top of my game, and wanted to be the one to break this story open.

"Still, I'm not screwin' around with that threat. Your mom's cookies are all I look forward to sometimes."

I frowned at that. "Talking about my mom's cookies sounds strangely sexual."

Bobby wrinkled his nose. "Don't make it weird."

I spent the rest of the evening on the scene as they dug for bodies. Hawke, his ground penetrating radar, and the cadaver dogs were right. There were six more bodies found, all at various depths. If this wasn't a serial killer, I wasn't sure what exactly it was.

Chapter Thirteen

I parked in front of the Gables' house, picked up my bag, and got out of my Jeep. I'd deliberately arrived early so that I would have some time with the Gables without the Murderoonies present. Edith, Margie, and Vera must have thought the same thing because they pulled in behind me in their murder van, complete with the logo on the side. The logo eyes followed me as the door opened and shut.

"Kate! I wasn't sure if you'd be here since you spent so much time at the development last night," Edith said, her tone perky and cutting all at once. She was jealous I'd been allowed inside the police tape, and hopeful that she'd get the Gables' Zundy story all to herself.

"I've been a journalist for years, Edith. I'm used to putting in long hours."

Vera got some equipment out of the back of the car, and Margie gave me a warm smile as she got out of the van. "We saw you with Drake and that handsome Hawke," Margie said. "I'd have stayed for them too."

"Yes," Edith said. "We watched them, and you, for most of

the night."

The Murderoonies had remained behind the fence at the development for hours, watching and reporting via Lives on their social media, even though they had nothing to report. They were there until almost ten PM when they accepted that there was no way they were getting into the scene.

Edith gave me a too sweet smile. "It must be so nice to have connections that get you into crime scenes no one else has access to."

"Plenty of people had access, Edith." I said, without stating the obvious, that she wasn't one of them. "I've spent a long time building networks with the Branson Falls police and other locals."

"Well, I'm sure that your romantic entanglements certainly help with that access," Edith said.

I had nothing nice to say about that, or anything Edith was spouting, really. So, I simply smiled and walked past her to the Gables' front porch. I knocked and Fern Gable opened the door. "Hi, Fern. It's nice to meet you. I'm Kate Saxee with *The Branson Tribune*."

Edith, who had been behind me the last time I saw her ten seconds ago, stepped in front of me. "And I'm Edith with The Murderoonies." She gestured behind us. "This is my partner Margie, and my producer, Vera. Thank you so much for seeing us."

Fern brightened at Edith's introduction, and invited us all inside. We sat in her sitting room, decorated in tones of white and brown, with overstuffed chairs covered in floral fabric. A cream-colored rug offered some softness to the hardwood throughout the rest of the room. Edith, determined to be at the center of something, sat smack dab in the middle of the couch, so I took one of the side chairs across from Fern, and Margie sat scrunched up next to Edith.

"Can you tell us about your interaction with Jeff Zundy?" I asked Fern. "I understand you met him because he and your son were roommates in college."

She nodded and repeated the same story Ella had already told me. Fern's son, Eric, had been going to school with Jeff and they were in the same social circles. Jeff had taken an interest in Mormonism early on in the year, and they were trying to convert him at the time. Eric would frequently come home on the weekends and invite Jeff to come with him. He'd stay for Sunday dinner, and sometimes even go with the Gable family to church in Branson Falls.

"I've felt guilty about it for years," Fern said, her voice quiet and carrying a slight tremble.

I furrowed my brow, confused. "Why would you feel guilty?"

She crossed her arms over her chest and ran her hands up and down her arms like she was cold. "Because we brought that evil here! Jeff loved Branson Falls and all the surrounding towns. He often commented on how friendly and accommodating everyone was. He was charming and I have no doubt he charmed several women around here to their deaths!"

I wondered how many people in town thought the women who went missing at that time had been victims of Jeff Zundy, and if this was common knowledge, why hadn't anyone said something to the authorities?

"Did women go missing around that time?" Margie asked, looking concerned.

I needed to ask Ella to look into that, and pull files for me from the *Tribune* archives.

Fern nodded vigorously. "More than one. Some of them weren't from here either. Jeff was smart about his victims. Branson is part of a big, rural county with lots of small towns, open land, and space to hide things. Especially back then before all the development started. No one knows how many bodies are actually hidden from here to Salt Lake."

That was unsettling. Other than Ella mentioning it, I hadn't heard about women going missing around that time. But I definitely wasn't alive then. Small towns were notorious for running on gossip, but if that gossip included something that would make the town or its occupants seem undesirable, the information would have been buried faster than when the LDS Church leadership tried to reverse the letter they sent to bishops and stake presidents saying that oral sex was an unholy practice and married couples shouldn't do it—it definitely wasn't allowed between the unmarried ones. And that letter had also happened before I was born.

Edith asked another question about the Branson Falls area. I texted Ella and asked her to check the *Tribune* archives and pull people who had gone missing while Zundy was known to be in Branson Falls.

"Did you get a sense that Jeff was interested in any of the women you saw him around," I asked Fern?

She opened her eyes wide and nodded slowly several times. "He was interested in everyone. Like I said, he was a charmer. People loved him and he knew exactly what to say and do to get people to think he was the greatest thing since sliced bread." Psychopaths tended to have that talent.

"Did you ever see him ask anyone out on dates?" I asked.

She leaned back in her chair, thinking about it for a moment. "Not that I remember, but he went to group outings and church sponsored dances and events when he was here with Eric."

I wrote that down in my notes, and texted Ella to look in the archives for photos as well. Maybe Jeff would show up in some of them.

We finished the interview with Fern and I thanked her for taking the time to talk to me. Edith did the same.

"If you need to know anything else, please don't hesitate to reach out," Fern said, closing the door behind us.

I watched Margie, Edith, and Vera as we made our way down the steps and walkway. Margie had been quiet most of the interview, and I'd noticed she was quiet a lot. I'd listened to a few episodes of their podcast and Margie spoke on the show, but not nearly as much as Edith. It was kind of like she was there to help prop Edith up.

Edith, on the other hand, looked like she'd gotten the story of the century. "That was great information. I can't wait to include it in the podcast."

It was new information, not great. And I wanted to find out more before I felt comfortable putting it in a news story. I vetted my sources and info—like a good journalist should.

"Our new episode about the bodies released today," Edith said, handing me a card with her name, contact information, and the podcast name on it—just in case I'd missed the giant logo on the van, and the welcome event the other night. She'd given me her card already so if this kept up, I'd have a collection before long. "You should give it a listen."

I gave her a smile that showed no teeth. "Have a good day, Edith. It was nice to see you, Margie, and Vera."

I got in my Jeep and immediately turned on the podcast. I placed an online order for cheesy breadsticks with extra cheese from Sticks and Pie for lunch, and listened while I drank the iced mocha I'd gotten from Beans and Things earlier this morning. I drove to pick up my food as the podcast intro played with Edith and Margie's voices proclaiming that they solved crimes in real time. The Murderoonies had titled this series of their episodes as *Bodies in Branson—Search for a Serial Killer*.

Edith's breathy, heavily edited voice came across my speakers.

"It was supposed to be a haven for people looking for space. People who wanted to spread their wings and roam on acres of their own quiet property. Instead, it's turned into a gruesome crime scene and a mystery that only the Murderoonies can help solve. We're on the scene and bringing you all the breaking news from Branson Falls, Utah, where *several* human remains have been found on a real estate development. Stay with us as we bring you all the latest details, including exclusive interviews, and information from sources that *no one* else has."

I rolled my eyes hard. I was pretty sure Edith's sources were the same as mine because she kept following me around.

The podcast went on for thirty minutes, but I took a break at minute fifteen to pick up my food. I drove to a park and ate in my heated SUV while I listened to the rest of the episode. It was basically regurgitating information from my interview with Grant that she'd crashed, and my online posts that I'd been writing as updates for the *Tribune* social media accounts. So that was sufficiently irritating. There was also a hefty amount of self-promotion, merch advertising, and a thank you to ALL the Murderoonies who had attended their arrival event at the hotel. Just when I thought it was almost over and couldn't get worse, Edith's tone turned teasing, like she had some juicy bit of gossip.

"In addition to investigating the human remains, we have a golden little side nugget of a mystery for you! Dylan Drake, Representative for Branson Falls in the Utah State House of Representatives, and the most eligible bachelor in Utah, is currently representing the property developers as their attorney. But, based on some things I've been hearing, *and* witnessing, chances are good he might be off the market. Tune in next time to see whose porch he was caught on a few mornings ago."

I groaned so loudly I was worried people might mistake it for another type of groan and that would cause even more rumors. Thank the goddesses I was inside my Jeep. This was just what I needed. An investigative podcast—and I put investigative in quotes—investigating my life. I already had The Ladies, who had dedicated their lives to that endeavor, and had been doing it for months. I didn't need a podcast with an international fanbase spreading rumors too. I bit the inside of my lip, thinking. Jackie had been involved in this somehow, I knew it. She was probably trying to give the Murderoonies something else to talk about that wasn't the dead bodies on her boyfriend's property. I wouldn't be surprised if she'd traded information with them: my dating history in exchange for the Murderoonies going easier on Grant and his development.

I closed my eyes, leaned my head back against the headrest on my seat, and took several box breaths. That didn't help, but swearing sure did.

I walked into the office and found Hawke sitting in my chair, his hair messy sexy, and wearing a dark, long sleeve shirt that hugged every muscle. It was hard not to stare. He was doing something on my computer and flashed me a heart-stopping smile when I walked in. "I would have invited you to lunch if I'd known you had some free time." I put my purse down and pulled my phone out of my pocket.

"Ella said you were at an interview so I thought I'd wait for you." He typed a few more things on the keyboard.

"What are you doing?"

"Securing things."

"We have IT people for that."

He gave me the courtesy of looking up and arching one brow. "They're not me."

Fair enough.

Ella came out from the back room, looking at some papers she was holding and mumbling something before saying, "Kate—" she glanced up, noticed Hawke, and stumbled a little. I couldn't blame her. He'd make royalty trip.

"Well, howdy Hawke! This is a nice surprise," she said.

"You didn't know he was here?"

"No, I've been workin' my fingers to the bone in the archive dungeon lookin' for the information you asked for."

"Thanks for doing that," I said.

Ella looked Hawke up and down. "I heard you've got some tattoos."

"I do," Hawke confirmed.

A thoughtful expression crossed her face and she put a finger up to her chin. "How would I go about seein' them?"

Hawke's lips twitched. "I'd have to take off my clothes."

Her eyes brightened and she held up her index finger. "Hold on, let me get my glasses."

I shook my head and laughed. "He's not stripping for you, Ella."

She pushed her lips into a pout. "But I want to see the tattoos. And everythin' else!"

"I don't blame you," I said, filling up my water bottle. "The whole package is impressive."

She stopped in her tracks. "You've seen 'em?" she asked, referring to the tattoos. Then gestured to the rest of Hawke. "And it?" she asked, referring to the package.

Not yet, but I wanted to. "I didn't say that."

Her eyes narrowed and she pointed at me. "You didn't not say it, either."

This could go on forever and I had questions I needed her to answer. "Did you find any missing persons?"

She pushed her brows together. "You gave me a big date range."

I took a drink from the reusable water bottle sitting on my desk. "I realize that, but we don't know the dating on the bodies yet, and I'm trying to figure out if anyone went missing around the same time Jeff Zundy was here. Fern Gables seems to think he killed multiple women in the area, and she blames her family for bringing him to Branson." Records weren't as thorough back then, but the *Tribune* had been around for a long time so I hoped Ella had been able to find some information.

"I was here during that time," Ella said. "Occasionally people would go missin', but a lot of times it was girls who'd gotten pregnant, or runaways."

She'd mentioned that before, and it still happened even today. Small Utah towns were brutal to women, especially women who had been identified as sinners. Few things marked an unmarried woman more than a pregnant belly. When I was in high school, girls who got pregnant and weren't shipped off to have the baby in secret somewhere else, were typically sent to an alternative school. It was explained as if they'd be more comfortable there, but I'd heard the real reason was that the administration didn't want other girls to see a pregnant classmate and get baby fever.

"I checked the whole county for the dates Zundy was here. The records I found show five teen girls went missin' durin' that time period, and eight women. One turned back up later. It also shows ten men who went missin' as well. It was assumed that the men got lost, or were in some kinda accident."

Ella put the papers down on the table and I rifled through them, reading as I went.

"Did you check homicides as well?" Hawke asked.

Ella's eyes widened like something had clicked in her head. "No! Dagnabbit. I'll work on those next."

"The remains could be bodies from people outside the county as well," Hawke said. "I can help check that on a wider scale."

Ella pointed at Hawke like he was her favorite conspirator. He probably was.

"Why homicides?" I asked. "Wouldn't that mean it was a murder and it had probably already been solved?"

"Nope," Ella said. "And there are lotsa murders. All over. Every day."

"In Branson?" I said, knowing full well that there weren't lots of murders here every day.

"People die all the time, Kate!" Ella threw her hands up to emphasize her point." For all kinds of reasons!"

I leaned against my desk while Hawke continued working magic on my computer. "I thought homicide rates have gone down in recent years. Is that wrong?"

"A homicide clearance rate means someone gets arrested. Not that it's solved." Hawke said. "And if police have a suspect, and the suspect dies or can't be located, police can clear the murder, so those numbers are also added to the clearance rate."

My jaw dropped. "Seriously?"

Hawke nodded. "It looks bad not to clear a case so police want to clear it, and most members of the general public don't understand the difference between solving and clearing. The two get lumped together in a lot of reporting and statistics so it seems like murders are being solved, but in reality, police solve fewer homicides now than ever before. It used to be easier to figure out who did it, but now it's harder. Ninety-three percent of murders were solved in the 1960s. Now it's about fifty percent."

"How is that possible," I asked, dumbfounded. "We have far more technology, and it's easier to catch people with everything from video surveillance and phone GPS, to DNA."

"We have more technology, but the world has changed," Hawke answered, leaning back in my chair and crossing his hands over his lower abs. "A lot of people think fingerprints solve everything, but it's not the exact science movies and TV shows lead you to believe it is. Forensic evidence is only a factor in finding suspects about eight percent of the time.

Forensic evidence is most often used to prove guilt after the police already have a suspect."

Ella nodded enthusiastically in agreement with Hawke. "It depends on where it happens, too. Murders in the home are usually easier to figure out 'cause they're often related to domestic violence. Women have the ability to be independent and leave those horse's butts now, so that's helped because they have the money and resources to get outta dangerous situations. But if it's a stranger homicide, those are lots harder to solve."

"Ella's right," Hawke said. "Most murders now are done by firearms. People are killed from a distance, so it's more difficult to figure out who did it, and what happened. But if someone kills their wife in a blind rage by stabbing them to death, that's easier because there's blood everywhere and it's not hard to make deductions on arrival at the scene."

"What about all the true crime stories you hear about police not being able to figure out what happened when they get there?" I asked. I'd been listening to some of The Murderoonies old podcasts, and a few other true crime podcasts as well to compare. The stories were often framed like the police couldn't figure it out, especially with cold cases.

Hawke tilted his head in acknowledgment. "Homicides are more solvable now, but a huge factor affects it—how fast police can arrive on the scene."

"Yep," Ella echoed. "The faster they get there, the better. Cases are more likely to get solved if there's a cop near the area who takes their police car home with them 'cause it means they can go directly to the scene instead of goin' to the station, switchin' cars, and then goin' to the crime."

"It gets them there faster," Hawke explained. "An officer

needs to get there as fast as possible and start talking to people before their stories change. Once people on the scene start talking to each other, initial thoughts and stories will evolve. Eighty-seven percent of homicides are solved by the first officer on the scene."

My eyes widened at that number. "I had no idea the stats were so high on that."

"But the officer has to get there fast enough to make deductions before stories and memories start to shift," Ella said.

"Police departments want to clear cases so their numbers look good," Hawke said. "Which means that some of those human remains on the Barret property could have been classified as something else—like a homicide, and written off as solved."

"I'm gonna go back and check on homicides," Ella said, grabbing a drink from the water cooler and a treat from the treat table. "Let me know what you find, Hawke. If you want to send me a pic of you shirtless, that wouldn't be bad either."

"Noted," Hawke said with a wide smile.

Ella smiled back like a cat that had gotten the cream, and walked toward the archive room.

I gave Hawke a look. "If you send her a half-naked photo of yourself, she'll probably have a stroke."

"It would be a great way to go!" Ella yelled.

Hawke couldn't hold back his laugh.

I got a piece of candy for each of us from the treat table and said, "I haven't even seen you naked, so Ella better not see that before I do."

Hawke's gaze turned predatory. "I'm up for it any time you are, Kitty Kate. Tonight even. We do have a date."

Shit. I'd forgotten about that. I hadn't slept last night, and neither had Hawke because we'd both been out in a field while police dug up bones.

"Did you forget?" Hawke asked.

I pursed my lips. "It's been a long week."

Hawke stood and leaned into me. "Why don't we do something easy and relax?"

That sounded like a great plan. "I can't think of anything better."

"I'll pick you up around six?"

"Perfect. I have a few things I need to do here first, and then I need to walk Gandalf before we go."

"I'll walk him with you when I get there," Hawke said, standing up.

I took a deep breath and felt my shoulders relax a little. Sometimes it was nice to know I had a person and wasn't carrying everything alone—even if it was only for a night. "I'll see you soon," I said.

"Don't forget to get a pic of his tattoos and package!" Ella yelled from the back room.

Hawke laughed and walked out the front door. For someone in her seventies, Ella had excellent hearing.

Chapter Fourteen

I watched Hawke leave, mostly because it was an excellent view, and then picked up my phone to call the farmer who had been leasing the Barret property before it was sold.

Wayne Post answered on the fourth ring. "Gawldangit! Who the heck is callin' me in the middle of the night?"

I checked the clock. It was three in the afternoon. "Hi Wayne, this is Kate Saxee with *The Branson Tribune*. I was hoping to ask you some questions about the old Barret property."

He coughed and snorted all at once, like he was disgusted but didn't know how to adequately convey that over the phone. "Damn Georgia and her kids. Sellin' it out from under me."

He'd gone straight to swears so it was clear he wasn't over it. "I was told they offered to sell the piece to you but you declined."

"That's 'cause the price they wanted was highway robbery! This is what happens when ya get city people involved. Come in here with all their tech computer money, stealin' land from hard workin' people. If Georgia's husband, Saul, had still been around, this wouldn't have been a problem. Damn woman and her damn daughter."

Women, getting blamed for everything since Eve. Clearly, he held Georgia and Bethany responsible, but not Jordan. "Did you have an agreement about the property with Saul?"

"Course I did!" He said, his voice rising like he was reliving his anger. "I had first right of refusal, and that land should've been mine."

"Did you have that in writing or in a legal document?" I asked.

He gave a revolted snort. "Heck no! Why in tarnation would I need that?"

"To make sure the land couldn't be sold out from under you." The exact thing he was saying had happened.

"It shouldn't have been sold out from under me because we're neighbors and honorin' agreements is the right thing to do!"

"Did you think you were going to get it for a different price than what the Barret's were asking?"

"Yes! I shoulda been allowed to pay what we agreed on years ago."

"The market has changed significantly since Saul died. That piece of property is worth a lot more now, and the developers were willing to pay for it."

"Dagnab Californians and city people again, tryin' to push all the farmers and rural people off the land so they can build McMansions." I could hear the disdain in his voice.

"You still think the Barret family should've sold you the property at the price you were quoted decades ago, from a man who's dead, and with no legal documentation it was ever offered for that price?"

"They should've honored their deals! And now look at it!" He started to laugh and that turned into a cough. "Bodies all over the place. Serves 'em right. If I'd bought it, the bodies would've stayed buried."

His wording stopped my note writing in my tracks. "Did you know there were bodies on the property?"

His voice took on a mysterious tone. "All land has secrets, Kate. I dare ya to find a property without 'em. Now I'm gonna go back to bed. You shouldn't call people so late." He hung up the phone.

Well, that was unexpected. I got the impression he knew more than he was saying, and I wondered if the Barret family, or Georgia's husband, Saul, had told him something about the property and the bodies. He seemed like he'd been close to Saul. I hadn't asked Georgia or Bethany much about Saul because he'd been dead for a long time and it seemed Saul's family relationships had been strained, but now I felt it was thread I needed to explore. A person could seem like the nicest human in the world but behind closed doors, their family could have a very different opinion of them. Studies showed one in twenty-five people were sociopaths, and based on how the Barret family had responded when I'd asked about Saul in the past, I wondered what Saul was truly capable of.

I still needed to talk to Jordan, but in all my interactions with the Barret family, they hadn't indicated to me that they knew anything about the bodies. In fact, Bethany had seemed eager to learn more, but maybe she was simply playing a part to avoid culpability. Saul was an addition to the mystery. It was hard to believe someone in the family didn't know about the bodies, especially now that the police had found nine of them. Nine bodies would be a difficult secret to keep.

I knew what Grant's development company had paid for the property, but I also opened a browser and looked up the price history. Grant paid *a lot* more than Wayne Post would have if he'd bought it before Saul Barret died. I sat staring at my computer screen and thinking until I was interrupted by Spence walking into the office.

"You look like you're in deep thought."

"I am. I just got off the phone with the farmer who was leasing the Barret property. He was angry."

"I imagine," Spence said, putting his bag down in his office. "He probably wanted the land for himself."

I lifted my hand and pointed my index finger. "Not only did he want it, but he thought he was entitled to it because of a verbal agreement he said he made with Georgia Barret's husband, Saul, decades ago. And he wanted it for the price it was worth then."

Spence's eyes went wide and he laughed as he walked to my desk. "That would have been quite the deal. The property is probably worth double what it was then."

"Four times the amount, actually." I showed him the property details sheet with the price history information.

Spence whistled. "Wayne was probably as upset as everyone else that someone from out of town was coming in and buying property he considered his own."

I had a theory about that and wanted Spence's take. "Have you noticed anyone treating you differently because you aren't from around here," I asked Spence.

His mouth went slack in a "you've got to be kidding" look. "Kate, I'm one of the only black people in this city. That alone means I'm treated differently. But being an outsider with different beliefs does as well. People weren't happy when I was brought on as the publisher of the *Tribune* instead of someone from Branson Falls or the surrounding areas. The problem is that most people who have the education for my job, or yours, don't want to live in a rural area. I think the town would have been content to let the same people who write the Community News run the whole newspaper."

I shuddered at the thought. "That would have been a nightmare." Every article would have contained the contents of Rachel's grocery list and Neil's garage sale finds. As well as a list of what every person in the article ate that week. Even with Spence, and now me, running things, I felt like there was still a lack of different perspectives simply because of the makeup of Branson Falls and the generations that had lived here and never left. If townspeople were in charge of the newspaper, it would read like a Mormon Ward newsletter. "How long did it take for people to accept you?"

"Years," Spence said. "Even now, I'm not sure I'm accepted as much as I'm tolerated. I'm not like them and they read that like a threat."

I'd grown up in Branson Falls for most of my life, so I'd been grandfathered in. People might not like me, what I now represented, or how I lived my life as an adult, but they didn't actively work to kick me out of town either. No one was purposely destroying my soda shop drinks, or starting groups like CFNP dedicated to keeping me out—though they might have destroyed my coffee with flour, and they did start the Facebook group about me. "I get harassed for not going to church, and for my coffee drinking and love life, but it's nothing like what you've experienced."

"There's definitely a hierarchy in Branson Falls," Spence said. "The longer you've lived here and have generations of family to show for it, as well as church records that match, the more power you have. What made you ask?"

I tapped my fingers against my thigh. "I have a theory," I said, taking a breath. "Remember when I was investigating the robberies last month and thought the thief might have been targeting people who hadn't lived here long?"

Spence nodded. "But the robberies were mostly random, right?"

"I'm not sure. The victims were chosen by Cadence's partner, and she never disclosed who that was. The disdain for outsiders and especially people with different beliefs was prevalent when I was young, but it's nothing compared to how it is now. People are angry. I've only been back in Branson for about six months, but I see it constantly. Even on the *Tribune's* Facebook page. If you're a transplant, people don't think you should be allowed to comment or have an opinion."

Spence shrugged. "That makes sense. I probably don't notice it as much because I've been living here for several years and I've become used to the attitude."

I grabbed my notebook and drew a picture for Spence. "Have you seen this symbol? It was painted on the sidewalk in multiple places a few days ago?"

"Yeah," he said, leaning against my desk and crossing his ankles over one another. "It's weird. And someone painted the same symbol on the old sheet metal plant so you see it as soon as you drive into Branson." The old sheet metal plant was basically a walking billboard used for vandals. My mom had made something similar for me as a kid where she installed a whiteboard on a wall, and that was the only wall I was allowed to draw on. The sheet metal plant was similar because it helped keep the graffiti concentrated.

"The symbol is from a group called Citizens For No Progress, or CFNP for short. I looked them up the other day on social media and their videos are crazy, and a little scary. They legitimately want things to go back in time. I think it's nostalgia for when they were younger, but even their kids and grandkids are participating because the opinions of the older generation are being passed down. CFNP is all over Utah, but it's especially prominent in rural communities. They're posting their signs and symbol, but not explaining it in order to get people to look them up. And also, because it makes them feel special to have knowledge others don't. They're anti-outsider, anti-newcomer, and definitely anti-new beliefs."

Spence put his finger up to his lips. "I've seen some of their videos, but didn't realize they were that organized, or that they were here in Branson."

"I think people who differ from the expected norm, and who didn't grow up here, are getting pushed out—especially if they've moved in recently. It feels like the town is being split into two camps. The old guard, and the new. It's easy for the old guard to make the new guard an "other" and dehumanize them when they don't know the new guard and have no interest in trying to understand who they actually are. Townspeople don't want new ideas here, so they're sabotaging the people who have them in one way or another." I lifted a finger ticking off my examples. "The flour attack at the grocery store. The vandalism at the coffee shop. The soda shop employees using cream that had gone bad, but only in the drinks of people who ordered coffee, had tattoos, and wore clothes deemed immodest. And now, the CFNP symbol on the sidewalks and sheet metal plant, reminding people of who's accepted, and who isn't."

Spence leaned back slightly and contemplated. "I mean, I could see it. But the only situation that was confirmed to be targeting people with different beliefs was the flour attack. The coffee shop has been a target of ire since it opened, and the soda shop employees said the sour milk was an accident."

I rolled my eyes. "An accident that only got put in the drinks of people who ordered coffee, and had beliefs different from the employee making it. I interviewed the kid at the soda shop and he admitted he didn't agree with what the customers had ordered, and he was not the least bit sorry about their sour milk. What if it's not just sour milk and flour attacks? What if the bodies were put on the Barret property as sabotage."

Spence pushed his brows together. "Wouldn't the police know that?"

I hadn't talked to Hawke or Bobby yet, so I wasn't sure. "Maybe, I'm sure there's some sort of dating they can do. But the land deal to buy the Barret property was in the works even before I moved back to Branson. It was plenty of time for someone to acquire some bodies and bury them there." Especially if they owned property right next door, like Wayne Post.

"What would the motive be?"

"To stop development. Maybe the land wouldn't be sold, and houses wouldn't be built there. New people would find somewhere else to live, and Branson Falls could continue to not change. And secrets would have been kept."

Spence inclined his head toward me as he thought about it. "I guess anything is possible. What made you think of this theory?"

I tapped my pen on a notepad. "I've been marinating on the idea since all of this started, but something Wayne mentioned on the call today caught my attention. He said if he'd gotten the land, the bodies would have stayed hidden."

Spence's forehead creased. "He knew about the bodies?"

I lifted my hands, palms up. "He wouldn't confirm or deny, but I thought his statement and the way he worded it were both suspicious. If he didn't put the bodies there, it makes me think he knew they were there, so maybe the Barret family has more information about the remains than they've let on."

"It sounds like something to keep looking into," Spence said.

"I plan on it."

I had about an hour before I needed to pick Gandalf up from my mom and dad's and get ready for Hawke to come over. I pulled up my browser and started researching more about the Murderoonies' first case: the women who had gone missing in Colorado. They'd been road tripping across the country in a camper van when family and friends stopped hearing from them. They were last seen by some neighboring campers who said they were going for a hike. Their camper was left abandoned, and their bodies were later found in the Colorado River.

Police had no clues or leads, but The Murderoonies had started investigating, asking for any evidence from people who had been in the area. The Murderoonies were eventually able to tie a social media post to the van, complete with an image of a man going through it. They asked for help from the true crime community again, and were able to identify the man in the photos. The women were killed by a guy who was squatting in a cabin in the mountains a mile away. It wasn't totally clear how The Murderoonies got their information, or how they put things together. But they'd solved the case and become darlings of the true crime podcast community. The Murderoonies had been covering crimes, and trying to solve them and replicate their original success, ever since.

A case where newly unearthed bodies might be the victims of a long-gone serial killer like Zundy would be too much for The Murderoonies to pass up. Frankly, I was surprised more true crime podcasts weren't also on the scene.

I looked at the clock and closed my computer. I had a puppy to pick up, a date to get ready for, and hopefully some investigating of my own...into what tattoos were under Hawke's clothes.

Chapter Fifteen

I got home early and texted Hawke to tell him Gandalf and I would be at the park.

The park was Gandalf's favorite place—probably because of all the smells, and the socks and food frequently left by kids. We walked there from my house every night—every night that I was home and not working, at least. There were a surprising number of people out for a night in November, but the sun was still up, and it wasn't as cold as usual this year.

A large group of teenagers were at the top of a grassy hill and sledding down it on blocks of ice. A kid came flying by me and almost took me out, like he was the bowling ball and I was the pin.

Ice blocking was both a wholesome, and strange, group date activity in Utah. And one I'd participated in as a teen on dates. People would put a small hand towel over a block of ice, sit on the top of it, and ride it down a grass covered hill. Sometimes they would have more than one block and race— like they seemed to be doing now.

Ice blocking was usually done by teenagers, and especially Mormon teens, who weren't supposed to date until they were sixteen years old, and even then, they were supposed to go on group dates until age eighteen. The reasoning behind the group dates was that kids were less likely to get in trouble—meaning have sex—if multiple people were there as witnesses and they could police each other. I'd always found the exact opposite to be true, and thought group settings were a great way to encourage people to make bad choices. And let's be honest, bad choices make the best stories.

As the kid almost took me out, I realized I knew the ice-capade. Keanu.

Keanu got up and waved his hands in apology. "So sorry, reporter lady! I wasn't aiming for you; these ice blocks are super slippery and hard to steer."

He came over to pet Gandalf on the head and Gandalf leaned into the scratches, not the least bit worried that his human had almost been run over by a mini-iceberg. I regarded them thoughtfully and realized my little dog would probably sell me for a potato chip and belly rubs.

"This isn't the usual crowd you run with," I said, noting that Keanu was with a group of young adults I knew went to church.

"They invited us, and they always have good treats, so we figured why not."

I lifted my brow. "They're probably trying to convert you. Next thing you know, they'll be throwing you in the baptismal font, calling it a baptism, and giving you a church calling."

Keanu busted up and leaned in conspiratorially. "Let's hope they ask me to bring refreshments to the next activity. They'll be brownies, and they'll be *magical*."

I grimaced. "I wouldn't. You saw what happened with the pot cookies."

He frowned. "I'm still sad about all that wasted weed."

A lot of people were, including some of the religious people in town who hadn't known they were taking drugs, but liked the effects and would have rather been left in the dark about the ingredients so they could continue to partake.

"Isn't it a little late in the year for ice blocking?" I asked, gesturing to the next round of kids sliding down the hill and laughing as they went. I was wearing gloves and a jacket. The temperature wasn't bad, but the wind gave the air a chill.

Keanu shrugged. "It's been unseasonably warm this autumn, Kate *Saxeeeeee*." He dragged my last name out with a sing song tone and a giggle.

My eyes widened, both because he'd used my real name instead of "Reporter Lady," and also because I didn't think the word "unseasonably" was in Keanu's vocabulary. He proved me wrong, and it wasn't the first time. I liked Keanu a lot. He'd helped me on a few cases since I'd moved back, and always provided more information than I thought he would. I'm not sure he ever really intended to, but was glad he did.

A kid came running down to grab Keanu's ice block so they could keep their race going.

"Hear about the bodies?" Keanu asked, kicking at a piece of ice that had fallen off.

I wrinkled my forehead. "The ones at the old Barret farm?" He must not follow social media or my *Tribune* posts because I'd been reporting on the bodies multiple times a day since they were found.

"Not just those," Keanu said.

My brows came together. "Are there other bodies I don't know about?"

Keanu nodded. "My buddy found some bones near Spartan Way."

I tilted my head in interest. I hadn't heard about that. And as long as my sources were being reliable, I was usually one of the first to learn about things like crimes, misdemeanors, and possible murders. "Did your friend call the police?"

Keanu scoffed. "Are you kiddin' me? He didn't wanna get in trouble."

I suppressed a sigh. "Okay, why don't you tell me where the bones are, and I'll go check it out. If it looks like we need the police there, I'll call them and your friend won't have to be involved."

Keanu lifted his shoulder. "Okay." He rattled off the area where his friend had seen the bones and I wrote the general directions down on my phone since he didn't have the exact address. "You'll text me if you find the body and it's a victim of the serial killer, right?" His voice was almost as eager as Ella's at the thought of the potential Jeff Zundy victims.

I nodded. "Sure will."

I continued on my walk with Gandalf, dodging the ice races and the frozen butts attached to the kids sitting on the blocks. I moved to a less inhabited side of the park where it was quieter and I could think.

The police were still investigating the bodies found on the development and so far, the only bodies identified had been men. The Murderoonies were convinced it was a serial killer and the work of Jeff Zundy—and kept promoting that on their podcast. The theory made for good entertainment, but I wasn't sure it was accurate. For one, if the bodies found were people who had gone missing, I was pretty sure they would have been reported as missing at the time. Ella wasn't done searching, and we didn't have Hawke's info yet either, but so far, we didn't have a lot of open missing persons cases. Then again, like Ella pointed out, girls around that age went "missing" all the time in towns like Branson Falls, and it was usually because their families wanted to cover up their pregnancy. Hawke was also right, the remains could belong to people missing from outside of Branson Falls, or their deaths could have been classified as something else.

"It's pretty brave of you to be walking out here all by yourself," a deep voice said from behind me.

I'd told Hawke that I'd be at the park with Gandalf. He'd found me, which wasn't surprising. He squatted down to pet Gandalf and Gandalf turned right over with belly rub expectations. Hawke laughed and followed the assignment.

"Luckily, I know self-defense thanks to an oversized GI Joe figurine who forced me to learn. And I'm carrying pepper spray. Also, it's dusk. The devil doesn't come out until midnight, or so I'm told."

Hawke's eyes flashed with amusement. "Why don't we go back to my house and test that theory?"

"Is that where we're going tonight?"

"Maybe."

I looked at my watch. "I thought you were meeting me at my house in an hour," I said.

"I got done early so I came to find you."

He'd never told me outright, but I suspected he could track my phone. At first I'd been pissed about it, but it had helped stop me from getting shot, so I'd made peace with it and decided the more help I had, the better. Since Hawke was exceptional at basically everything, and hot as hell, I was fine with his assistance.

Hawke stood and we kept walking so Gandalf could get his exercise. Puppies have more energy than toddlers.

We heard yelling in the distance and watched as two teens racing down the hill tumbled off their ice butt slides. They got up, laughing uncontrollably, and I shook my head. "No one could pay me enough to sit on a freezing block of ice and ride it down a hill in November."

"What about riding other things?" Hawke asked with a quirk of his lips.

I'd walked right into that one. "I guess it depends," I said, trying to decide how far I wanted to go with this.

His eyes sparked with anticipation. "On what?"

"The temperature of the ride."

He stopped and moved close to me, his muscular body towering over mine. He leaned down and put his lips on my neck, then started kissing his way up to my ear where he whispered in a husky voice, "It would start warm and soft. Then it would move to steamy. And would end with sweltering."

We were in the middle of a park where teenagers were riding ice down hills and I was ready to jump on Hawke right there in public. I needed to cool down, and fast—without the aid of sitting on frozen water. "I know we have a date tonight and I know you have things planned, but I got lead from Keanu about something and I need to check on it. Do you want to go search for some bones with me?"

He smiled slowly. "That line wouldn't work on a lot of men, Kitty Kate. But I'm one of them."

I grinned. "I know."

"Don't think we're done having the conversation about heat," he said.

A rush of anticipation shot straight to my core. "Oh, I won't."

He grabbed my hand and we finished the walk back to my house where we got in Hawke's sexy, dark blue '67 Shelby Mustang named Roxy, with thick white stripes running over the hood, roof, and trunk, and drove to Spartan Way.

We walked around the general location Keanu had given me, but didn't see any obvious bones or dead bodies. We were searching an area in the field, near a For Sale sign. Gandalf kept pulling at the leash, which he was not supposed to do, and he knew it.

"What's your deal, little guy?" I asked, trying to pet him and calm him down.

"He's a puppy," Hawke said.

I shot Hawke a look for trying to justify Gandalf's bad behavior. "A puppy who learned not to pull on his leash in his puppy classes." He pulled again, trying to get to something in the dirt. "He's usually really good at commands and not acting out."

Hawke pulled back his bottom lip with his teeth like he was assessing something in a field, then moved toward Gandalf. He crouched down and let Gandalf smell his hand until Gandalf backed down and let the leash lag. Then Hawke reached over to move some weeds around in the area Gandalf was pulling toward. It took about thirty seconds before

Hawke motioned me over. I looked down, and saw what appeared to be bones.

My jaw dropped. "Holy shit, is that what I think it is?" Keanu's friend had been right!

Hawke moved a few more weeds and nodded. "That looks like a human leg bone."

"You've got to be kidding me."

Hawke shook his head and sighed. "I wish I was, because I have a feeling our night just took a very unromantic turn."

Later I'd have the capacity to be disappointed about that. Right now, I was too excited about scooping the Murderoonies, and also because my dog had uncovered the evidence. "Is my dog a cadaver dog?" I asked, momentarily stunned. "Because I think he's a cadaver dog!"

Hawke looked up at me with his half smile that made me want to kiss him senseless. "Your mom is going to love this."

I groaned. "Oh, hell," I said, thinking of all the trouble she could get in if Gandalf really could scent dead bodies. She'd take him out every day and turn him into her own personal body finder. It had all the makings of multiple Catasophies.

Hawke laughed. "Most dogs are pretty good at scenting dead things," Hawke said. "But cadaver dogs are specially trained. I'm not a forensic anthropologist so I'm not exactly sure what this is, but we should get the police out here in case. I'm not going to disturb the scene any more than we already have."

"How do you know so much about cadaver dogs?" I asked.

He gave me a look.

"Never mind," I said.

Hawke placed a call to Bobby and the police were at the scene in less than ten minutes. It took Bobby all of five minutes to confirm the bones were bones, and they were going to have to secure the scene.

"I hate to do this, but I should probably stay and help with the crime scene," Hawke said, taking me aside. "I have resources they need."

I nodded, the disappointment finally settling in because our plans had been ruined. Again.

"You can take the Mustang home," he said, handing me the keys.

I widened my eyes. "Are you kidding me?"

He looked at me like I might be crazy. "No."

"Do you know how long I've wanted to drive this? Like, since the first moment I saw it!"

"All you had to do was ask."

I smiled and ran my tongue over my lips. "Good to know. I'll be asking for a lot of things going forward."

His eyes took on a dangerous sparkle. "I look forward to saying yes to those, too."

I tilted my head. "I mean, you might be agreeing too soon. What if I want to drive your Ferrari that I've never seen."

"There are a lot of things you've never seen, Kitty Kate. I'm happy to show you all of them."

My cheeks got pinker the longer we talked. I could make excuses for it with the cold, but Hawke knew better so there was no point.

I took the keys and my magic little murder sniffing dog and started to walk away, but turned around. I shouldn't have asked because I knew it would make me even more depressed, but I did anyway. "Hawke, what were we going to do tonight for our date?"

He took a breath like he was wistful about it as well. "Dinner, wine, and a massage were involved."

I couldn't hide my disappointment. "That sounds nice."

"It will happen another night. I'll make sure of it. Maybe we can utilize the red dress you wore to the auction again."

"I mean, it was a bit torn."

His eyes sparked. "Good. I'll tear it the rest of the way next time."

My stomach flipped and I couldn't hide my smile at that.

As I pulled away from the scene, a squirrel and raccoon showed up via their white sedan. The Speedy Superheroes had arrived. Bobby would be thrilled. The Murderoonies would probably show up shortly as well. We all had more helpers than we wanted on this case.

I started Hawke's throaty Mustang and maintained enough self-control not to rev the engine until I got a full block away. I pulled it into my garage where it would be safe all night, and then went inside, showered, and fell fast asleep with Gandalf cuddled into the nook of my arm.

Chapter Sixteen

"I heard there was another body found last night," my mom said, opening the door before I could even knock. Her towel was over her shoulder and her hand was on her hip. "What do you know?"

Hawke had left me a voicemail this morning commenting on my use of the Mustang engine, and also saying they should know more about the bones in the next few days. "Not much." I said, watching Gandalf run over and make circles around my mom's legs until she picked him up. "I got a tip about the bones last night so Hawke and I went over with Gandalf to check it out. Gandalf found the bones immediately."

She froze and almost dropped my dog. "Wait one whole minute," she said, her eyes getting wider. I could practically see the wheels turning in her head and knew nothing good would come of this. "Are you saying my grandpuppy can smell dead bodies and hunt *murderers*?" I wasn't sure if she was horrified, intrigued, or both. I suspected both.

I couldn't blame her because I'd been enthralled with the idea last night as well, but like most things, I knew my mom was going take this information and make it into something much bigger than it probably should be.

I gave Gandalf some little ear rubs and his eyes rolled back in his head like he was in heaven. "I'm saying he can smell dead things, not find the person who killed the dead. The murderer could have been a coyote, and the victim a deer for all we know." Hawke and Bobby both thought the bones were human, but that wasn't public knowledge yet, and I didn't want any info getting out that the Murderoonies could try and steal. Especially when I was the one who broke the story about the bones on the *Tribune* social media pages last night.

My mom got a look in her eyes that told me she was getting an idea. That look always terrified me. "Imagine the side hustle we could have!"

My forehead formed a lot of lines. "Who's *we*?"

"Me! And Gandalf, of course! Who else?"

I raised my hands in the air, palms out. "Far be it for me to think I have a say in my dog's future career."

She went on like I hadn't said a thing. "Do you know how much influencer dogs make? It's a crazy amount! Gandalf could be an influencer and a murder solver!"

I scratched the corner of my mouth. "Paw P.I. murder investigations isn't something I had in mind when I adopted him."

Her voice went up an octave. "That's because you didn't know about his talents! And Paw P.I. is a great name for our business! I'm going to make him a shirt!"

She'd been making Gandalf clothes since I brought him home from the animal rescue. He had a better wardrobe than I did.

"I think he'd be very happy chasing his frisbee and playing with his toys in your back yard instead."

Her eyes went wide with disbelief and she shook her head. "But that's not his calling! Clearly!"

I wasn't going to win this. "Okay. Make him another outfit, but he's a puppy and not a dead body sniffing dog. Let him play and enjoy his life."

She gave me a smile that told me she was placating me and she had other plans. I was late for work, so I didn't have time to argue and hoped that Gandalf would forgive her for whatever scheme she was coming up with.

"Heard Hawke's Mustang was at your house all night last night," Ella said as she walked into the main office and saw me at my desk.

I threw my hands in the air. "How the hell do people know about that? His car was parked in my garage!"

"Your garage has windows."

"Are you saying The Ladies are trespassing and sneaking around my house every night to spy on me and my guests?"

Ella shrugged like it wasn't a big deal. "Yeah, pretty much. What was he doin' there all night?"

I moved some papers on my desk. "He wasn't there. We were walking Gandalf when I got a tip about a body being found on Spartan Way. We drove over to check it out and Gandalf found the bones. We called Bobby, and Hawke stayed to help, so he let me take his Mustang home. I put it in the garage so it would be safe and hidden from Lady spies, but clearly, I need to install some sort of shocking fence to keep people off my property."

Ella's brows pinched. "That wouldn't be very nice."

"Neither is a bunch of busy bodies peeping in my windows!"

Ella wrinkled her nose at that perspective. "His car's still there."

"Because he's been helping the police at the crime scene all night. But at this rate, I'm going to tell him to leave it so The Ladies have no idea when he's coming and going."

Ella slitted her eyes. "That's also a dirty trick."

My voice rose because I was so freaking pissed. "It's not even close to as dirty of a trick as what The Ladies put me through on the daily."

Ella moved her head from side-to-side like she agreed, but didn't want to come out and say so since she was technically one of The Ladies. "How's he gettin' around if he doesn't have his car?"

I lifted a shoulder. "He's probably driving his Audi R8, motorcycle, one of his Ferraris, or another vehicle I haven't been introduced to yet."

Ella's jaw went slack and her eyes were as big as saucers. "He owns all those cars?"

"Those are the ones I know about, but he owns more than that. He has a garage as big as a warehouse. And who knows what vehicles he has in other locations. I don't think this house is his only piece of real estate."

Ella pushed her lips out. "What do you think he does for a livin' to afford all those cars?"

"Other than he's some sort of independent contractor, I

have no idea. And I've checked." And I could find nothing, despite all of my resources and even calling in favors.

"I bet it's Only Fans," Ella said, nodding like she'd solved the mystery.

I laughed. A lot. But to be honest, I'd absolutely pay for that content. "I think it's something more in the moral grey area than that. How do you know about Only Fans anyway?"

Ella thrust her chin out. "I've been alive a long time, and my husband's been unalive for years. I'm old, not dead."

Now it was my turn for my jaw to drop. "You've been on Only Fans?"

She shrugged.

"Number one, that's *super* Mormon illegal." Even though Mormon dudes were some of the highest consumers of pornography in the world, it was against the rules of the religion. At one point, Utah even had a Porn Czar—a position funded by taxpayers at the Utah State government level and a person whose job description had been "obscenity and pornography complaints ombudsman," for real. The position was eliminated after relentless worldwide mocking and the state really wanted people to forget it had ever existed. I tried to bring it up often.

"Who's gonna know about it?" Ella justified. "It's not like I'm tellin' my bishop." Technically, she was supposed to. And if she did, she'd have to repent and promise not to do it again.

"They passed a law making it so you can't even view porn in Utah without registering a digital identification card, or using a third-party verification service—and I wouldn't put it past the state to share that info with the church," I warned her. "How are you watching it?"

"A VPN."

I blinked, stunned. "I didn't know you even knew what that was."

"Hawke probably helped her figure it out," Spence said, coming in from the back room and picking up a doughnut from the treat table.

Ella laughed. "Nope, I Googled it when they passed the stupid law."

Of course she did. She was more tech savvy than a lot of forty-year-olds I knew.

"It's how I access the dark web too."

I gave her a look. "What in the world are you doing on the dark web?"

She moved her shoulders in a little dance. "Lotsa good tips and gossip on there. It's where real true crime happens."

I had no idea what it would be like to have so much spare time that I would actually want to search for things to investigate on a place like the dark web, where getting accurate info was definitely not easy.

"You wanna find out where the bodies are buried, that's where ya go," Ella said.

That caught my attention. "Where do you usually search?"

"The vermin site on Tor. Lotsa juicy details there."

I made a note and would be checking it shortly.

What Spence said earlier caught my attention though. "Why do you say Hawke probably helped? What do you know about his job?"

Spence took a bite of his doughnut before answering. "Rumors mostly. But I know he has contracts with governments."

The 'S' there struck me. "Governments? Or just the US government?"

"Governments," he said, emphasizing the 's.'

"What does he do for them?" I asked.

"I have no idea. But I've heard he's excellent at it, and is considered the go-to for his line of work, whatever that actually is."

Contracts with governments made me think about why he'd chosen to settle in Branson Falls, of all places. A theory started to form. I needed to ask Hawke about all of this. Maybe the next time I saw him, or on our make-up date for the date the dead body discovery had waylaid, which was a make-up date for the one where I'd been left hot and bothered in the parking lot.

Ella changed the subject, "Sure is a lotta bodies bein' found all over the place."

"Yeah, it's odd," Spence said.

"It makes my theory about sabotage even more compelling," I pointed out.

"Who's tryin' to sabotage people?" Ella asked.

I took a sip of my salted caramel mocha. "Anyone who didn't want homes to be built here, or new people with different beliefs to move in," I said. "Every time a body is found, they have to stop all development work and investigate. And property for sale doesn't look as appealing if human remains are found on it." When I got home last night, I'd looked up information on the property with the new bones. "The property on Spartan Way used to be a farm. It was also for sale and under contract with a real estate developer from Salt Lake City. Maybe people are trying to stop the land from being sold and more homes from being built because they want to keep small town Branson Falls small." My money was on CFNP for that, but I wasn't sure they were organized enough to find and hide bodies.

"Oh, like the CFNP," Ella said, nodding.

My eyes flew to her. "You know about them?"

"Course I do. Their logo's all over the sidewalks, old sheet metal plant, and even stickers on cars. They've been recruitin' people at church."

That shouldn't have surprised me, but I hadn't considered it until now. "How many people in Branson are part of this group?"

"Heaps. People don't want new people comin' in, takin' land, tellin' 'em what to do, and changin' their way of life."

"Which is ironic considering most of the people I've seen who are upset are also members of the church, and Mormons are kind of known for going into places, attempting to take over entire cities to get them to believe in their religion, and kicking out anyone who doesn't fall in line. Like when the Mormon saints settled in Independence, Missouri, in 1831, and leaders instructed church members to buy every parcel of land between their temple and the state's western border, but to keep it quiet and not print the command because the general public couldn't know about their takeover plans…yet."

Ella wrinkled her nose. "I wouldn't know anythin' about that."

"Most Mormons don't." Which was a choice. Many of them deliberately chose not to learn church history that might make their church look bad, or make them question their beliefs. Just like the marijuana in the cookies—they'd rather not know than have to decide what they'd do with the actual truth. "CFNP is basically doing the same thing to new people moving into small Utah towns that was done to Mormons when they migrated west and kept getting kicked out of places because no one wanted them there."

Ella shrugged in agreement, and leaned toward me as she pulled out her phone. She started showing me some of the short form social media videos CFNP members had made. One was a protest in Salt Lake. Another was of people yelling during a city council meeting about home prices, outsiders, and land being stolen. I thought I recognized someone in the video.

"Can I see that?" I asked, putting my palm out for Ella's phone. She handed it to me. I rewatched the video, then paused it when I got to the part where I thought I recognized someone. It was Wayne Post, the farmer who had been leasing the Barret property and wanted to buy it. He was wearing a button with the CFNP symbol, and leading the yelling. But the thing that surprised me the most was the person standing next to him. Jordan Barret, Georgia Barret's son.

I called Jordan Barret again, but got his voice mail. I left a message asking him to call me back as soon as possible and telling him it was urgent. I couldn't figure out why Jordan would be at the CFNP meeting. He was part of the Barret family trust and as such, had benefited from the sale. Maybe he was at the CFNP meeting for something else? I had no idea and needed to talk to him to find out more.

I did more research into the property on Spartan Way, then I accessed my Tor browser and entered the dark web. I'd been a journalist for years and the dark web was something I'd had to access in the past for stories. You could only access it through Tor because the browser was encrypted and kept everything anonymous. It's why so much illegal activity happened on the browser. Regular internet browsers tracked people and didn't offer anonymity like Tor. The dark web could be a dangerous place if you didn't know what you were doing. Frankly, it scared me a little that Ella was on it. I didn't want someone to take advantage of her.

I typed in the website Ella told me about and started looking through some of the posts. People were offering tips about getting rid of bodies, others were offering hit man jobs. Some were obvious about it, others were trying to cover it up and make it look like pest control, hence the vermin name in the domain. I knew law enforcement accessed the dark web, and wondered how much they were monitoring sites like this one. It seemed like a hotbed of information and potential violent criminals to chase down. I scrolled through several posts until I came to one that caught my attention. It said: *"Need to bury some secrets? I know someone who's been doing it for years. They have nine jobs under their belt, and know how to keep things covered up."*

I replied to the post in a private message and asked for more information. I'd see if they answered. In the meantime, I took a screenshot of the post, including the web address and link. If anyone had some magic that could track this person down, it would be Hawke.

When Jordan still hadn't called me back, I grabbed his address from my laptop and left to see if I could talk to him in person. His house was a yellow two-story on the north side of town. The yard was covered in leaves, but it looked well-kept. A late model white sedan was in the driveway. I rang the video doorbell and could hear movement on the other side, but the door didn't open. I knocked again. Still nothing.

The fact that he was avoiding me, and had been all week, made me even more suspicious. I took out one of my business cards and wrote a note on the back asking Jordan to call me as soon as possible. I left it in the door, and waved at the doorbell camera, trying to look friendly and unintimidating. Then I crossed my fingers that Jordan would call.

I stopped by Fry Guy to grab some lunch and got some for Spence and Ella, too. While I was waiting in the drive-thru, I got a call from Bobby.

"I have news," Bobby said.

"I'm a news repository," I said back. "What do you know?"

"We have initial tests back on the bodies. They're all male."

I almost dropped the phone. "All nine of them?"

"All. The first three were men so we had a suspicion the others might be as well. Gender can be determined pretty easily, so we asked for that info as soon as possible. Identifyin' the bodies will take a bit longer, though we did get a name on the first body."

I inhaled a short, quick breath. "What's the name?"

Bobby paused. "I'm only tellin' ya this because we've already notified the family and there's gonna be a news conference in a few days where we announce it. We hope to have more names by then as well."

I was on pins and needles. "Don't keep me in suspense, Bobby! What's the name?"

"Larry Caldwell."

The name sounded familiar, but I couldn't place why. "You're the best, Bobby. Thanks for letting me know."

"I have more info for you too."

My eyes widened. "It's like reporter Christmas! Lay it on me."

"The bones on the Barret property had been buried and the remains had been there a while. But the dirt around the body on Spartan Way had recently been disturbed. Like someone had dug up the area to put the bones there. The bones were also well-preserved, and didn't look like they'd decomposed on that site."

"How could you tell that?"

"Hawke has tech that can do anything."

I wasn't the least bit surprised to hear that.

"So, someone put the bones there deliberately?" I asked.

"That's the theory. And that bit of info is still off the record, so keep it to yourself."

"I will, and I'll make sure my mom brings you cookies," I said.

"I knew the day would have a bright spot. Watch for the news conference release, and I'll talk to you soon, Kate."

I hung up right as I got to the window and picked up the food.

I put lunch on the treat table and started separating it, then called for Spence and Ella.

Spence walked out of his office with his lips pulled tight. "What's wrong?" I asked, concern creating lines between my eyebrows. I was going to have to start getting Botox soon, or those lines would become a problem.

He pushed one side of his mouth out, elongating the

grimace and making me even more worried. "Have you heard the latest Murderoonies update?"

I hadn't. I'd been a little busy investigating, so listening to their podcast with information they'd likely gotten from me, wasn't on the top of my priority list. "No, why?"

Spence pulled it up as Ella walked in the room. "It's short."

Edith's voice came through the microphone. "A quick little tidbit for our Murderoonies! Another body was found last night in Branson Falls on a completely different property! The body was found by a name you'll recognize, journalist and editor of *The Branson Tribune*, Kate Saxee. We hear her dog played a key role in the discovery. On another note, she was there with Hawke, a mysterious and very attractive local resident who's been helping the police with the investigation on the Barret property. That Kate is a busy, busy girl! If you remember, she's also tied to another very eligible bachelor, Utah politician and lawyer, Dylan Drake. We'll be keeping an eye on these three and their love triangle, and bringing you more info about the bodies, Jeff Zundy—and Kate's love life—as we know it. Until next time, happy murder investigating!"

I closed my eyes and took ten very deep breaths to try and calm my nervous system. It didn't help. But stabbing the Murderoonies might. "I'm going to try very hard to refrain from murdering them," I said.

"At least they gave you and Gandalf credit for finding the remains," Spence offered.

The look I gave him did not radiate appreciation. "I'll bet you a thousand dollars I don't have that The Ladies have something to do with this, and are supplying the Murderoonies with information about me. Jackie Wall wants to take pressure off her boyfriend, Grant, and she's willing to throw anyone under the bus to do it. Especially someone she dislikes anyway, like me."

"Do you want me to post the before and after picture of her boob job?" Ella asked, unwrapping her sandwich, and popping a fry in her mouth.

That made me smile a little. I shook my head. "No, that would make me as bad as Jackie is. I just need to remind her that I have pics of her doing a flour-covered walk of shame."

Ella's eyes widened. "You do?"

I nodded, dipping my own fry into the fry sauce. "It would be wise for her to remember that. I've already threatened her with it once, but she wasn't aware I have receipts to back it up."

"I'll tell her," Ella offered.

"I'll tell her next time I see her," I said.

"Brother Love's Traveling Salvation Show" started ringing from my phone. "Hey," I answered with a smile.

"We have a date tonight," Drake said.

"I haven't forgotten."

"I'll pick you up at six."

"I'll be ready, and dressed for the mountains in November."

"I have a blanket, and I'll definitely be keeping you warm. See you soon, Katie."

Drake hung up and I stared at my phone for several seconds.

"Who was that?" Ella asked.

"Drake. We have a date tonight."

The look she gave me made me think she could also use some Botox. "But you just had a date with Hawke."

I wrinkled my nose. "That's how dating works. I see different people at different times."

She put a finger to her lips, assessing. "You're like those penguins at the aquarium in the city who can't decide who they want to mate with."

I wasn't sure whether I was offended at being compared to the penguins, or flattered. They were adorable and I loved watching their social media updates. Ava was auditioning for the role of homewrecker, and Roto was a bit of player. I was invested. "I'm just trying to live my best life, like Poppy."

Ella widened her eyes in way that indicated I was definitely doing that. "Where ya goin' on the date with Drake?"

I took a bite of my hamburger. "The full moon lift ride at the ski resort."

"You're goin' on the full moon lift ride?" Ella asked, her tone excited. "*Together?*"

"Yes," I said, trying not to make it sound as scandalous as Drake had pitched it.

"It's a date with Drake! A Drake date!" Ella's voice was sing-songy and full of insinuation. "In the dark! On a mountain! In the cold! You're gonna do it, I know it."

I closed my eyes, shook my head, and finished my lunch. "We're not doing anything."

"Wanna bet?"

"And we're definitely not doing anything on a ski lift, thirty feet above the ground. That would be dangerous."

"Anythin' is possible."

"How do you know about the ride?" I asked, trying desperately to change the subject.

Ella balled up her sandwich wrapper and threw it away. "I used to go with my husband. It's been warm this year, so they extended the ride an extra month. But it's the last night for the season, and I sure ain't missin' it!" Ella said.

I heard the front door open and Hawke's shoulders filled the entire doorway as he walked in. He took up a lot of space.

"Hey," I said with a wide smile.

He flashed me one back. "Hey, yourself."

"Did you get any sleep last night?" I asked.

"Not much, and not for the reason I wish I'd lost sleep." His tone was full of insinuation.

I stole a glance at Ella and Spence, who were both right there and happily listening in. Hawke didn't let that go unnoticed. He flashed them an unapologetic grin. "Hi, Ella and Spence."

Spence sliced his head down in acknowledgment, and Ella's mouth spread wide. "Heya, Hawke! What do ya know about VPNs?"

I bit the inside of my lip, curious to hear his answer. His lips moved into a sly smile. "What do you know about VPNs, Ella?"

She looked at him like she was trying to ascertain how much she should trust him. She was far safer giving that info to Hawke than she would be to Utah State House of Representatives member and adult entertainment regulator, Drake.

"She's been using one to access restricted content," I supplied.

Hawke's lips spread into a full-on smile. "That's a good way to go somewhere you're not supposed to be."

"Do you often go places you aren't supposed to be, Hawke?" I asked.

His eyes sparked. "As much as possible."

I was hoping to get information from him with that

response, but he always managed to answer questions without really answering questions. It was a talent of his, and not one that I, as a reporter, appreciated.

That made me think of CFNP. "If I gave them to you, could you access information from some videos?"

"Probably. It depends on what information you're looking for."

"I'd like to slow some social media videos down and see if we can identify as many people as possible in them."

I'd already identified Jordan Barret and Wayne Post in the video Ella had shown me, but there were a lot of other CFNP videos I hadn't seen. I wanted to know if there was anyone else in the videos that I recognized, and who might be connected to CFNP and the Barret property.

"I can do that," Hawke said. "Send me the videos."

"Can you also track down someone posting on the dark web?"

He slitted his eyes. "What are you up to, Kitty Kate?"

"Investigating. Can you do it?"

"It's not easy. It's literally built for anonymity. But send me the information and I'll see what I can find."

"Thanks," I said, throwing my lunch trash away. "Was there anything else you needed?"

He shook his head. "Just wanted to see you."

My heart and stomach both did flips and I grinned like a goofball as I stared at him and he stared back. Spence cleared his throat, probably because it looked like I was having eye sex with Hawke, and I broke our gaze. I glanced back and saw that Hawke had not looked away because Hawke didn't care if people saw us having eye sex, or any type of sex for that matter.

"Do you want your car back?" I asked Hawke.

"Eventually."

"I guess you don't really need it when you have so many other vehicles to choose from."

He sliced his head down once. "I do, but Roxy is special. And I have to put her away for the winter soon."

That made sense. He wouldn't want to get salt on the car, and Utah's winter roads would be frosted with the stuff.

"When are you gonna name a car after Kate?" Ella asked.

Hawke smiled. "Who says I haven't already?"

Surprised lines formed on my forehead. "Have you?"

"I guess you'll have to come over and find out." With that invitation hanging in the air, he turned and walked out the door.

Chapter Seventeen

Drake and I settled into our seat on the lift ride. I was dressed in jeans, a black sweater, a black winter coat, and a warm grey beanie cap. The mountains are always colder after the sun goes down, and wind is almost constant. The air definitely had a bite to it tonight. Our chair had barely started its climb up the mountain when we heard screaming. A lot of it. And not for the under-the-blanket reasons I'd been promised.

"Someone's angry," Drake observed, his tone amused.

The lift stopped. We'd barely made it off the platform. There was so much yelling that I thought for sure it was a toddler. "It's probably past their bedtime. I don't think I'd bring a kid on here," I said. "I'd spend the whole time trying to make sure they didn't make a break for it and jump off the lift."

Drake looked around the lift to where the noise was coming from and paused. "I don't think that's a toddler..." His voice trailed off.

I looked behind me and to the left, toward the location of

the noise…the same spot where the lift ride was supposed to end.

"Is that Ella?" Drake asked.

Now that I was paying attention, I could clearly hear her voice and the arguments she was making. We were two chairs in front of her, going up. She was going down, and theoretically, she should be getting *off* the chair lift.

"You've already been on once, Ma'am." The poor kid couldn't be more than twenty, and wasn't equipped to deal with the tenacity and sheer stubbornness of Ella.

She huffed. "I refuse to get off because you shortened the ride when you added this fancy new lift! The ride used to be twice as long, and you're chargin' the same price! I'm stayin' on to get what I paid for!"

"That's definitely Ella," I said. "I saw her in the office earlier today and she told me she was going on the ride tonight."

"Well, I should thank her because she's going to make the ride longer for us," Drake said, slipping his arm around me and tucking me into his side. He smelled like cedar trees and fresh air. It was intoxicating.

I should maybe feel guilty about the arm and the tucking, especially after the eye sex with Hawke earlier today, but it was cold, and even if it hadn't been, I didn't feel bad. I wasn't ashamed about making sure I made an informed decision when I was ready. "She told me that she used to go on the ride with her husband every year. She still goes." My heart broke a little thinking about it.

Drake looked over at me, his eyes soft. We were still close enough to the bottom of the ride that he could talk to the employees. He turned to the woman operating our side of the lift and flashed her his politican's smile. "Avery," he said, his tone inviting. "Will you let the office know I'll pay for her to go again?" he nodded toward Ella.

Avery's lips spread into a shy smile. "Sure thing, Drake."

I wasn't sure whether to be touched by Drake's gesture for Ella, or bothered by the fact that a teenager—along with the rest of the women in the state—seemed to have a crush on him.

"What is she, sixteen?" I asked. "How does she even know you?"

He lifted a shoulder. "I met her buying the lift tickets, and she's seen me on the news."

Of course she had. Drake was charming AF. It was only a matter of time before he'd be off in Washington, DC, being a politician there. I considered what that life would look like, and if it was one I'd want to be part of. I wasn't sure.

The lift began to move again and I glanced back. Ella was two chairs behind us, and still seated. She looked very pleased with herself, like she'd won the argument. I was sure Drake would let her believe that, and not tell her he'd paid for her second ticket.

I moved the heavy blanket and made sure it covered us both, and then asked Drake, "How are Grant and his partners handling things?"

He cocked his head to the side. "As best as they can. Now that they have one body identified, it helps with the investors."

"Bobby told me the body was Larry Caldwell."

"Yeah, Grace is having a hard time."

Grace Caldwell? I hadn't had time to look up Larry's relatives yet. "That's why the name sounded familiar. I met Grace at the assisted living facility. Bethany said she visits Georgia a lot."

Drake tilted his head. "Makes sense. They were friends. Larry and Saul knew each other."

Huh. I wondered if Larry pissed Saul off and that's how he ended up dead.

"What's going on with the investors?"

Drake scrubbed a hand over his chin. "GCR doesn't always take investment money on projects, but they have some investors on this one. Having to answer to the investors is a big part of the stress."

"Are the investors blaming GCR for not doing enough due diligence?"

Drake shook his head. "No, GCR had the land looked at, but it's not like there's a service you can hire to find human remains before you buy a piece of property."

"Maybe there should be," I said. "Actually, don't mention that to my mom. Ever since Gandalf found the bones on Spartan Way, she thinks he's a murder sniffing dog and she's trying to start a side hustle with him searching for dead bodies."

Drake laughed. "She could probably make it work."

"Don't encourage her," I said. "How are the investors pressuring Grant and his partners?"

Drake took a long breath, and pressed his lips together. "If I tell you something off the record, will you keep it off the record and not report on it, or do anything that indicates you have this knowledge? At least not until I tell you that you can?"

Little sparks of excitement started going off in my chest. "Of course. My sources are always confidential."

"GCR has an offer from someone who wants to buy the development."

I blinked, surprised. "When did the offer come in?"

He shook his head. "I can't say, but it was recent."

"Before or after the bodies were found?"

"Can't say that either."

My mind was spinning. It could be all sorts of people, but the ones at the top of my list were Wayne Post, or the CFNP.

Drake continued, "The investors want Grant to get the infrastructure in and then sell. GCR has done that before—sold property once they've already started the development process. But it's not easy, and they usually take a loss."

I knew they'd sold property before because I'd found some information about it in my research, but that kind of practice wasn't unheard of in the development world. "Are they going to take more of a loss by keeping it?" I asked.

"Maybe. It's a shitty situation because it was a really good investment. I even considered buying in."

"Why didn't you invest?"

"I saw more of the numbers and felt like something was off. They got a really good deal on it."

I nodded. "I agree, but it was still a significant amount."

"It was, but I've lived here my whole life and knew the Barret's could have gotten a lot more for it, so I backed out. I avoid things that seem too good to be true."

So did I. And I had two men in my life who fit that "too good to be true" description perfectly. They both made it seem like everything would be cupcakes and rainbows, but no relationship was ever like that all the time. I should know, I'd almost married an asshat who'd promised me the world and then screwed someone on the side. My heart couldn't handle the disappointment and it was one of the reasons I wasn't in a rush.

"Why are you looking at me like that? What are you thinking?" Drake asked.

I waved off his comment and tried to stop my thoughts from writing themselves on my face—a difficult feat. "Nothing."

"I don't believe you."

I shrugged. I wasn't about to expand on my emotions or the indecision that came with them. That way lay vulnerability. And lots of it. He was trained to read body language and facial expressions, and my poker face was not stellar. Another point in the Botox column since it could help freeze my expression.

"I heard about Gandalf finding the bones," he said, bringing up our conversation from earlier about my mom and Paw P.I.

"I got a tip while I was walking him and went to check it out. It will be interesting to see if they're somehow connected to the bones on the Barret property. My gut says no."

"Why?"

"The bones on Spartan Way weren't buried deep. It almost looked like someone had put them there recently."

"Is that what Hawke thought too?"

My jaw went tight for several seconds. "So, you heard I was with him?"

"Apparently his car is still at your house."

I swore under my breath. "The freaking Ladies think they're the gossip police."

"Maybe they're trying to keep you safe from him."

I gave a disbelieving laugh. "That's the last thing they care about doing." I couldn't help wondering how long Drake and Hawke were going to be able to handle me dating them both. I knew I wasn't ready to make a decision, and didn't know when I would be. We'd had this discussion earlier in the week, but I felt I needed to have it again. "You know I was with Hawke at the Halloween party." It was a statement because I knew he already knew that.

He shifted in the chair, pulling me closer. "Not for long. And the rest of the night you were with me."

"Not the *whole* night," I said, making sure to emphasize the word "whole." I did spend the rest of the party with him. It had been reported about with heaps of judgment in the Facebook group The Ladies used to keep track of me. I wasn't sure what The Ladies had done with their lives before I arrived back in town because it seemed tracking me was their full-time job. Hawke had managed to infiltrate the group. The fact that he'd been surprised about me going back to the party indicated he hadn't seen the Facebook group gossip while he was gone.

"It could have been the whole night," Drake said with a slow smile.

I took a deep breath. "That wouldn't have been a good idea." For many reasons. Including the fact that minutes prior to running into Drake, I was being relieved of items from my costume in public by another man entirely, and would have happily stripped Hawke naked if Hawke's phone hadn't gone off when it did.

Plus, despite the rumors about Drake's experience with women, I really wasn't sure how much of that was true, and his religion meant he'd get in a lot of trouble for having sex. I didn't know if either one of us could handle the guilt if I deflowered him. Sex outside of marriage was a sin he'd have to confess to his bishop. That would get Drake's temple recommend revoked for a time...maybe—men in the church tended to get away with a lot. Definitely a lot more than women did.

Most people believed sex was a sin Drake had already committed though, and no one seemed too concerned about whether or not he was continuing to partake of it. I got the impression that people assumed his carnal appetites were ravenous based on the fact that he looked the way he did, and a lot of married men in the church were living vicariously through him. He was getting to experience what the rest of them wouldn't have until they made it to the top level of the Celestial Kingdom—as many women as they wanted.

"I don't see why not?" Drake stated matter-of-factly.

"We've been over those reasons repeatedly. And again, I'd just been with Hawke! Doesn't that bother you?"

A muscle feathered at his jaw. "I like a challenge. May the best man win."

"Oh, brother." I fought back an eye roll at that. It was one of the things I'd been worried about after hearing them both talk earlier this week. "What's with you two? I've asked the question before, but neither one of you will tell me, and I'd like to know. What secret do you both have on each other?"

"You'd have to ask him why he has a problem with me. But I know my problems with him."

"Then why don't you tell me what those are?"

He pressed his lips into a line before answering, "I have. He's dangerous and if push came to shove, I don't think he'd put you first."

"Yeah, but why do you think that. What happened to give you that opinion?"

"You're a journalist. Investigate."

I glared at him and my blood started to simmer. "You might regret that. I like a challenge too, and who knows what skeletons I'll find in your closet."

He lifted a shoulder, unconcerned. "I have nothing to hide. Does Hawke?"

Hawke likely had a warehouse full of skeletons, not a closet. They didn't scare me, though, and he seemed to be opening up the more we got to know each other. "If you have nothing to hide, why don't you just tell me?"

"Because it's not only my story to tell, and I try not to tell the stories of others. I'm not ashamed of what you'll find. Hawke might be though."

I'd asked the question thinking I would get non-answers like I had in the past, but Drake had unknowingly given me a hint and direction to follow. I'd tried finding information on Hawke before and it had led to dead end after dead end. There was a reason Hawke had a mansion for a house, and an even bigger garage, with cars that most people would only ever dream of—in his early thirties. He'd never come out and told me his title, or the name of his business, but it felt a lot like a mercenary. I'd even asked him about it and he'd neither confirmed nor denied it. He'd admitted to killing people, but that could be taken in a lot of ways—like did he kill them with his own hands, or did they die because of something he was a part of or took responsibility for?

He was also exceptional at security, and only keeping info in the public realm that he wanted to be there. But Drake was easier to investigate. Much easier. He was Branson's state representative, one of Utah's most sought-after bachelors, and a politician whose moves were tracked almost as well as The

Ladies tracked me. If Hawke had gotten involved in something with Drake, maybe I really could get some information about them both via researching Drake.

"I take that to mean you two were involved in something together?" I asked.

Drake's lips formed a line. "Not exactly. We were involved with the same organization for a time."

Drake was a well-known philanthropist who sat on multiple non-profit boards. Not to mention his day job as a very successful lawyer, as well as his political affiliations. The list of organizations Drake could be referencing was long, but it narrowed down my search. And I was definitely going to search.

The wind blew my hair and I shivered as I tried to get it out of my face.

Drake slowly took off his gloves and gently tucked my hair behind my ear. He put his warm hand on the side of my head, turning my face toward his, and my whole body tingled. He leaned over and kissed me, his lips pressing into mine, gentle at first and then with more force. My breath started to quicken as his hands went up my side. "This probably isn't a good idea," I said, breaking the kiss. "Anyone can see us."

He held my gaze. "Trust me when I tell you that I could not care less."

And in that moment, I decided I didn't care either.

"Oooo-eee!!" Ella exclaimed when I got into the office to start the work week. "I was behind you on that lift and I saw everythin'!"

Dammit! In the heat of the moment, I'd forgotten she was there, and probably had her phone out recording it. "I even got pics and vids!"

I knew it. Dammit again. "You shouldn't take photos and videos of people without their permission. Especially when those people are your friends. A *friend* would delete the pictures and videos they secretly took."

She gave me the most affronted look. "I will not."

I pursed my lips. "I better not hear about those pics and videos being posted in The Ladies Facebook group."

"Why would I share that with them?" she asked innocently.

"Because it's gossip, and it's exclusive gossip that only you have."

She thought about it for a minute. "True. But it's you, and my loyalty to you overrides getting acknowledged for the scoop."

I was touched. But not entirely convinced she was going to keep the information to herself.

"Besides, Diane Graves was there and got pics too, so it's already been posted."

I was no longer touched. And my swearing count for the day quadrupled because I knew that of the selective group of people who had access to the group, Hawke was one of them. He wasn't on a work emergency. He was home now, and paying attention. I wasn't sure how he'd react.

"What, exactly, did Diane post?"

"Not much. Just some blurry pics with you two cuddled up. And one of you smoochin'. And maybe doin' some other stuff under the blanket, but she was on the other side of the lift goin' down and too far away to get a good pic. People were lamentin' the fact that you were both movin' and her pic was unfocused."

I took a deep breath and hoped that rest of the week would be better than the way my Monday morning had currently started.

I got a doughnut from the treat table, and settled in to edit the stories from our other reporters, and work on updating the human remains story before it went to print tonight. I was a couple of hours into the task when I got a call from Annie. "Hey," I said, surprised to hear her voice. "What's going on?"

"You should get over to the new hotel. There's a situation."

"Where the Murderoonies are staying?"

"Yeah, but it doesn't have anything to do with them...at least I don't think it does. I'm here for an unrelated call, but there's a scene."

"I'm intrigued. I'll head over."

I pulled into the hotel parking lot, which was already overflowing thanks to the Murderoonies staying there. I found a parking spot and saw Annie's ambulance in the front of the hotel, but that's not where the commotion seemed to stem from.

There was a crowd around the back of the hotel. Some were holding signs telling people to get out of town, and others were yelling. There were a line of electric cars waiting to charge. The chargers had only been installed in the last year. They were fast chargers, right off the freeway, and the only electric vehicle chargers in the area within fifty miles.

Because of that, the hotel was a popular electric car charging location.

I got closer and saw that the issue seemed to be a bunch of huge trucks parked in the electric car charging parking spots, revving their engines, and blowing dark smoke from their exhausts. I stood back and got some pictures.

Utah had some of the worst air quality in the nation, especially during winter thanks to inversions where the mountains created a bowl-like effect with the valleys sitting at the bottom. The air pollution got trapped under the clouds in the bottom of the bowl for everyone to breathe. Study after study showed that the pollution severely affected people's health, especially the elderly and kids, and could even cause heart attacks, birth defects, respiratory issues, and other serious problems. The truck owners didn't seem to care about the health issues they were contributing to with their exhausts, and even seemed to take pride in it. The trucks were deliberately parked in the charging spots so the electric cars couldn't charge.

Three of the people in the waiting electric cars were trying to talk to the group of men standing in front of their trucks. There were five truck owners, and I recognized a couple of them as people I'd known growing up, including a guy who was a few years older than me, Jason Rife.

"Listen, we just need to charge our cars," one of the EV owners said. "You clearly don't need chargers. We don't park in front of your gas station pumps, why are you parking in front of our chargers?"

Jason smirked and replied, "If you parked in front of our gas pump, we'd move to another pump because they're everywhere."

Another EV driver spoke up this time. "Gas is fine, but it's not the only option. It's good to have different fuel types. How are EVs hurting you?"

Jason's buddy, Harvey, threw his arm out, pointing at the cars. "They're takin' away our rights!" he yelled. "Just like they're takin' away our land!"

The EV drivers all looked at one another, confusion written across their faces. "How?" the EV driver asked, genuinely curious.

"Cause they are! Dang government's tryin' to make car makers stop usin' gas engines. It's gonna take jobs! Hoity-toity people comin' in here, takin' over our towns, buyin' our property, and tellin' us how to live. It ain't right!"

Ah, so this was fear related. Fear was a powerful manipulation tool and studies showed it could even change the brain. Enough exposure to fear-based beliefs, and people could easily be controlled by the things they were told to be afraid of. People will prioritize their safety and survival every time, so it was easy to see how fear was driving people who felt threatened by change, and it wasn't only happening in Utah.

I moved forward, getting the attention of Jason, Harvey, and their three friends blocking the electric vehicle chargers, as well as the EV owners waiting to charge their cars. "I'm Kate Saxee with *The Branson Tribune*." I addressed the truck drivers first. "Do you want to tell me why you're blocking the EV chargers?"

"Cause we can, Kate," Jason said. He was wearing a t-shirt that read: If I want your opinion, I'll tell it to you.

"It's our right," one of the guys I didn't recognize answered, spitting on the ground right in front of me in a way that indicated he thought about as much of women as he did electric vehicles.

"But your rights are infringing on other people's rights," I pointed out.

"That ain't really my problem," Harvey answered.

I looked at the EV owners. "Have you faced this issue before?" I wasn't sure how big of a problem this was, but I'd read about it in other states.

"Sometimes," a woman EV owner answered. "It usually happens in smaller communities, not bigger cities."

"There are probably more chargers in bigger cities too," I said.

She nodded.

I turned back to Jason, Harvey, and their buddies. "Do you think you're making a point this way?"

Jason nodded. "Yep."

There was no arguing with that.

One of the truck owners left our group and went to his truck and revved it, the black smoke almost choking everyone standing around. "How do you get away with that?" I asked, fanning my face and coughing. "You're required to have your emissions tested yearly, and that exhaust certainly doesn't pass."

He gave a smug grin. "Cars and trucks older than twenty-five years can be classified as antiques, and they don't have emissions rules."

Well, that probably needed to change. Maybe the Utah state legislature should take that up instead of trying to ban books and regulate people's private lives.

I saw a patrol car pull in with lights flashing. Bobby got

out and started shaking his head. I could see him mentally questioning his life choices.

"You have to move," Bobby told the truck owners.

"Free country," Jason shot back.

Bobby pushed his lips out and nodded. "Sure is, but this here is private property and the owners of the hotel say you're makin' things difficult for their guests. Ya can't be here, blockin' the electric car chargers."

The five guys grumbled and swore, but still didn't move.

Bobby took a wide stance and crossed his arms across his chest. "I'm happy to call a tow truck for all your vehicles after I take ya into the station and book ya into jail, but I'd really rather avoid the paperwork, so let's make this easy on all of us."

The men grumbled some more, but the threat of their trucks being towed was more of a deterrent than arrest, so they reluctantly went over to their vehicles and started to move. As the trucks left the electric vehicle spaces, I noticed that several of them had CFNP stickers on their windows and bumpers. The movement was more widespread than I realized, and seemed to be gaining popularity every day. I didn't see an end to it on either side. People weren't going to stop moving to small communities like Branson Falls. Differences and belief systems would continue to be challenged because of it. And the people who wanted things to stay status quo would keep pushing back.

Annie came over while we watched the electric vehicles pull into the charging stations. "That was unexpected," she said. "People are posturing and trying to prove a point. I'm sure all the anti-progress groups don't help the situation."

"I agree. Some of the stuff I've seen from Citizens for No Progress is scary."

Annie's eyes went wide and she nodded rapidly. "The group is unhinged."

I closed my notebook and stored my pen. "HOTBS is on again tonight and I'm watching it with Phyllis. Will I see you there?"

"Wouldn't miss it," Annie said with a smile.

"I'll see you tonight, then."

I wanted to talk to Hawke about CFNP, and especially the fact that charger-blocker, Harvey, brought up people taking their land. I had some thoughts and wanted his perspective. I wasn't far from his house, so I called him.

"Are you home?" I asked when he answered the phone.

"I am, actually."

"I need your help. I'll be there in about ten minutes."

"I'll see you soon," he said and hung up.

As I started to walk to my SUV, I stopped to put my phone back in my purse and heard a tense voice say, "Don't do that."

I stopped, wondering if someone needed help.

The voice continued, "They won't agree to it."

I looked around and saw Vera, the Murderoonies producer, pacing on the walkway by the side of the hotel. She was on her phone.

"Take care of it, and figure out a way to manage the information. It's what we pay you to do, Aslow."

She hung up the phone without another word and walked in the hotel side door she was next to.

I wondered what needed to be taken care of. And more importantly, who was the Aslow she mentioned, and why did it sound familiar?

Chapter Eighteen

I made the turn down Hawke's driveway.

I'd been to Hawke's house before. For a self-defense lesson, as well as a lesson in clothing removal. The later tutorial was cut short by some stolen farm equipment. His home was located at the end of a private asphalt road, nestled in the belly of a mountain that I was certain he owned, along with all the land around it. Hawke was thorough about everything, but especially security. His house was a formidable red brick structure, three levels, with a white front portico and white trim accents. His gym was almost as big as his house, and his garage, housing cars that I'd only ever seen in online lists of "cars you wish you could afford," was even bigger than that. I'd been in a few of those cars and wouldn't turn down the chance to take any ride Hawke offered.

I rang the doorbell and waited for more than a minute. No one answered. He'd said he was home though, so he must be here somewhere. I stepped off the porch and moved to the side of the house. I heard a loud, rhythmic thumping noise coming from an area beyond the garage and nestled in trees. I frowned, immediately suspicious of what could be making said rhythmic thumping noises, and followed it.

I walked around the corner and came upon a half-naked Hawke. I froze and forgot to breathe. I knew he was built like a superhero, but this was the first time I'd gotten a glimpse of what was under his shirt. He was wearing dark blue jeans that sat low on his hips. Low enough that if he had also been wearing underwear, I would have seen it. I didn't, and he wasn't. His sun-kissed skin was stretched over rock hard ab muscles, and his arms were as big as some men's thighs. His entire body looked like it had been sculpted by a master artist.

He had a tattoo on his upper arm that extended over his shoulder and onto his back. I couldn't see the design well from where I was standing, but what I could see looked like storm clouds, lightning, and mountains. I'd seen peeks of that tattoo under his shirt sleeve before, and had vowed to see the rest of it. I could cross viewing it off my bucket list, though I was eager to do a more thorough, hands-on inspection.

And to top it all off, he was holding an axe. Scratch that, he was *swinging* an axe and chopping wood. Like an actual lumberjack. However, I imagined most lumberjacks didn't cord wood shirtless. Then again…my mind trailed off into at least a dozen different 'naked' and 'wood' related scenarios before Hawke's swinging distracted me again. Add wood fireplace replenisher to the ever-growing list of Hawke's talents.

"I can't believe you don't hire people for that," I said.

I expected to startle him but instead he simply looked up and gave me that slow, sexy smile. "It's a good workout. Some guys pay a lot of money to pretend to do work like this."

Ah, so he *had* seen the full moon lift ride pics and videos in The Ladies Facebook group. And he wasn't opposed to pointing out Drake's shortcomings—of which I was sure Hawke had a list or five. To be fair, Drake had grown up on a farm and had plenty of muscles as well, but I didn't point that out.

"Were you chopping wood half naked before you knew I was coming? Or did you take your shirt off once I called?"

He grinned and I couldn't stop staring at his broad shoulders, wide chest, and the muscles he was using to swing the axe, or the sheen of sweat that covered all of that exposed skin.

"Is it distracting?" he asked.

"No," I lied.

He smiled wider and pulled his bottom lip back with his teeth. "You're lying."

I shrugged and grinned back. "It seems a little cold for shirtless swinging."

"I'm working up a sweat. Want to try?"

I licked my lips, trying to decide how far to take this. "I have some experience with wood."

His eyes flashed, part heat, part excitement. "Let me give you some more." He dropped the axe and reached his arm out, offering me his hand. I took it, and was immediately against him, his hard chest crushed to mine. I suddenly cared very little about the bite of cold in the air as Hawke's lips pressed to mine in a searing kiss. His lips were warm and his body even hotter. I could feel the hard planes of his chest and stomach as he explored my mouth with his tongue and my body with his large hands, slipping them under my shirt and making his way up to my bra. I let my fingers trail over his abs, and then I let them slide lower—around to his back, and the waistband of his jeans. My fingers slipped under it, and he was definitely going commando. I smiled into the kiss and started to move my hands to the front of his jeans when my phone went off, playing "Forever in Blue Jeans."

I groaned, and not with pleasure.

Another phone call interrupting us. Story of my life.

I broke the kiss, leaning my forehead against his and swearing before lifting my phone to my ear.

"Hi, Spence."

"There's a CFNP event going on at the fairgrounds right now," Spence said. "I think it's in response to the electric car charger situation earlier."

I lifted my head and stepped back, while still keeping a hand on Hawke's hard chest. "Do you think I could get in without being noticed?" I asked. I'd been wanting to attend a CFNP event in person and see if it was as crazy as the videos on social media.

"It sounds like a big crowd," Spence said. I'm not sure if you'd be noticed. And even if you are, they're at a public event in a space owned by the county. And you're there as a member of the press. They don't have the authority to tell you that you can't be there."

Given their past history, I was pretty sure CFNP thought they had the authority to do anything they wanted. "I'm going to try and get in." Hopefully I wouldn't get kicked out.

I hung up the phone, briefly closed my eyes, and gave Hawke a disappointed sigh.

Before I could even explain, he said, "Where do you need to go?"

That was a really nice thing about Hawke. I never had to explain things when it came to the unexpected with my job, and he completely understood because he had to deal with it in his job too.

"The fairgrounds. There's an impromptu CFNP meeting going on and I need to be there."

"Then let's go," he said, pulling on his dark green t-shirt that molded to his body like a second skin.

"You're coming with me?"

"Always, Kitty Kate," he said with a wink. "Follow me."

I walked next to him as we hiked up a slight incline to get to his garage.

"Bodies, serial killers, and a hate group. Next thing you know, you won't be able to tell Branson Falls from Salt Lake City," Hawke said.

"I think that's part of the problem. And part of the reason for the bodies and the hate groups. People don't like uncertainty, and will do almost anything to stop it, especially when it threatens their safety and security."

"That's the truth," Hawke agreed.

"Branson Falls is supposed to be a quiet place—at least it always was when I was growing up. I think that sense of nostalgia is what the people who are from here are trying to retain."

Hawke's lips stretched into a slow smile. "The places that are supposed to be quiet are usually the ones I'm the most suspicious of."

"Is that why you built a house here? You thought all the secrets would be good for your business—whatever it is?"

"I built a house here because I heard you were coming back," he said, playfulness dancing across his expression.

My lips tipped up and I shook my head. Hawke was just as charming as Drake and I couldn't deny it.

"Wait here and I'll grab a vehicle." I couldn't wait to see what magic car he chose from his giant garage this time.

He pulled out of the building in a matte black-on-black Jeep Wrangler with custom shocks for traversing all kinds of terrain, and thick tires sporting a tread that looked capable of scaling the steepest mountain in Moab, Utah. He'd put on a black ball cap, and that combined with the green long-sleeved t-shirt, jeans, and work boots was disarming in a way that authoritative cargo pant and muscle shirt wearing Hawke was not. This Hawke looked like the president of a college frat, and there was something about the combination that made all my hormones lose their minds. It probably had something to do with my inner child, and probably needed consultation from a therapist, but for now, I was fine with letting it ride. He was sin incarnate and I was holding onto that temptation with both hands.

"Hop in." His eyes flashed with promise.

I opened the door and settled in the seat.

"Buckle up," he said, his voice low. The insinuation in those words was tangible.

I took a breath and got a whiff of sand, sweat, and pheromones that were all Hawke. This was a horrible idea. I should have driven myself. There was a good chance we wouldn't even make it to the fairgrounds at this rate and I needed to be at the event for my job. I needed something else to concentrate on.

"What did you mean when you said you'd heard of me?" I asked. "We'd never met until six months ago when Chelsea Bradford's body was found at the lake."

"I hadn't met you, but I'd heard of you. And we'd been in the same room together."

I stared at him, my lower jaw threatening to drop right off my face. "No way. I absolutely would have remembered you." There was no reality in which Ryker Hawkins and I had been in the same room together and I had not noticed. He was impossible to miss, and my ovaries would have gotten the memo before my eyes did.

"It was a news conference for a rescue mission I was involved with a couple of years ago. You were one of the reporters there."

I thought back to stories I'd covered that could fit, and one immediately came to mind. "The Ambassador who was kidnapped?"

He nodded.

"That was you?"

"Me, and some others. Things like that are usually a team endeavor."

I shook my head in complete disbelief. "I can't believe you were part of that rescue, and can't believe you remembered I was at the news conference."

"You asked hard questions and didn't back down. I noticed."

"Thanks," I said, surprised and flattered at the same time. "Seems like you would have tried to get to know me before moving your whole life here though. I was dating my ex then."

"You were, but I play to win, Kitty Kate."

Hawke was way too strategic to have moved for a woman he didn't even know. "You built this behemoth of a house long before I decided to move back."

He grinned. "Maybe I was hoping you'd come back."

Again, he was far too smart and logical for that. "I think I know why you actually moved here." It was a hunch that I took some time to research yesterday since Sunday had been quiet and I'd actually gotten a day off. While I couldn't find out much about Hawke in general, I knew enough rumors about him from things Spence, Bobby, Drake, and others had said to look into those. And I'd found a connection.

One of Hawke's eyebrows shot up. "I'm all ears."

I turned toward him so I could read his reaction. "One of the biggest defense companies in the United States has contracts with the U.S. Military. That defense company has a very large presence near Branson Falls. I think you work with them."

He eyed me for several long seconds, but gave nothing away. "Why would you think that?"

"Just a hunch." He'd told me about his military background, though he was still so young that I knew he hadn't stayed in the service long. He hadn't told me much else though. Like how he managed to afford the house, cars, and property he did. If he worked with defense contractors as part of his business, that would certainly help explain it. Their contracts were in the billions.

Hawke rolled his tongue along the inside of his cheek before answering. "As hunches go, it's not a bad one."

That surprised me. "So you do work with them?"

"I work with a lot of people."

"The US government?"

"Lots of governments."

"What do you do for them?"

He paused for a long moment and seemed like he was very carefully trying to decide what to say. "If someone had contracts with defense contractors or the military, for whatever reason, it would be very likely that those contracts, and what the person did for those entities, would be classified. Even if the person wanted to tell someone about it, they couldn't."

I nodded once, understanding. "So, if someone worked with defense contractors or the military, would it be the only thing they did?"

Hawke turned into the fairgrounds parking lot and parked next to a lot of large trucks. He was right to have brought the Jeep. The Ferrari would have drawn too much attention, and Hawke drew enough of that all on his own. "Depends on the person. I'm involved in a lot of things."

"But you can't talk about them."

"Some I can. Some I can't."

"And if I find out more information and have questions?"

Hawke turned to look me and held my gaze. "I'll answer what I can. I always will."

To say the CFNP crowd was riled up was an understatement.

There were hundreds of people at the event, and I recognized a lot of them. I wondered if this had been an impromptu gathering, or planned. If it was impromptu, I was impressed with their attendance results.

The event had already started. There was a guy speaking on a raised platform at the front of the building with other men sitting behind him, including the Barret's farmer neighbor, Wayne Post. The speaker was someone I recognized from some of the CFNP videos I'd seen, but he wasn't local.

"We're committed to keepin' our land, and our heritage! And stoppin' the newcomers from tryin' to overtake our beliefs! Today it's electric cars, tomorrow it'll be your houses! Your property! Your jobs! And your way of life!"

The crowd responded immediately with eardrum bursting cheers.

I tried not to let my expression show it, but I was stunned by the fearmongering. It was like the guy speaking had taken a course in Brainwashing for Dummies, and had excelled.

I turned to Hawke, who managed to assess the situation while keeping his face neutral—without Botox. It was impressive. "Do you know him?"

Hawke nodded. "Zack Turk. He's an entrepreneur and has been helping to fund CFNP across multiple states, but he lives in Utah."

Zack continued, "They don't get to dictate the way we live in Branson Falls, or anywhere! If people want to live here, they have to conform! They don't get to make our town into the place they came from!" he shouted.

Other people weren't allowed to dictate the way he lived, but he was allowed to dictate it to other people? I wondered if he understood that he sounded liked a complete hypocrite. I doubted he had the self-awareness.

The men behind him on the platform jumped up and cheered. Wayne Post stepped to the microphone and shouted, "And they don't get our land! We're takin' back the property that keeps gettin' stolen from us!"

That fit in with my theory that Wayne Post, or the CFNP, were responsible for the offer on GCR's development of the Barret property. And since I'd seen Jordan in a video at a CFNP event as well, maybe he'd helped orchestrate putting the bodies there.

Wayne started chanting, "Kick 'em out! Kick 'em out! No

new people! No new ideas!" The crowd immediately joined in and it was like a weird combination of a high school pep rally and documentaries I'd watched on cult indoctrination.

I discreetly took some videos and photos, and took notes as I watched the rest of the event that seemed to have the sole purpose of getting people angry for the sake of being angry. I was certain that what was underneath that anger was a lot of emotions, and would be better dealt with by talking through it and trying to reach compromises that could help everyone instead of dividing us all into "others" and us vs. them. But anger was easier than self-reflection and mutual understanding. The whole thing left me feeling disturbed and sad.

The event was winding down when I noticed a surprising person make their way to the stage to talk to the event organizers. "That's Jordan Barret," I said as Jordan walked up to Wayne and Zack and shook their hands. The three of them looked like they were old friends.

"This is an interesting development," Hawke said, tracking their moves as closely as I was.

I'd been trying to reach Jordan for a week, and now he was right here. I was about to make my way to the stage and ask them all some questions, but the three of them disappeared behind a curtain. A burly man stood in front of the curtain, his hands at his sides near his weapons.

"What are the chances that I can get past their security and behind that curtain to talk to those three?" I asked Hawke.

Hawke cocked his head, considering. "Not great alone, but you have me, so it's a matter of how much carnage you want to cause."

I had no doubt Hawke was capable of it, but the building had enough contention running through it without me adding more. "I'll talk to them when we're less likely to end up as part of the news story."

Hawke and I walked out to his Jeep and started the drive back to his house.

"Remember when you asked me to slow down some of the CFNP videos to see if more people could be identified?"

"Yeah. Were you able to do that already?"

"A few of them. I recognized a lot of the people from those videos here today."

I sighed. "I guess that shouldn't be a surprise, but it's disappointing. Anyone you think might have had something to do with GCR or the bodies on the property?"

"Not that I saw, but like I said, I was only able to go through a few. The flour bandit seems pretty committed to attending though."

I nodded. "I saw him in one of the first videos. It's one of the things that made me think there was a connection between CFNP and people in Branson who were trying to stop new people from moving in."

Hawke draped a hand over the steering wheel and glanced at me. "What did you need my help with earlier."

Ah yes, the reason I'd stopped by his house that had nothing to do with seeing him star in the lumberjack fantasies that I hadn't even known I had. "It was a question about the CFNP, actually. Do you think CFNP has the cash availability to purchase property. Especially a piece like the Barret property?"

Hawke lifted his hand to his face and ran his thumb across his jawline. "Probably. They're becoming more popular and public-facing now, but they've been around for a few years and have wealthy backers. Zack Turk is one of the many wealthy people who fund them. Why?"

"Wayne Post is involved with them, clearly," I said, gesturing back toward the fairgrounds and the event. "He wanted the Barret property and couldn't get it at the price Saul Barret had agreed to sell it to him for—decades ago. But I bet he could get a screaming deal on that property now."

"Because the land is less valuable with all the press the bodies have received," Hawke said. "That makes sense. Do you think Wayne, and even CFNP, knew about the bodies?"

"That's the multi-million-dollar question. I looked into CFNP to try and get more information about their operations, funding, and members, but they've buried the information in a ton of red tape. It's hard to track."

He licked his lips. "Not for me. Let me see what I can find."

"You're full of all kinds of talents."

"You haven't seen anything yet," he promised.

Hawke dropped me off. "You sure you don't want to stay? I can take off my shirt again, and yours too."

I closed my eyes, wishing I could. "If I had time, I would take you up on that offer."

He gave a long sigh. "Then I guess we'll both be disappointed."

That we would. "One of these days, we're both going to have time to escape somewhere," I said.

"I'm going to hold you to that."

I hoped he would.

Chapter Nineteen

I got back to the office and filled Spence in on CFNP, and my idea that they could be trying to get land back that's being sold, but at lower rates. Then I looked up info on Zack Turks. He owned several companies in Utah that catered to farming. He'd sold some of the businesses, and had done very well. The CFNP crowd was his target business demographic, so I wasn't surprised to know he helped to fund them.

I also researched some information on The Murderoonies and their business ventures. Vera sounded like she was talking to a business associate on the phone when I overheard her, so I wondered what else they were involved in. It looked like they owned some real estate—probably their studio in Salt Lake City, and some other buildings. They were also tied to a corporation that looked like it held other business entities. As I was looking through the information, a call came in from Bobby.

"Don't tell me it's more bodies, Bobby," I said when I answered, still scrolling through documents.

"Not yet," he said. "But it could be. Get over to your mom and dad's house."

I pulled up to my mom and dad's house and a police car was already on the scene, parked across the street. I saw a familiar bright yellow Hummer next to the cruiser. And a familiar matte black Jeep that I'd been sitting in an hour ago was parked in my parents' driveway. What in the world were Drake and Hawke both doing here? And why did they arrive before I did?

I got out of my Jeep and immediately noticed my mom's festive—or anti-festive, depending on who you talked to—yard décor had changed.

The witches had moved.

My parents had a large, circular grey stone patio in their front yard. It had a pergola over it, and sat higher than the rest of the yard, so it almost looked like a stage. As a kid, that's exactly what I'd made it into, performing concerts for all of my adoring fans—the bugs in my mom's rose bushes, and the voles in the rock wall. A black, circular stone firepit sat in the middle of the patio. The patio was located on the most noticeable area of my mom and dad's large lot.

Previously, my mom's inflatable witches were parked on the lawn, near the front door. The witches were now placed around the black fire pit like it was their cauldron. A four-foot-tall sign was posted like a little mini billboard in front of the patio, clearly visible to all of my parents' neighbors. The sign had a pitch-black background, with my mom's name painted in a beautiful cursive, glittery, hot pink font that caught the sunlight from every direction. The second word was bold white and capitalized. The third and fourth words were smaller, but still blazing white. It said: *Sophie's Satanic Sunday Sermons.* A glittering pink pitchfork was below the words, and the sign was crowned with two sparkling pink devil horns.

I took a very deep breath. This would not end well. I'd say it was about to be a Catasophie, but it felt like it had gone far beyond that.

My mom was standing near her display, a sly little smile on her lips as she watched me survey her meticulous staging.

"What's going on here?" I asked, gesturing to the inflatables strategically placed around the cauldron, and the sign that was probably going to be the cause of the next Utah War.

She puffed her chest up and folded her arms across it. "Since my neighbor seems to think my witches are satanic, I decided to hold a weekly event. Don't you like the name?"

Oh, good lord.

It was like a train wreck and I couldn't stop staring. "You're going to get yourself in so much trouble with this."

She shook her head with substantial force. "Nope. I checked with the city and I'm in complete compliance."

"They approved of that specific sign?" I asked, pointing. The glitter pink was blinding.

She pressed her lips together. "Approve is a strong word. They didn't say yes, and didn't say no. But there aren't any laws against signs."

She was about to force one to be put into place.

"How long has that sign been up?" I asked.

She gave a self-satisfied smile. "I put it up last night."

Well, at least the whole neighborhood probably hadn't seen it yet since it was likely dark when she debuted it.

"And installed a spotlight. The glitter on the sign really pops with the illumination." She pulled a clicker out of her pocket and turned the light on.

So everyone *had* already seen it. She probably bought the spotlight advertised as "capable of being seen from space." Even in the middle of the day, the light managed to outdo the sun.

"Have you heard from your neighbor, Gladys, yet?"

My mom's eyes narrowed and she looked like she wanted to commit murder. "That old bat came knocking on my door last night and again this morning, demanding I take the sign down because it was an affront to her eyes. Frankly, it's not my problem that her eyes find so many things offensive."

"You know this isn't going to end, right?" I asked. "She's going to keep pressuring you to take the witches down."

"And I'm going to keep adding to my display. It's my property."

I shook my head. "What does Dad think of this?"

"He's in complete support because it makes me happy." She paused. "And also because I told him I'd make his favorite cookies."

"So, you bribed him for his support?"

"I didn't bribe. I made an enticing offer."

"That's the same thing."

I heard a door slam. Hard. And saw Gladys from across the street, wearing tan linen slacks and a flowery red blouse. She came storming across her yard and her aim seemed to be straight for my mom.

In the spotlight, she looked like an avenging angel. She

crossed the street with the speed of someone flying, and I half expected her to pull out a sword like the angel who allegedly threatened Joseph Smith with it if he didn't start practicing polygamy. Only Gladys' sword would be used to slash my mom's witches, and cut down her sign.

A man followed close behind her, but not quite at the same clip as Gladys, and I'd recognize that shoulder span anywhere. Drake. Bobby was right behind Drake.

"You're tryin' to ensorcell people!" Gladys shouted, coming up to my mom and stopping a couple of feet in front of her.

My mom put her hands on her hips, daggers shooting from her eyes. "You don't even know what that word means, Gladys."

I saw movement from the house and my dad came out of the garage. Another large set of shoulders I'd recognize anywhere followed him. Hawke.

Gladys marched over to the sign and gestured to my mom's display with sharp movements. "It's the holidays! And almost Christmas! And here you are, turnin' your yard into Lucifer's playground!"

My mom's whole stance changed and her legs moved shoulder width apart like she was getting ready for a fight. "That's right, Gladys," my mom said, her tone low and threatening. I'd heard that tone many times growing up and knew it was *not* one to screw around with. "I'm building an amusement park for Lucifer and the one-third of heaven that followed him. You should thank me because maybe it will keep all those fallen angels busy so they aren't doing what they're supposed to be doing—tempting you."

Gladys glared at her and I could almost see the steam coming out of her ears. "You're an agent of Satan, Sophie

Saxee." She paused. "In fact, you're even worse than an agent of Satan. You're *Korihor!*"

I gasped at the insult, and Drake raised his hand, rubbing his thumb and forefinger across his forehead as he let out a long-suffering sigh. Korihor is the Mormon version of the Antichrist, so that was the insult equivalent of a nuclear bomb.

My mom's eyes looked like they were on fire and her voice got even lower, and more calm. "Are you calling me Korihor?"

My stomach knotted and I couldn't remember a time I'd felt more tense—and I'd almost been shot three times in the past six months.

"If the horns fit!" Now Gladys was confusing Mormon beliefs about the devil, but to be honest, a lot of people did.

My mom lifted a finger and pointed it straight at Gladys like it was an angel's sword of her own. "If Jesus Christ arrived right now, I bet he'd choose my lawn over yours, Gladys Simpson, because mine isn't fertilized with judgment!"

Gladys started shaking like she was unstable and might actually explode. "You're askin' for it, Sophie."

My mom got right up in her face and stared her down with terrifying efficiency. "I dare you."

I sensed that punches were about to be thrown and that would look a lot like *The Golden Girls* MMA, so I got between them. "Let's settle down, ladies."

Drake stepped in. "Gladys, why don't we go talk over here."

My dad wrapped an arm around my mom's waist and dragged her away, literally kicking and screaming.

Hawke stood to the side, trying very, very hard not to laugh.

I looked at him. "I don't know what was more ridiculous, the accusation that my mom was the Antichrist, or the idea that Jesus cares about what lawn he stands on."

"Personally, I liked "Lucifer's playground" and hope your mom adds another sign."

"Don't encourage her."

Bobby talked to Gladys, and Drake came over to talk to me and Hawke.

"What are you two doing here anyway?" I asked Hawke and Drake.

"I was here helping your dad with his car," Hawke said.

"Gladys told me Satan had possessed a neighbor and called me to come over and figure out how to manage the situation. She thought maybe I could pass a law, or cast out the adversary."

"So now you perform exorcisms?" I asked.

"I mean, she should have been able to do it herself. She just had to raise her hand to the square." Mormons believe they can cast out evil by raising their hand at a ninety-degree angle to make a square, and saying "In the name of Jesus Christ, make this thing happen." I'd tried it multiple times as a kid and since Jackie Wall and Amber Kane were still as awful as ever, I could confirm with surety that it did not work.

"She probably thought she needed your extra priesthood power," I said.

Bobby walked over. "I'm gettin' to see you multiple times today."

"Lucky me," I said. "Did you get the situation with my mom and Gladys figured out?"

Bobby shook his head. "I don't think that'll ever be resolved. There's no law sayin' your mom can't have yard décor. And there's no law sayin' Gladys can't be mad about it or retaliate with her own décor."

"So it's going to be a yard-off?"

"I guess, unless someone can convince 'em both to back down." He gave me a pointed look.

I put my hands up in front of me, palms out. "I'm not getting in the middle of this so you should probably be prepared for more calls."

Bobby lifted a shoulder. "I don't mind. These calls always come with cookies. As long as you don't try to get them taken away from me again, Kate."

"As long as you all keep me informed so I don't get scooped by podcasts, cookies are on the table all around."

Drake's eyes sparked at that, and Hawke licked his lips. "Promises, promises, Kitty Kate."

I blew out a breath, unwilling to get into that discussion here, with *everyone*. I changed the subject to something I'd been thinking about ever since I saw Jordan hanging out with Wayne Post at the CFNP event. "Did anyone ever talk to the excavator about how he found the bodies on the Barret property?"

Bobby looked at me like I might be a few French fries short of a Happy Meal. "Yeah. From diggin'."

"No, not that. I mean, why did he have someone there watching while he dug. It seems weird, and it's not common. Did someone warn him he might come across human remains?"

Bobby shrugged. "I didn't ask."

I turned to Drake. "Do you know anything about the excavator?"

He shook his head. "Just that Grant and GCR had used him for developments in the past."

I made a mental note to get in touch with Jory, the excavator, ASAP. Jordan Barret or Wayne Post could have known the bodies were there because they put them there, and then could have warned the excavator to be careful during the dig.

My phone dinged in my pocket. "I should probably get back to work."

"Thanks for the other night," Drake said.

I stared at him. Hard. "Yeah, the *lift ride* was fun." I said the "lift ride" part slower so Hawke didn't think I'd spent the night with Drake.

"I still need to come get my car from your garage," Hawke said.

I rolled my eyes. "You both need to stop the dick measuring. It doesn't impress me."

"That's because you haven't seen it yet," they both said at the same time. Then gave each other a strange look.

So now they both knew that I hadn't seen either one of them naked. It was going to be even more competitive now.

"I have some interviews to get to," I said. I walked away to check on my mom, who seemed to be taking the Agent of Satan title in stride and was probably already designing a shirt, and the next sign to add to her collection. My dad looked tired. He usually did.

I gave them a hug, ran to the back yard to give Gandalf some pets and throw his ball, then grabbed some cookies for myself on the way out.

After the situation with my mom, I drove straight over to the Barret property. Grant's BMW was parked in front of the temporary office.

I knocked on the door and stepped inside. "Hi, Grant. I have a few more questions if you have time?"

"Sure," he said, motioning to the seat in front of him.

I settled in and pulled my phone out to take notes. "Talk to me about your investors on this development. Are they people you've worked with before?"

"Yeah," he said. "Most of them, at least, but not all."

That "not all" part is what interested me. "You trust them and don't think any of them would try to sabotage you in any way?"

He put his hand up to his mouth, thinking. "I don't see why they would. It would be their own money they'd lose."

"And you trust everyone you work with?"

He scrunched up his forehead, like he was confused by my line of questioning. "As much as I can. I wouldn't work with them otherwise."

"Have you heard of the group, CFNP?"

His eyes widened. "The group trying to stop developers from buying land? Yeah. They're a pain in my butt."

"What about Wayne Post and Jordan Barret?"

He pressed his lips together. "Wayne was not happy we got this property instead of him. And Jordan didn't want to sell."

"Did you ever find out why Jordan didn't want to sell?"

"He thought the land was a good investment and wanted to keep it in the family. Bethany and Georgia disagreed. We tried to work with him to come to some kind of compromise, but nothing panned out. Why do you ask?"

"It's a lead I'm chasing," I said. I wanted to see how he'd

react to the next bit of information. "Wayne and Jordan are both involved with CFNP."

Grant's eyes widened. "I did not know that."

I believed him. "Do you think CFNP could have something to do with the bodies on your property?"

Grant pressed his lips together and lifted one shoulder. "I think CFNP is capable of anything."

Good to know. "How are things going with the project. Have you heard any more about what's happening or timelines?"

"I know the police are having a news conference tomorrow to go over what they've found. I hope that means they've identified the bodies so the families can have some closure, and we can figure out what to do next."

Thanks to Drake, I knew the information about someone interested in buying the development, but I couldn't mention that without implicating Drake so I tried a different way. "What to do next makes it seem like you're not planning to continue developing the property. Is that the case?"

He ran his fingers over his arm in a pacifying gesture. "We aren't sure. We're exploring options with our investors."

I nodded, knowing he wasn't going to give me more information at the moment. "Let me know what you decide."

Grant nodded. "And let me know if you find out more about CFNP. I might try to get some information myself."

"Keep me posted," I said.

I walked out the door and ran into Jory, the excavator. "Hey! I was going to call you, Jory. How are you doing?"

He leaned against the railing for the stairs to the GCR office. "I'd be better if I was able to dig up some dirt."

"Hopefully soon. The police have a news conference about

the bodies tomorrow. Speaking of that, I remember you said you had your son with you as a spotter. Is that normal when you're digging, or were you looking for something specific?"

He lifted his arm, bringing it across his body and scratching his other arm, almost like he was uncomfortable. "I always bring him along. Never know what you're gonna find when you start movin' dirt."

Huh. I wondered how many bodies he'd come across in his dirt relocations. "How did you decide where to start digging the day the bodies were found?"

His eyes widened slightly and he shifted his weight "I just do what I'm told."

"By Grant?"

"By GCR and their investors. They had a plat map and phases. We started on phase one."

That was helpful information as well. Especially because that plat map was public, so if someone wanted to bury bodies in places the bodies would be immediately found, it would be easy to look at the map.

Jory opened the door and went inside to talk to Grant.

When I arrived back at the office, a van sporting two wide eyes was parked in front of the *Tribune* and Edith walked out the front door with her trademark skip in her step. "Oh, Kate! I'm so excited about our joint Live event!"

"What Live event?" I asked.

She pushed her brows together, confused. "The news conference is tomorrow morning so we're doing an event tomorrow night. We're going to premiere the Jeff Zundy episode and go over all the details so far. Then we're having a live Q&A. We thought it would be good to have all the major players in one place. Chloe talked to Spence about it and he said you'd be there, and the *Tribune* would stream it Live at the same time we are."

I forced a smile while firmly committing to harm Spence. "I've been in and out of the office today, so he hasn't been able to talk to me about it."

"Well," she said, her tone perky as ever. "Don't you worry about a thing! You're not used to all this technology or Lives, so Chloe will send over the talking points and it will help raise engagement on all of our socials. It's a win for everyone!"

Sure sounded like it. Had she insinuated that I was an idiot and didn't know how technology, Lives, or social media worked? Because that's what it seemed like. I wondered if I could get Botox by tomorrow, and have it go into effect that fast.

"I'll see you at the event!"

"Sounds peachy," I said back, not trying to hide my sarcasm.

I walked in the door and Spence was standing there, waiting.

I stared at him all the way to my desk where I dropped my purse and put my hands on my hips. "How would you like to die, Spence?"

He lifted his index finger and waved it back and forth in a no-no gesture. "You probably don't want to make threats like that, Kate. You never know who's listening."

"I've turned off my phone's GPS and tracking info, and know all about burying bodies so I'm not overly concerned. I can't believe you agreed to a joint Murderoonies / *Tribune* event."

He put his hands in his pockets and leaned against the wall. "It's good for all of us. The Murderoonies bring a huge audience, and the exposure helps us out, especially because you're the one who's been doing all the investigating. You're going to come out of this looking great. The Murderoonies need you."

I slitted my eyes, suspicious. "You're just trying to flatter me so you aren't lethally harmed."

He raised his hands palms up. "I do care about my life."

I finished editing some articles and finalized the layout. Then I did a couple of social media posts before picking up Gandalf, and heading home to watch HOTBS with Annie and Phyllis.

Annie brought mint brownies, Phyllis made her delicious homemade hot chocolate with marshmallows, and I brought a charcuterie board with some vegetables, dip, and hummus. As dinner went, it wasn't a bad menu. We were ready for the hot mess express.

We got our plates and sat in Phyllis's living room.

"I heard there was a CFNP meeting after the hotel incident today," Annie said, stacking a cracker with cheese.

I nodded. "I was there. It was insane. Everyone was so against change, and it's all fear based. I've never seen anything like it. The event was almost cult-like."

"Lotsa people are involved with them," Phyllis said, pointing a carrot at me. "Especially people at church."

"I recognized a lot of them. Including Jordan Barret, which I thought was odd since he benefitted from the property sale."

"I was surprised the Barrets wanted the land sold," Phyllis said. "With Saul Barret, all kinds of secrets could've been buried there."

My ears perked up. "What do you know about Saul?" I asked, taking a bite of my own cracker and cheese.

She lifted a shoulder. "You hear things."

"Hear things like what?"

She shook her head. "Like the Barrets had a lotta secrets."

Phyllis got a notification on her phone. "Oh! It's a Murderoonies update! I've been waitin' for this! Can we listen to it before we watch Homemakers of the Beehive State?"

Clearly, my HOTBS acronym hadn't caught on with everyone yet.

"Sure," Annie said.

I hadn't listened to the latest episode and needed to before the Live event tomorrow that I'd been volunteered for. This would be one less thing I had to do later tonight. "Let's hear it."

Phyllis pulled it up on her phone. The haunting intro played and then Edith's voice slid across the microphone introducing herself, and Margie's voice did the same. Edith jumped right into the podcast.

"Today we have a special guest! The face and paws behind Paw P.I., Sophie Saxee, and her grandpuppy, Gandalf!"

I almost choked on the sliced meat and cracker I was eating.

"You okay?" Phyllis asked, stopping the recording.

I nodded and took a drink. "I didn't know my mom was going on the show, or that my dog was the subject."

"Do you want to keep listening?" Annie asked.

"Oh, I definitely want to hear this so I can find out what damage control needs to be done."

Phyllis turned the episode back on.

"Sophie is Gandalf's grandma, correct, Sophie?" Edith asked.

"I am!" my mom said with more enthusiasm than a Mormon Relief Society President.

"Gandalf belongs to another character we know from previous podcasts. *Branson Tribune* editor, and your daughter, Kate Saxee."

"That's true," my mom confirmed.

"I understand you spend a lot of time with Gandalf."

"I puppy-sit him during the day and most times Kate's at work. She works so much and doesn't want to leave him home alone. She's a good dog mom."

"Gandalf was instrumental in helping find the most recent body on Spartan Way. Why don't you tell us about Gandalf's role, Sophie."

I closed my eyes and pressed my fingers to my temples as the recording continued with my mom explaining Gandalf's murder sniffing abilities and a list of offerings people could hire him for. We had discussed Paw P.I. and I'd mentioned it in jest, but I didn't realize she'd already incorporated her side hustle and gotten Gandalf a guest spot on the podcast that was currently a royal pain in my ass. I was also beyond irritated that Edith had called me a "character," as if I was fictional and she'd made me up for her show.

I texted my dad.

> Have you heard this.

He texted back almost immediately.

> More times than you know.

I was sure my mom was very proud of that recording.

"**My sources tell me Kate's dating two extremely eligible bachelors: the politician we all know and love, Dylan Drake. And Hawke, who doesn't seem to have a last name or any public career information that we could find, but is very involved with the human remains investigation on the GCR property development,**" Edith said. "**How do you feel about Kate's relationships?**"

"**Oh, Drake and Hawke are both delightful,**" my mom supplied. "**And hunky too!**"

I put my palm to my forehead and took several deep breaths.

"**Who do you think she'll end up with?**"

My mom paused. "I couldn't say, but hope she'll be happy when she eventually decides."

"**Who do you think Kate's leaning toward?**"

"**Hmm, I don't know about that. They both spend a lot of time at her house, though.**"

"**I heard Hawke's car has been there for a few days. Has he moved in?**"

"**Not that I know of. I've seen his house and she'd probably want to move in with him instead. It's like a royal estate!**"

I was going to kill my mother, right along with Spence.

"**Well, that sounds exciting. We couldn't find out much

about Hawke, or what Hawke does for a living. Do you know?"

"He owns a business. He's pretty private about it."

"What about Dylan Drake. It's my understanding that Kate is no longer a member of the LDS church. That complicates a relationship with him, doesn't it?"

My mom paused. "It can. It probably depends on the person. He seems interested in Katie though."

Katie, Mom? Seriously?

"Do you really think he'd be with a non-member? It probably wouldn't be great for his career. Or do you think he'd try to get her to come back to the fold?"

"I'm not sure what his plans are, but he's a very smart man and I'm certain he's thought things through."

"Does Kate even want a relationship?"

"She's very outgoing and committed to her job. She's been hurt in the past, so I think she's being careful and taking her time. She wants a partner, but it would have to be someone who valued her independence as much as she does."

"She's given you a hint about who she wants to be with though, right? You're her mom. You have to know."

"I think she's figuring things out. She's only been back for six months or so. I don't expect her to get engaged soon. But they'd both make an excellent son-in-law!"

"Will you invite us to the wedding?" Edith asked.

"Of course!"

I closed my eyes and wanted to bang my head against the wall repeatedly.

"That didn't go in the direction I thought it would," Annie said, drinking her hot chocolate like she'd just been given a lot of tea, and she had. The Ladies were probably already posting gossip updates in their group.

"Me either. I thought they were going to talk about the bodies," Phyllis said, sounding a bit disappointed.

"Police haven't released the latest information for Edith to speculate on yet. The Murderoonies don't have anything else to talk about, so they were looking for filler. I became the B story earlier this week. I think Jackie Wall and The Ladies had something to do with that. Then Gandalf finding the bones and my mom starting Paw P.I. fell into their lap like a freaking gift. They used it to get more gossip about me and my love life, and my mom was so excited to be on the show that she probably didn't even realize what she was saying, or that millions of people would hear it."

"Yeah," Phyllis said with a nod. "People sure have had a lot of opinions about you and your boyfriends in the comments of the episodes the last few days."

I sighed. I was definitely not pleased about being dragged into the Murderoonies' plotline.

"Why don't we turn on the show and try to get lost in other people's drama instead of mine," I suggested.

Annie nodded and Phyllis turned HOTBS on. It was a lot more dramatic than my life, and I hoped it stayed that way.

I got home about an hour and half later and was greeted by Gandalf jumping up and down, and bringing me toys. I threw his ball as a text from Hawke popped up.

> You might want to listen to this.

A link was below the text. I clicked on it and the Murderoonies latest podcast pulled up.

> I already have.

> Now everyone thinks my dog is gone from my house most of the time, but you're there ravishing me instead. Fantastic. Your presence is probably a better deterrent than a dog.

His response was lighting fast.

> I definitely bite harder.

Weirdly, that was both threatening and arousing.

> I'm not sure how to feel about that.

> We'll have to try it and see.

I hearted that response and wondered if the innuendo we constantly threw around would ever have time for follow-through. Maybe if our jobs allowed it eventually.

It had been a really long day and I needed to deal with my mom, but I didn't have the energy at the moment. I jumped in the shower to wash the day off, and then climbed into bed where Gandalf, who didn't bite, snuggled up next to me.

Chapter Twenty

I knocked on my parents' door the next morning as Gandalf ran circles around my legs. Drop off was going to be dicey today because I had a bone to pick with my mother.

She opened the door with a smile and opened her mouth like she was about to jump into a recap of her glory days as a true crime podcast guest.

I held up my hand to stop her. "We need to have a discussion about boundaries."

"What are you talking about?" she said, her eyes going wide in an attempt to look innocent.

"You turned Gandalf into your business partner."

She smiled big and petted him. "He loves it! He gets so many pets and compliments on his Paw P.I. shirt, and we're already investigating things!"

I had no idea what they were investigating, but had bigger things to discuss. "Then you told the whole world I'm usually not home during the day, which is a security risk."

She frowned. "I'm sure it's fine. You have that fancy security system, and Hawke's there."

"No! He's not! And that's the biggest issue! You told every person with ears that I'm dating Drake and Hawke!"

She lifted her shoulder. "You are."

I took a deep breath and fought back a scream. "But the whole world didn't need to know that!"

The lines at the corners of her eyes got deeper and she looked at me like she didn't know what she'd done wrong. "Everyone in town already knows that. Why does it matter?"

"Because everyone in town didn't know that. They were speculating and I purposely hadn't confirmed or denied the rumors because it's nobody's business. It's personal, and you went into a lot of detail about things you don't even know, said I could be living with Hawke, and even insinuated I'm going to marry one of them! I don't want my life becoming a side story to this murder investigation, but the Murderoonies needed a plot to keep their listeners engaged while they're waiting for more information to come out about the case, and you contributed to it with a ton of personal information about me."

Her lips turned down, and the lines at the corners of her eyes became more prominent. "I'm sorry, Kate. I didn't mean to share things I shouldn't have. I'll be more careful in the future. I was just so excited to be interviewed, and I'm used to Branson where everyone knows everything."

I pushed my thumb and forefinger to the bridge of my nose, trying to calm down. "If you know something about my personal life, I need you to keep it a secret, okay?"

"Okay, I'll be more careful going forward."

Gandalf went running through the house to find a toy and brought one back to us. I gave him pets and kisses, and told him to be a good boy while I was gone, then threw his toy. "Thanks for taking care of him."

"You're welcome! We have a busy day of investigations! Laney Quint wants Gandalf to search for their daughter's lost doll, and Bryce Card wants Gandalf to walk some property he's thinking of buying and see if Gandalf smells any dead things."

I gave her a look. "He's not a trained cadaver dog so that might be a problem if Bryce buys the property and eventually does find dead things."

"He signed a waiver I printed off a legal website, so Gandalf can't be sued."

Well at least we had that going for us.

"Have a good day! Hopefully you learn a lot at the news conference. Let me know if Cuddles the dragon and her sidekick will be necessary!"

Last time she wore that costume, she'd been a bit of a menace, so I couldn't imagine a scenario in which Cuddles would have to be called into action again, but you never know what might happen.

"Love you," I said. I hugged her and petted Gandalf one last time before I left for the assisted living facility. The news conference didn't start for two hours, and I wanted to talk to Bethany and Georgia about the bodies, and see if I could finally get ahold of Jordan.

I knew Bethany usually spent time with Georgia in the mornings because Georgia's memory was better, and hoped she would be there today. I heard voices coming from the room and knocked. Bethany opened the door, a look of happy surprise on her face.

I said hello to her and Georgia before pulling Bethany aside. "Have the police talked to you about the news conference today?"

"No," Bethany said. "But I heard there was going to be one, and I plan on attending."

"Police have identified some of the bodies and they're going to announce the names."

Bethany's eyes widened. "I wonder who they are? I've been hoping that we'd find out more soon."

"Is there any chance that Jordan, or even your dad, knew about the bodies on your land?" I asked.

Bethany looked off in the distance like she was trying to remember something or make a connection in her head. "Not that I know of. You'd have to talk to Jordan, but I can't imagine he knows anything. My dad's been gone a long time."

"And good riddance!" Georgia piped up.

"Mom!" Bethany gasped, and gave a nervous laugh. "Don't say those things." Bethany looked back to me. "It's everything going on with her memory. Sometimes she doesn't have a filter."

Bethany guided us toward the door. "I'll be right back, Mom." We stepped into the hall and spoke in hushed tones.

Georgia's response made me wonder even more about Saul. "You mentioned not having a great relationship with your dad. Do you mind if I ask why the relationship was strained?"

She paused and pressed her lips together, trying to decide what to say. "He wasn't a nice man, and life wasn't easy because of it. I would say that none of us were too upset when he passed away."

That was harsh, but understandable if things had been as bad as she indicated. And it echoed some of what Ella and Phyllis had said about what kind of man Saul was. "I've heard he didn't have the best reputation, and might have been a bit controlling."

Bethany gave a short, derisive laugh. "That's an understatement. My mom changed a lot when he passed away. She was finally able to figure out who she was and what she wanted. That mattered a great deal to her, and so did helping other women who had been in the same situations as she had. She volunteered for women's organizations until her health started to decline. I don't like to speak ill of the dead, but all of our lives improved after he was gone, and my mom was a different, much happier person."

That made sense. Georgia had married young and probably went along with whatever Saul told her to because she felt she had no choice—and she'd committed to doing that in the LDS temple wedding ceremony.

"How much do you know about the relationship between your dad and Wayne Post?" I asked.

Bethany shrugged. "They were good friends, which is probably why my dad had offered to let Wayne buy the property."

I wanted to ask about Saul's relationship with Larry Caldwell, but the info wasn't public yet.

I was still trying to figure out how the bodies got on the Barret farm, who put them there, and who knew about them. It could have been Wayne Post, Jordan, the CFNP, Saul, or someone else. I wasn't sure, but I was getting closer to figuring it out, I could feel it. "This might be a sensitive question to answer, but do you think your dad could have had something to do with the bodies on your old property."

Bethany leaned against the wall and looked at the ground for several seconds before meeting my eyes. "You know, I've thought about that a lot since all of this happened. I honestly don't know. But it wouldn't surprise me if he'd been involved."

I was surprised to hear her admit that, and felt awful that she'd grown up with a father who made her feel like he was capable of killing someone. "You think your dad was a murderer?"

"I think my dad had a lot of problems, and I think a lot of people are capable of a lot of things."

I couldn't disagree with that. "Thanks for your time, Bethany. I'll see you at the news conference?"

"I'll be there, and hopefully we'll all get some answers."

I walked out the door, convinced that Bethany hadn't known about the bodies. Maybe Georgia did, but her memory wasn't reliable enough to get solid answers or leads. As the automatic doors opened for me to walk out of the building, I saw the person I'd been trying to get an interview with for more than a week. Jordan Barret. He was standing with Grace Caldwell—the woman I'd met the first time I'd visited Georgia, and Larry Caldwell's wife—and two other women I recognized from my time reporting in Salt Lake City: Rochelle Hart and Trixie Barton. Jordan's hands were in the air and Grace was pointing at him, angrily. Rochelle's lips were turned down in a frown, and Trixie had her arms crossed around her like she was giving herself a hug. Their voices were raised, but not enough for me to hear what they were saying from where I was standing.

I walked closer and heard Grace say, "Jordan wouldn't allow that."

Rochelle noticed me and made a gesture telling them all to quiet down.

"Hi, Grace," I said, knowing full well that the identity of one of the bodies about to be announced at the news conference was her husband. I could understand why that would make her upset. What I couldn't understand was what Jordan Barret had to do with it.

Grace pasted on a smile that was even faker than the ones I gave The Ladies. "Kate. So nice to see you again. Were you here visiting Georgia?"

"I was. I had some questions that Bethany was able to answer."

Grace, Rochelle, Trixie, and Jordan all looked at each other with concern.

I turned to Jordan. "Jordan! It's so nice to see you. I'm Kate Saxee with *The Branson Tribune*, and I've been trying to reach you for days to talk about the property and get your perspective. Do you have some time now?"

He looked like a deer caught in the headlights. "Nope. Sure don't. In fact, I have to leave to do something for my mom. I'll talk to you ladies later."

He ran off. I thought about trying to catch him, but he was literally running, and he was much faster than I was. I would find him later today though, and we would definitely talk.

I turned to Grace, Rochelle, and Trixie. "Well, that was abrupt. How are you ladies doing? The bodies must have been a shock."

"You have no idea," Rochelle said.

"Did your husbands all know each other?" I asked.

"They did," Trixie answered. "They were friends."

I looked at Grace. She was wringing her hands and her eyes were watching Jordan on his sprint. Something was going on between her and Jordan, and since her husband's body had been found on the property, I wanted to know what.

"Grace, can I talk to you privately?"

She looked at me, taking her attention off of Jordan. "Sure," she said with a smile that didn't reach her eyes. She turned to Rochelle and Trixie. "I'll be back, girls."

We moved down the sidewalk, out of earshot. "I want to express my condolences. I know your husband is one of the names being announced at the news conference. I'm so sorry."

"Thank you," she answered.

"Do you know what happened to him?" I asked.

She looked up at me, still worrying her hands together. "He went missing on a hunting trip twenty years ago."

"And you never knew where he was?"

"No."

"Weren't your husband and Saul Barret friends?"

She rubbed the back of her neck like she was distressed. "I thought so, but maybe not." Her tone indicated that she thought Saul might have been involved in Larry's death.

"This must be a shock. Do the police know what happened?"

"They haven't told me what they've found. I hope they announce more at the news conference. Speaking of that, I should probably get over there."

I looked at my watch. "Yeah, me too. I'm sorry for your loss, and for the trauma this must be bringing up again."

"Thank you," she said, and touched my arm as she walked away.

I watched her leave and saw her stop next to Rochelle and Trixie. They spoke in hushed tones, and made several glances my way. Something was up, and I hoped I'd find out more at the news conference.

I stopped by the *Tribune* to check on the Live talking points that Edith said she was going to send over to Spence. Sure enough, he had them. I read through the points and added my own notes with things I wanted to make sure to bring up.

Ella came out of the back room. "I thought I heard your voice! I have some more missing persons names for you," Ella said.

"Thanks, Ella." I took the list from her.

"I have a few. I narrowed it down, and Hawke helped with names outside of the county."

My eyes scanned through the names and froze. "Erold Hart and Lane Barton," I said, glancing up. "They wouldn't happen to be related to Rochelle Hart and Trixie Barton, would they?"

Ella seemed surprised. "Yeah, they were. Erold was married to Rochelle and Trixie was married to Lane. Erold went missin' twenty-one years ago, and Lane went missin' twenty-two years ago. They were from Salt Lake, but they were friends with a bunch of other families like the Caldwells and the Barrets, so people in Branson Falls knew them. How did you know they were related to Rochelle and Trixie?"

I grabbed the papers and my keys. "Call it a hunch. I have to get to the news conference."

"I'll see you there!" she said.

THE DEVIL SHOPS ON SUNDAY

The news conference went exactly like I thought it would. Bobby announced the names of three of the bodies: Larry Caldwell, and two other names I didn't recognize, but would research when I got back to the office.

He also said there had been rumors about a serial killer, but the police were confident that wasn't the case. Based on the shouting and boos from the the Murderoonies section, they disagreed with law enforcement's assessment, and wanted to know who the police thought killed that many people if it wasn't a serial killer.

Bobby shut things down pretty quickly, and didn't take questions. That made the Murderoonies and their fandom even more upset. I was glad no one had access to flour like the flour bandit, or other foods like Mrs. Olsen, because they probably would have thrown it all directly at Bobby.

I pulled Bobby aside after the news conference was over.

"I saw Jordan Barret having a tense conversation with Grace Caldwell, Rochelle Hart, and Trixie Barton this morning."

Bobby's eyes went wide.

"Did you know Rochelle and Trixie's husbands both went missing? Rochelle's husband went missing twenty-one years ago, and Trixie's husband went missing twenty-two years ago."

Bobby leaned back on his heels. "I knew they went missin', but I was young. You think they're two of the bodies on the property?"

I sliced my head down once. "I do. They were friends with Saul Barret. So was Larry Caldwell. When you get the rest of the identifications back, I think Erold Hart and Lane Barton will be two of them."

Bobby chewed on his bottom lip, thinking through it. "What does Jordan have to do with it?"

"I think Jordan knew about the bodies being there. Maybe Saul told him, or even had Jordan help bury them."

"Interestin'," Bobby said. "That falls into line with some of what we've seen from the scene and our investigation. It looked like the people who were buried on the property all died somewhere else and were moved and buried on the land."

That made sense. I just wasn't sure why they'd done it.

"I'm gonna make some calls and see if we can expedite the identifications of the rest of the bodies now that we have two more possible names." He patted me on the shoulder. "Good work, Kate."

I smiled. "Thanks. Let me know what you find out, and I'll let you know when I have more info."

Bobby nodded as another officer came to talk to him. I left the building to go back to the *Tribune* and look more at Ella and Hawke's list.

Hawke's motorcycle was parked next to my Jeep. He was leaning against my door, checking something on his phone when I arrived.

"From now on, I'll have to listen to the latest Murderoonies episode to figure out what's going on between us," he said, putting his phone in his pocket.

I shook my head and sighed. "I talked to my mom about

that. She won't be going on any more podcasts discussing my…friendships. And I've asked her not to discuss them at all. With anyone."

"Is that what this is? A friendship?"

I shrugged. "I'm not sure how to define it. What do you think it is?"

He gave that slow, tantalizing smile that always made me wish he were wearing fewer clothes. "It can be anything you want it to be, Kitty Kate."

"That was a non-answer if I've ever heard one, and an answer you've given me before."

"I'm just waiting for you to decide what you want."

"What I want? A relationship isn't one way, you know. It takes honesty, communication, vulnerability, commitment, and time. From both parties."

"You know what I want."

"I actually don't."

"You."

"But what does that mean?"

"You tell me."

I threw my hands in the air. "I can't deal with the non-answers!" I opened my Jeep and put my bag inside. "Were you able to look up the financial history on the GCR investors and Jordan Barret?"

Hawke nodded. "I'm still waiting on some of the investors, but should have info back later today. I do have Jordan Barret's records though, and emailed them to you."

I pulled up my email and started looking through it. "He had some large deposits at irregular intervals."

"I noticed that," Hawke said.

An idea was percolating in my head. "Can you check the

accounts of Grace Caldwell, Rochelle Hart, and Trixie Barton to see if they had the same amounts taken out of any of their financial accounts around the same time?"

Hawke gave me a look of understanding. "I can. I'll get back to you in a couple of hours." Hawke grabbed his helmet, and took off on his bike.

I walked into the *Tribune* office and immediately opened my laptop. I picked up the list of missing persons Ella had given me to check it against the other two names that had been released during the news conference. I didn't see any names that corresponded, so that was a bit deflating, but I was still sure I was on the right track with Jordan.

Spence came out of his office. "It sounds like the news conference was a bit uneventful."

"We got two names we didn't have before," I said. "When it was over, I talked to Bobby privately and told him a theory I have."

"What theory is that?" Spence asked.

I explained what had happened at the assisted living center with Jordan, Grace, Rochelle, and Trixie.

"Grace's husband, Rochelle's husband, and Trixie's husband were all friends."

"And they all went missing?" Spence asked. "That's suspicious."

"I thought the same thing. So, I did a little more digging. Not only were they friends. They were friends with Saul Barret."

Spence put his fist up to his chin in a thinking pose. "You

think Saul killed them and buried their bodies, and others on his land?"

"What better way to guarantee that bodies don't get accidentally unearthed than to put them on your own property, that you aren't ever planning to sell?"

"But then he died and they did sell," Spence said.

"Exactly. Saul died twenty years ago. Grace said Larry went missing on a hunting trip twenty years ago, Erold went missing twenty-one years ago, and Lane went missing twenty-two years ago. Saul could have killed them."

"And Jordan could have helped to bury the bodies," Spence said.

I nodded, thinking through all the pieces in my head. "Maybe Saul started killing people and when he died, Jordan continued it. We don't have identification and ages on all the bodies yet, though, so maybe they were all victims of Saul."

"Have you talked to people who knew him?" Spence asked. "Do you think Saul had it in him to commit murder?"

"Georgia's memory isn't good enough to get reliable information. But I talked to Bethany and she said Saul was not a nice man, and no one in their family was sad when he died. I still can't reach Jordan, but saw him at the assisted living center. He ran away from me. He was at the CFNP meeting and seemed very friendly with Wayne Post, and the main speaker who's one of the CFNP funders. I think Jordan is in this up to his eyeballs."

"Maybe Jordan moved the bodies to the property," Spence suggested.

I leaned back in my chair, the wheels in my head turning. "That's a good thought." If CFNP needed bodies, maybe Jordan knew where to find some because of his dad.

"You probably need to talk to him."

"I'm planning on it. One way or another."

Ella came in the door. She'd been at the news conference and had stayed longer than me—probably to socialize and theorize with the Murderoonies.

Spence pointed to a paper sitting in front of me. "I put the talking points for the Live event tonight on your desk," Spence said.

"I saw," I said with a little bit of a glare.

He put his hands up. "It's good for the paper, and you know it."

"I know," I relented. "But I don't have to like it."

"You'll be on stage, obviously," Spence said. "But I'll be taking care of the camera, and our staff will be managing the Live feed."

I read through the points, which seemed to be mostly Jeff Zundy related. "I see they're still focusing on the serial killer angle."

Ella piped up, "It's a lotta bodies all in one place. The same person had to be involved."

"Maybe." But I had some theories, and Jordan Barret was on top. It looked like he'd buried, or helped to bury the bodies of Grace, Rochelle, and Trixie's husbands. And based on what I'd seen at the assisted living facility, they all knew it, so it seemed like they were in on it together somehow. But I wasn't sure what the motive was, or who killed them.

"Is your love life on the talking points?" Ella asked, peering over my shoulder to look at the card.

"No, and it better not be. I'll shut that shit down fast."

"People saw you holdin' hands with Hawke the other

night. There's pics in The Ladies group about you," Ella said, getting a doughnut from the treat table.

I heaved a sigh. "Who took that photo?"

"Cami Pine's daughter was ice blockin'. She had her phone."

Phones and social media were going to be the death of me one day. And my dog would probably be able to find my bones.

My phone started ringing with "Play Me." I answered and Hawke went straight to business. "I sent you an email and you need to open it now."

"Okay," I said, clicking on the message that popped up from Hawke. It was a list of transactions.

"What am I looking at here?" I asked him.

"The first page is a list of high value transactions from Jordan's bank account. They're all deposits." I nodded. I'd seen these already.

"There are nine transactions of five thousand dollars each, over the course of the last twenty-five years."

I paused at that. I hadn't counted the transactions previously. "So Jordan, who is forty-two years old, has been getting paid the same amount to do something for decades, nine times," I said. "And there were nine bodies."

"Exactly. Now go to the next page."

"There's a transaction from Grace Caldwell, for five thousand dollars. A debit." I read the information and then flipped back to the page with Jordan's transaction history. "The debit happened on the day before the deposit into Jordan's account occurred."

"Yes," Hawke said. "Another interesting thing is the date of the transaction. It's a different date than when Larry was reported missing."

He was right. Grace told me her husband went missing on a hunting trip twenty years ago, but the transaction happened twenty-two years ago.

"Why do you think there's a discrepancy in the dates?"

"You'll have to ask Jordan Barret," Hawke said. "Rochelle and Trixie both had debits from their accounts within a week of Jordan depositing another five thousand dollars. I'll email those files to you now."

I stared at the information. I knew Jordan had been involved with this, I just didn't know how. "It looks like these women all buried their husbands' bodies, and Jordan helped them. For a fee."

"That's how I'm reading it."

The date discrepancy between when the financial transactions happened and when the bodies were reported missing was odd. I chewed on my lip as I thought. "Did you ever find out more about the government card that was found with Larry Caldwell's body?"

Hawke paused. "I did. It was an old Veteran's Affairs card."

The wheels were turning in my head. "That helps. Thanks."

"No problem. I also sent you the list of investors and financial info for Grant's company. And," he paused dramatically, "I found some info about the dark web post you were looking for."

My eyes widened. "You're full of information today."

"I try."

I saw the email ping and pulled it up.

"Great. I've got some leads to chase before tonight. Will I see you at the Live event?"

"I wouldn't miss seeing you in action."

I grinned. "I owe you."

"I know. And I'll collect."

I wasn't upset about that.

I looked through the email about the GCR Development investors and recognized a familiar name. Trent Aslow. He was listed as the real estate broker who worked with GCR, and I remembered Grant mentioning his name. Aslow was also the same name Vera from the Murderoonies had said when she was talking on the phone about handling things.

I looked through the information Hawke had sent about the dark web post next, and gasped. Everything was starting to make sense.

I grabbed my bag. I had two people I needed to talk to before the event started. Jordan Barret was on top of that list, and this time, I wasn't taking no for an answer.

Chapter Twenty-One

The Live event was held at the high school in the auditorium, which said a lot about expected attendance numbers. Black curtains hung as a background, and there was a huge Murderoonies sign on the stage, and another *Tribune* sign that wasn't nearly as big. I wondered where that had come from because I'd never seen it before.

A red couch, the same color as the blood in the Murderoonies logo, was on the stage for Edith and Margie. Another grey couch was angled across from it for me. Side tables sat on the end of each couch with drinks for everyone on stage. I was going to need it, I'd been running non-stop all day, but I was excited to reveal everything I'd found out. I adjusted my black linen pants, and my white, cap sleeve silk shirt as I listened to the rumble of noise from the audience and waited for the curtains to open. We were all wearing microphones attached to our shirts.

"Did you understand the talking points?" Edith asked me.

"I think I got it," I said with smile.

The curtains opened and I walked on stage with Edith and

Margie, all of us waving. I looked to Spence in the back of the auditorium. He nodded once, indicating he knew the plan.

We introduced ourselves, and then Edith moved forward and explained the program for the evening. She finished with an enthusiastic, "Let's get this Live event started!" The crowd responded with cheers.

The event began with the most recent Murderoonies episode, detailing a summary of the bodies being found on GCR's development in Branson Falls, and then going into the history of Jeff Zundy, his time in Branson Falls, and information from Fern Gables. They made a case for how remains on the development could have, and very likely were, his victims. The end of the episode listed the victim names from the news conference this morning. I listened to the whole thing, which was a regurgitation of information from the past week and half, knowing full-well how wrong their theories were. When the podcast ended, Edith opened it up to discussion among the three of us.

"Why do you think the bodies are victims of a serial killer?" I asked.

Edith laughed like I was adorable. "Did you listen to the podcast, Kate? I think we made it pretty clear. Maybe we need to play it for you again?"

The crowd laughed, and I gave her a smile that showed no teeth.

"You've been convinced this was Jeff Zundy from the start," I said. "Did you pursue any other leads?"

Edith gave a sputtering laugh. "Of course we asked questions. That's what we do. But the signs all point to Jeff Zundy." Because that's where they wanted the evidence to point.

"It wasn't a serial killer," I told her.

Edith gave me a look that said 'bless your heart.' "All of those bodies on one property and you're telling me murder wasn't involved?"

"Oh no. Some of them were murdered. Others weren't."

"Really?" Edith said like she was placating me. "And how would you know that?"

I ran a hand down my pants like I was smoothing them, but really it was a signal for Spence to get ready. "Because I know who buried the bodies."

A gasp flowed through the crowd.

"How?" Edith sputtered, sitting up straighter in her seat.

"Investigating." I waved my hand at the back to indicate to Spence that he should start the video recording I'd gotten that afternoon.

"To be clear," I said before the video started, "I recorded this earlier today. The subject is aware that I have it, and that I'm playing it now. The police have also already received a copy."

Jordan Barret's face filled the screen and murmurs went through the audience.

"I'm recording now," I said, sitting so we could both be seen in the camera shot.

Jordan shifted in his chair. "Okay."

"Here's what I know. I know you were working with Grace Caldwell, whose husband, Larry Caldwell, went missing twenty years ago."

Jordan pressed his lips together.

"On June tenth, twenty-two years ago, there was a deduction of five thousand dollars from Grace Caldwell's bank account. On June eleventh, there was a deposit of five thousand dollars made into your

bank account. Grace's husband wasn't reported missing until almost two years later."

Jordan shifted uncomfortably in his chair.

"I also have a list of missing persons for the past fifty years, and I know you were working with Rochelle Hart and Trixie Barton. Both of their husbands also went missing, and I have transaction records showing corresponding deductions from their accounts and deposits into your account."

Jordan worried his hands together.

"There are six other transaction records of the same amount in your account over the last twenty-five years, and coincidentally, there were six other bodies found on your family's property, now the GCR home development." I looked down at my notes and then back up. *"Can you tell me how the bodies ended up on your family's property?"*

Jordan ran his palms up and down his thighs. "I'd rather not, but I guess I don't have much of a choice anymore."

I gave him a prompt to get him talking. "I have reports from several people saying that your dad wasn't a very nice person."

He took a deep breath. "Those reports are accurate. My dad was a horrible human."

"Did your dad have something to do with any of the bodies on your family's property, Jordan?"

He shook his head. "Not my dad." He paused and chewed on his lip. "My mom."

The entire audience listening gasped.

It took me a minute on the recording to rein in my own shock. Georgia Barret was not someone I'd thought capable of murder, and not someone I'd even considered. I thought back to our first conversation though, and some of the things she'd said about her husband, and then when I saw her earlier today as well. She didn't seem fond of him, but I'd written it off as challenges with her memory. I shouldn't have.

"My dad was an emotionally and physically abusive asshole. He was emotionally and physically abusive to me, my mom, and Bethany. My mom didn't feel like she had anyone to go to. Her family told her to work it out because she was in this for eternity and she didn't have a choice. Her church leaders told her the same thing. When he died of a heart attack, we were all relieved. My mom was finally able to live the life she'd wanted, and figure out who she was. She was also relieved because it meant her kids were safe. Everything changed for the better after he was gone."

I'd wondered if Georgia had more to do with Saul's death than anyone previously thought.

"He died young. Do you think it was of natural causes?"

Jordan looked right at me when he answered, *"I think he had a heart attack, and he deserved it."*

Okay then.

Jordan looked out the window before turning back to me. *"There were other men who also deserved it. My mom hadn't had the support she needed to escape the situation with my dad. But she had friends, and knew of other women who were in the same abusive situations she'd been in. My mom wanted to help those women, and came up with a solution. We'd bury their bodies on our property where they'd never be found."*

"So, they were murdered?" I asked.

He shook his head. *"I didn't ask questions, I just helped them hide the bodies when they came to me for assistance. I didn't want any other kids to go through the hell I had growing up."*

"Were all the men you buried abusive?"

He shook his head again. *"My mom also had some friends who were counting on their husband's Social Security and Veteran's*

Affairs payments to get them by. As long as their husbands were alive, the women still got payments in higher amounts. When their husbands died, they'd call me and I'd help them get rid of the bodies. They told people their husbands were gone somewhere, or sick, until they couldn't pull off the lie anymore. At that point, their husbands were reported as missing. The higher payments stopped, but they'd saved enough to be able to keep going for a while."

"But you took money from them to help."

"I didn't want to. But the first woman I helped insisted, and told others about the fee. It set a precedent and the transaction made it seem more legit."

"How did people know to find you?"

Body burying wasn't something you could advertise on social media.

"The dark web. People started posting on Tor about my services handling vermin. Word got around, and I was able to help several women."

"Did you kill any of those men?" I asked.

"No," he stated firmly. *"And I didn't ask how any of them died. I just made sure they were buried and wouldn't be found again."*

"And you thought you could control that because your family trust required a majority agreement to sell, and you didn't plan to sell the land."

He swallowed hard and nodded. *"My mom obviously knew about the bodies, and was actively helping her friends. But when her memory began to deteriorate, she forgot that there could be issues if a developer started digging up the property. I'd helped keep the womens' secrets for years, and wanted to make sure the bodies stayed buried. My mom voted to sell with Bethany, and there was nothing I could do to stop it. I tried."*

"With Citizens For No Progress?" I asked.

He nodded and ran a hand through his hair.

"For most of this investigation, I thought you were working with Citizens For No Progress, especially after I saw you at the CFNP event a few days ago. What's your connection to them?"

"Once it looked like the sale was going to go through, I enlisted the help of CFNP to hide bodies on other properties. They had access to bodies that had been donated to science. I thought it might take the heat off of me, my family, and the women we'd tried to help if more bodies were found in other places."

"What was CFNP getting out of it?"

"Their goal is to stop the growth going on in small towns, and discourage people from moving in. They thought a bunch of people found dead on new properties in Branson Falls would discourage buyers."

"Wayne Post was helping you. What did he have to do with all of this?"

"He was friends with my dad and wanted the land but couldn't afford it. He's also a big supporter of CFNP. Wayne and I worked with CFNP to come up with our plan. We thought if the bodies were found, GCR would sell the land at a reduced rate and Wayne would be able to get it for a price closer to the one my dad had promised him."

I waved at Spence to stop the recording.

It was so quiet that you could hear a pin drop. Edith's face looked ashen, and Margie was shocked. I'd dropped a bomb that people were still trying to recover from, but I wasn't done.

"I don't know what to say." Edith's tone was distressed and her expression was a combination of concern and confusion.

"I know, it's a shock." I paused to give her a few seconds to catch her breath. "I need to ask you some questions, Edith."

She looked up at me, worry lines forming on her forehead.

"How did you know about the bodies on the property, Edith?"

Her eyes were clear and she still seemed as bewildered as ever. "We heard about them from a message that Vera got on our tip line."

"That's right," I said. "Vera mentioned that the tip you got, leading you to Branson Falls, was anonymous. Did the tip include the number of bodies?"

Edith pinched her brows together. "I don't think so."

"Then how did you know the number of bodies that would be found?" I asked.

"What do you mean?" Edith answered.

"When you had your event at the hotel, Vera said you thought you should investigate the case because there could be nine bodies found."

Edith wrung her hands together. "I-I-I don't know. I thought she was spouting numbers."

"But there were exactly nine bodies found. Did the tip line tell you that?"

Edith looked a little worried now. "I don't remember where I heard it, but I must have heard it somewhere."

I turned to Vera who was standing off stage and addressed her, "Do you remember, Vera? How did you know the number?"

Vera stiffened, then schooled her expression as she took long, deliberate strides onto the stage. She attempted an innocent look and shook her head slightly. "I can't recall exactly what the tip line said."

"How did you know the number?"

"You're not the only one who can investigate, Kate," she said with an air of superiority.

"You're right. But I've got a bit more experience with it than you do. Do you want to tell everyone who the owner of DAB Enterprises is?"

Every part of her body froze and then she tried to recover. "It's a Murderoonies company. We have a lot of them."

"Talk to me about Trent Aslow, Vera."

She licked her lips and swallowed. "He's our real estate broker."

"Trent Aslow works in the same office as Eddie Prestman, the real estate broker for the Barret family," I said, watching her reaction closely. "Eddie is engaged to Bethany Barret."

Vera pressed her lips together. She knew things were unraveling and it was live so there was nothing she could do about it.

"Trent is also the broker for Grant and GCR Development."

She lifted her shoulder like she didn't know anything about that, but I knew she did.

I moved around her. "You've been wanting to expand The Murderoonies empire, haven't you?"

She crossed her arms over her chest. "We're always looking for ways to grow our business."

"And you wanted to develop property with a Murderoonies spin."

"Again, we're always looking for ways to grow."

I scanned the audience in the general direction where I knew he was sitting. "Trent, do you want to come up?"

Trent Aslow stood from the back of the auditorium and came to the stage.

I signaled Spence, and he started the recording with Jordan again.

"Did Bethany know about the bodies?" I asked.

Jordan lifted his shoulders. "She said she didn't, but I don't know if I believe that. She's the reason the land was sold."

"Because of her fiancé?"

"Yeah. He told one of the other brokers he worked with about the property, and they pitched it to their clients."

"Are you talking about broker, Trent Aslow?"

Jordan nodded.

"So, Trent pitched your family farm to GCR Development and that's why they bought it?"

Jordan shook his head. "No. First, he pitched it to DAB Enterprises."

I watched my jaw drop on the camera because I knew full well who DAB Enterprises was. I'd been looking at their name on the investor list for GCR Development and the Barret property.

"The Murderoonies?"

Jordan nodded. "Yep."

"But the Murderoonies didn't buy it, GCR did."

"That was part of the plan."

I waved to Spence, and he shut the recording off again as shocked voices rumbled through the audience.

I directed my attention to the crowd.

"I talked to Trent a couple of hours ago. Again, Trent works at the same real estate brokerage as Eddie Prestman, Bethany Barret's fiancé." I paused to let that information sink in just in case people had missed it when I'd mentioned it to Vera. "Do you want to tell everyone what you told me Trent?"

Trent took a microphone that one of our *Tribune* staff

members brought out on stage. "Eddie contacted me a little over a year ago and said he had some information. He'd come across Georgia Barret's journal where she confessed to helping women hide their husbands' bodies and using her property to do it. I remembered Vera mentioning a dark web tip about the same thing. The two situations were very similar. I put two-and-two together, and talked to Vera about my suspicions."

I shifted my stance toward Vera. "Did you read the journal, Vera?"

She pressed her lips tight, trying to decide how she wanted to answer. I could almost see the calculations in her head before she decided to own it. "I did. We'd heard rumors about a female vigilante helping women hide dead bodies and we wanted to cover the story. Someone sent us a tip about it from a posting on the dark web. We'd been looking for the location and had a few people researching. When Trent reached out, I was confident the Barret farm was the same property referred to in the dark web tip we received," Vera said. "I told Trent to try and buy the land."

Trent continued, "I talked to Eddie about brokering the deal. But the Barrets wanted more than the Murderoonies could spend. So, I approached Grant and GCR Development instead. Then we brought on the Murderoonies as a large investor in the project so they'd still be able to have some say. Based on Georgia's journal, we knew the general areas where the bodies were buried, and as investors, we were able to give input into the development phases. We knew the bodies could be found while the land was being excavated, and that fit perfectly with The Murderoonies' plan to have a true crime housing development and community. They knew if there was enough press, GCR might not want the development anymore. Once all the bodies were found, they put an offer in under one of their other company names to buy the piece from GCR."

I looked over and Edith's face was ashen white. "I-I-I don't know what to say. I didn't know about any of this." She waved her arms around to encompass it all. "I swear it." She looked so horrified that I believed her. Margie's face had taken on a green tint like she was going to be sick.

"Why not be honest about it from the beginning and tell GCR Development about your suspicions and your interest in it being a true crime development? You could have partnered with them from the start."

"Because then it wouldn't have had the real true crime that had happened on it with the investigation as well. Our numbers have been great on this case! People love visiting a place with a story, especially if it's a story they feel like they're a part of."

It's what the Murderoonies had built their whole business around.

She turned to the audience. "This is an incredible community and you're all a part of it! Let's keep building it and solve more crimes in real time together!"

The audience erupted with some jeering, and others cheering. Some people looked absolutely furious at being used and tricked, others looked like they couldn't wait to buy a lot on the development. Edith and Margie were completely stunned, and Vera started toward them.

I saw Grant stand up from the back room and walk out, his phone to his ear. He was already trying to manage this situation, and I didn't blame him. There was a lot that would need to be worked out.

Drake came up from the back of the room. He leaned in so I could hear his deep voice over all the commotion in the audience. "I have to go help Grant, but this was great work. You're incredible at what you do."

"Thanks," I said, truly appreciative of the compliment.

"Can I take you to dinner to celebrate your skills?"

I took in the auditorium and the mayhem going on. "I think I'll be here covering this for a while, unfortunately."

He ran his tongue across his lips. "What if I want to bring you home later?"

Drake liked to say things like that, but I didn't think he'd ever really follow through. "I dare you, but not tonight."

His eyes lit up. "You think I won't accept that dare, but I will.

"We'll see."

"Yes, you will." Drake walked away to go take care of his clients.

I looked around the auditorium. People were yelling at each other, some looked ready to start a brawl, and others seemed excited.

Edith and Margie were arguing loudly with Vera. Chole was there too, and it looked like they were trying to decide whether or not to turn off the Live feed. Their numbers were probably through the roof, so I was guessing they'd leave it on.

I felt a large arm snake around my back, and the smell of the beach came with it. I smiled and leaned in to the touch.

"You're a little like your mom, you know," Hawke said.

I narrowed my eyes. "What's that supposed to mean?"

"You showed up today and everything turned to chaos."

I grinned and ran my tongue over my teeth. "I think that means I did my job."

He met my eyes and held them. "That," he gestured to the stage, and me, "was one of the most impressive things I've seen, Kitty Kate. And I'm hard to impress. I can't believe you got Jordan on video."

I smiled and tried not to preen. That was a huge compliment coming from someone like Hawke. "When I started dropping information about his bank transactions, he knew it was over. He agreed to go on camera because I told him cooperating and admitting culpability might help when the information came out, and it was coming out with or without his side of the story."

Hawke's eyes trailed over me and he slowly licked his lips. "You're kind of threatening, and it's kind of a turn on."

The corners of my lips ticked up. "I feel the same way about you."

"Want to do something about that?" he asked with a raised eyebrow.

I saw Spence coming toward me and knew I'd be here a while. "I'd like that, but I don't think it's going to happen tonight."

He let his lips linger right next to my ear and in a husky voice he said, "Soon then, Kitty Kate," he promised. "It will be soon."

Chapter Twenty-Two

I spent the next few days writing articles about the bodies with all the details I'd discovered. Spence and our *Tribune* staff were manning our social media, which had exploded since the Live.

The day, and week, was nearing the end. I leaned back in my office chair and lifted my arms in the air, hands clasped, to stretch my shoulders out.

Ella came out of the back room, carrying her purse and ready to go home. We were all exhausted. "Everyone thinks you're a dang hero!" Ella said, stopping by my desk.

"She kind of is," Spence admitted.

I laughed. "You're all going to give me a big head."

"What's going on with the Murderoonies?" Spence asked Ella. "Have you heard anything since Kate's live takedown?"

Ella's eyes went huge. "They basically became the subject of their own true crime podcast! It was a dumpster fire in the comments and chat, and it's still goin' on today. Almost everyone's split into two camps: people who are pissed, and people who want to invest in the property and buy a house!"

"Which camp are you in?" I asked her.

She pushed her lips out, thinking about it. "I'm not gonna lie, I was mad they tricked us. But I wouldn't mind livin' next to fellow true crime enthusiasts! Think of all the fun we'd have!"

"I thought Grant, Chris, and Ryan would be furious," I said. "They were at first, but they've had so much interest in the lots now that they're raising prices and their profits are probably going to be triple what they projected. You have to hand it to the Murderoonies—they knew what they were doing."

"Will there be any consequences for the Murderoonies?" Spence asked.

I shook my head. "Not that I can tell. Technically, they didn't do anything wrong. GCR might have tried to sue them if this had affected the development negatively, but all the extra press and the Live got everyone talking about it, and that's great for GCR's business."

"But their serial killer case went up in smoke," Spence said.

I cocked my head to the side. "They were wrong about the bodies being Jeff Zundy victims, but thanks to Fern Gables and her interview, the Murderoonies now have a lot of missing women to investigate, and they're doing a whole series on that."

"It's so excitin'!" Ella said, unable to contain herself. "It's gonna be popular."

"Speaking of bodies and missing persons, what's going on with Jordan?" Spence asked. "Is he going to jail?"

I shook my head. "Jordan is in trouble for burying the bodies in unmarked graves, and facilitating the whole scheme, including taking money for it. Drake is representing him, but given the circumstances and that he was a minor when all of this started, had suffered severe abuse, and was doing it at the direction of his mom, Drake doesn't think he'll go to jail."

"What about Georgia?" Ella asked. "Are the police gonna look into Saul's death? Everyone's wonderin' if he really died of a heart attack."

I'd had the same question. "It was decades ago. There's no real way to investigate it now, or prove anything. He was buried in an actual cemetery and if they tried to exhume his body, there would be little left to evaluate. Georgia's health is in serious decline, and everyone failed her when she was trying to get help while going through Saul's abuse. Charging her with something would make things even worse. Personally, I think it's best to let that particular mystery remain unsolved."

Spence grabbed some candy from the treat table and gave a piece to all of us. "What about the other women who had their husbands buried?"

"I'm not sure. They're still identifying bodies, but from what I've heard, some of the women are already dead. The other women who are still alive could be charged with Social Security or VA fraud if they were still accepting the higher government payments after their spouses died."

Ella popped a piece of candy into her mouth. "Have you heard from Bethany? Are she and her scheming fiancé still together?"

Spence grimaced. "I haven't heard anything, but I don't imagine that's going to go over well. The guy she's supposed to marry read her mom's private journal and used it as leverage to sell their family property. Property that he knew had bodies buried on it and would cause a lot of problems, embarrassment, and even legal issues if the bodies were unearthed. She trusted him and he betrayed her. I don't know what it would take for her to get that trust back."

I nodded, agreeing with Spence. Trust was vital to relationships and if the same thing had happened to me that happened to Bethany, I'd be out immediately.

"Did the CFNP have anythin' to say after the Live and Jordan's truth bombs?" Ella asked.

"They posted some videos and made some statements about fighting the good fight and staying strong for the cause," Spence said. "They admitted to helping Jordan plant bodies on other properties because they thought the bodies would deter people from moving to Branson Falls. It seems like it did the opposite. GCR is purchasing another piece of property to start developing soon."

I'd talked to Grant and knew that even with the dumpster fire that happened on his first Branson Falls development, he wasn't deterred. Given the response to the Live, and interest in the lots, he was excited to get another piece of property built out. Some people would be upset, but the key to success is adaptation, and people can't stop progress, even when they try to join a group claiming to do that in its name.

CFNP seemed to still be going strong, but this situation had highlighted the divide happening in Branson Falls, and some people were reaching out, trying to learn more about each other, and build bridges. Caring for others was something I'd admired about my hometown growing up, and I hoped those roots would be what people were inspired to get back to. I also hoped it would put a spotlight on the issues of "others" and "us vs. them" in other places as well, and would be a spark for change, more acceptance, and for people to try and find a way to understand each other, and come together.

"One thing that hasn't died down is the interest in your love life," Ella said. "The Live was still runnin' when Drake and Hawke both came up to you on stage."

I frowned. "Hopefully the interest in that will die down eventually."

Ella pressed her lips together and looked from one side of the room to the other without moving her head. "Don't hold your breath." She patted me on the shoulder before saying goodnight, and walking out the door.

I finished up the story I was working on and stood to stretch.

Spence came out of his office. "Do you want to come over for dinner soon?"

My eyes widened with surprise. "Dinner with you and the new boyfriend?"

A tinge of red flushed Spence's dark skin and I laughed. "Did you just *blush?*"

"Don't make me uninvite you," Spence said, his tone joking.

"I would love to finally meet him." I picked up my iced coffee and took a drink. "Where do you want to go, and when?"

"I'm sure you'll be busy this weekend, so next Friday? It would be best if we did it at our house. That way we'll avoid the inevitable rumors."

My eyes widened in surprise. "Have you seen The Ladies' Facebook group about me? I guarantee the rumors would reflect poorly on me, not you."

He laughed. "You're probably right, but this way, we all stay out of the line of fire."

"Why would I be busy this weekend?" I asked, gathering my things, and closing my laptop.

Spence seemed to catch his breath and then waved his hand in front of him. "It's been a long couple of weeks and I think we could all use some downtime."

I couldn't argue with that. "Okay, I'll see you next Friday night then. What can I bring?"

"Just yourself. Xander is a chef and will handle everything."

"He's a chef?" My eyes went wide. "And you didn't tell me that? Good lord, I love him already! My grilled cheeses are about to get an upgrade!"

Spence laughed. "I'm sure he'll be amused to hear that."

I opened the door to my house and took a deep breath as I stepped inside, happy to be home. It had been a long couple of weeks and I was ready for a break. I always felt like my house was my sanctuary.

With my hours the past few days, Gandalf had been staying with my parents. He was probably so full of cheese and treats that he was going to burst. My mom was supposed to drop him off tonight after their latest Paw P.I. job.

I put some dishes away, and washed out my coffee cup. It was nice to have a few quiet minutes to breathe.

A knock sounded on the door. So much for that minute. I hoped it wasn't a salesperson, or the Mormon missionaries. They were basically the same thing.

I opened the door and Hawke's wide shoulders filled the frame.

I didn't even get a chance to say hello as he moved toward me, purpose and heat in his gaze. He put one hand on my hip, and the other on the side of my face and pulled me to him. His lips met mine and I sank into the kiss, his tongue exploring my mouth as his hands explored my body. We kissed for what seemed like minutes and I was disappointed when he eventually pulled away.

"What was that for?" I asked, breathless.

"A reminder."

"Of what."

"Everything we could have."

Everything we could have was all fine and good, but the problem was that it wasn't *everything*. It was everything when it was convenient for Hawke's schedule. When there wasn't a work emergency, and work wasn't a priority. To be fair, I'd done the same thing to him with my own job repeatedly. Also, he was in the business of keeping secrets, and I was in the business of asking questions and exposing secrets. I wasn't sure how to make a relationship work with our careers, and I was still trying to decide if I was ready for a relationship at all. There were a lot of unanswered questions and things to address.

I stepped back.

"Are you here to pick up your Mustang?"

He very slowly and deliberately shook his head. "I'm here to pick you up, like I promised."

"Pick me up to go where? Dinner?"

He ran his tongue over his lips. "That too. Somewhere far,

far away, where we can't be interrupted by work. And somewhere warm. Where you won't need clothes."

My eyes went wide. "But I have Gandalf. And work."

"Already taken care of," he said.

"How?"

"Your mom owes me, and so does Spence."

It was an invitation I couldn't say no to, but if Drake had made it, I probably wouldn't have said no to that either.

Hawke's phone rang and I closed my eyes, preparing for more disappointment.

He answered, "Handle it."

There was a pause.

"I'm busy. Handle it."

He hung up the phone and slid it into his pocket.

"Do you need to take that?" I asked, gesturing to the call.

"I need to take you," he said, and pressed his lips hard to mine as he dragged me out the door to wherever warm place we were going—with only the clothes on my back.

The End

Watch for Devilishly Short #2 coming July 2024!

and

Book 5, *The Devil Gets Divorced*, coming Fall 2024!
Available for pre-order in my author store soon!
www.angelacorbettshop.com

Author's Note

I've planned for my Kate Saxee Mystery Series to be long...at least twenty books. It's important to me for my characters to grow, change, make mistakes, and even change their minds—just like in real life. In the Kate Saxee world, Kate's only been back in Branson Falls for about six months. She's definitely not ready to choose the person she'll end up with forever, but I promise you she's going to have a great time figuring it out. ;-) I hope you'll stick around and join Kate on her journey. I love this series, and I'll keep writing it as long as my characters have stories to tell. Book 5, *The Devil Gets Divorced*, will be out in Fall 2024, and you can pre-order the eBook in my author store soon! www.angelacorbettshop.com

Acknowledgments

There are many people who help make my author business run so I don't lose my mind, and I appreciate every one of them. Thanks to my cover designer, Ink and Circuit Designs, for always taking my ideas and hitting them out of the park. Thanks to my editors, proofreaders, and beta readers. I can't catch everything on my own, but I try, and my team picks up what I miss. Also, I want to give an enormous thank you to the fantastic team that runs my recently opened author store. They help manage things so I can have more time to write.

Thanks to Cody Martens, the wizard of real estate and my friend, who answered my questions about dead bodies and disclosure laws. For real, if you ever buy a house in Utah, ask if someone died in it first because they don't legally have to tell you if you don't get curious! Another huge thanks to Officer Friendly, a long-time friend, police officer in the Salt Lake City area, and former SWAT member who answered about a thousand dead body and crime scene questions for me. He also explained the sheer amazingness of the dogs they use in police work, and the dogs are incredible! I've taken license with some things for the sake of the story, so if you're a police officer or realtor and think anything is incorrect, please know any mistakes are my own.

And most importantly, to Dan, for being my best friend, soul mate, and the one person on earth I know I can always rely on. I'm an author, but this is also a business and the business side takes far more time and energy than I wish it did. When

I'm feeling overwhelmed and just need to get words in, Dan steps in to help, and he's my biggest cheerleader. He's also a brilliant tech wizard, and an extremely smart and talented software developer. He knows all things tech, so I'm indebted to him for his brilliance and for not minding the notepad at dinner so I can take notes while he answers my millions of daily questions. I love you with my whole soul.

Last of all, thank you to you, the readers, for being supportive and loving this series and the characters as much as I do. I can't wait for you to read *Devilishly Short #2*, in July, and *The Devil Gets Divorced*, coming in fall 2024!

Books by
Angela Corbett/Destiny Ford

<u>Kate Saxee Mystery Series</u>

The Devil Drinks Coffee

Devilishly Short #1

The Devil Wears Tank Tops

The Devil Has Tattoos

The Devil Shops on Sunday

Devilishly Short #2 (Coming Soon)

<u>Tempting Series</u>

Tempting Sydney

Chasing Brynn

Convincing Courtney (Coming Soon)

<u>A Dude Reads Romance Series</u>

A Dude Reads Romance-Tempting Sydney

A Dude Reads Romance-Chasing Brynn

<u>Hollywood Crush Series</u>

A-List

<u>Fractured Fairy Tale Series</u>

Withering Woods

Scattered Cinders

<u>Emblem of Eternity Trilogy</u>

Eternal Starling

Eternal Echoes

For special sneak peeks, giveaways, and super secret news, join Angela's newsletter!

http://eepurl.com/KhLAn

If you enjoyed reading *The Devil Shops on Sunday*, please help others enjoy this book too by recommending it, and reviewing it on Amazon, Barnes and Noble, Google Play, iBooks, or Goodreads. You can also review it in my author store at www.angelacorbettshop.com. If you do write a review, please send me a message through my website so I can thank you personally! www.angelacorbett.com

xoxo,
Ang

About the Author

Angela Corbett is a *USA Today* bestselling author, and a graduate of Westminster College where she double majored in communication and sociology and minored in business. She has worked as a journalist, freelance writer, and director of communications and marketing. She lives in Utah with her extremely supportive husband, and their sweet Pug-Zu, S'more. She loves classic cars, traveling, puppies, and can be bribed with handbags, and mochas from The People's Coffee. She's the author of Young Adult, New Adult, and Adult fiction —with lots of kissing. She writes under two names: Angela Corbett, and Destiny Ford.

http://www.angelacorbett.com/

Join my newsletter to get a free book!
http://eepurl.com/KhLAn

- facebook.com/AuthorAngelaCorbett
- x.com/angcorbett
- instagram.com/byangcorbett
- tiktok.com/@authorangelacorbett

Made in the USA
Coppell, TX
17 November 2024